Daughters of the Valley

by Leah Banicki

Wildflowers – Book 3

Daughters of the Valley

By Leah Banicki

©2014 – published by Leah Banicki

Book 3 of Wildflowers Series

https://www.facebook.com/Leah.Banicki.Novelist

All bible references are used from King James Version, used with permission from Bible Gateway. All verses can be found at https://www.biblegateway.com/

Preface

Oregon City

Oregon City was a small community in the Willamette Valley, with humble beginnings. Started by trappers and a few rugged pioneers who wanted a chance to make their own civilization in the wilderness of Oregon.

By 1850, despite the California Gold Rush stealing good men from the lumber camps, wool mills and small farms, the town was blossoming. Not in the way the East would have considered prosperous, with their bustling cities and train travel. But in the way a small community grows with small business and resources. One family at a time, coming and building a foundation from God's green earth up into something worthy of respecting.

Living on the frontier means you had to rely on your own hard work, and then also the small community around you. Selfishness and community never did go together well.

Men and women worked side-by-side to make things safe from the weather, the cold winters and the wildlife.

One lesson the West was bound to learn was relying on their women more than they ever had previously. A woman was more than just a plaything. She was to be respected for more than just childbearing and cooking up a hearty meal. Women were the helpmates that God had designed.

Woman could be a moral compass when men tend toward argument and stubborn will. They can be a fount of ideas when things go wrong. They can be another set of arms to help with clearing the land and tending the crop. They are there to raise up the next generation to be strong and hard working, taught from their mother's lap the ways of God and the ways of the land.

As many families traveled the Oregon Trail west they must have known the value of every person that made that long hard journey. Every man, woman and child were needed to carve out a place in that rugged frontier.

Chapter One

October 20th, 1850
Angela Fahey

Angela Fahey was anxious. She lay in bed listening to the quiet house. She was currently living with her best friend, Corinne Grant, and Corrine's husband Lucas. The cabin was roomy and even had an entire wing for the housekeeper, Violet, who Angela heard puttering around in the kitchen making breakfast. She felt strange being between two worlds again.

She was again waiting for her future. She had stability in a temporary situation but she wanted to settle into some more permanent roots. She was more than ready for change.

Angela stretched and climbed from her bed, knowing she needed to do something useful with herself.

She brushed her hair a little too quickly, ripping through some snarls in her wavy red hair. She made two hasty braids and wrapped them quickly around each other in a trick that Violet had taught her. Her hair was neat and put away, exactly what she wanted. In her world control wasn't always easy to find. She would take it where she could find it.

With a skirt and blouse on, she quietly padded in her stockinged feet to the kitchen to help Violet.

"Any chance you need help?" Angela offered. She saw Violet pouring coffee into a mug from the tall pot.

"Sorry Angie, I just finished up." Violet smiled sweetly then handed the full mug over to Angela.

"You are always finished. You know that?" Angie teased. Angela was always impressed by Violet's work ethic. She wore a smile and always had a cheery word for everyone. Her bread was the best in the county or farther, and she shared recipes with everyone she could. Violet was a generous soul with pale blue eyes and joy bubbling out of her.

Angela put fresh cream and sugar into the coffee. She and Violet visited at the table while the house stirred. Usually their mornings were spent this way with Violet teaching Angela cooking techniques and bread baking skills. As well as the every day household things that Angela hadn't learned in her bizarre childhood at the work orphanage.

Three days a week the ranch next door brought buckets of fresh milk from the dairy cows. Violet and Angela would strain it, separate the cream and some days they would churn it for butter. The ranch next door had more than enough and the owner was Corinne's father, John Harpole. Having family for neighbors made everyone feel safe and everyone helped each other. Violet pitched in to feed the ranchers and harvesters during the harvest and planting seasons. John's new wife Marie shared her love and support throughout the year for Corinne's newlywed household. Marie may have been Corinne's stepmother but she became the surrogate mother for every young lady of the area. The West was no place to be without support. Her first son, Cooper, was the pet of everyone. He was now nine years old and with his sidekick Pepper, the Australian Shepherd, he filled all the water barrels every day and was learning his stepfather's business of running a ranch.

After a few minutes of a visit with Violet, Angela made a plate for herself. Violet ate quickly and sat crocheting quietly while they waited for Corinne and Lucas to make an appearance.

Corinne and Lucas were dressed and ready soon thereafter and the plans for Saturday were thoroughly made. Corinne and Lucas were going to walk their land and tie string around trees to be cleared for more crops in the coming years. Their acreage was mostly on the opposite side of the creek and they had a lot of work to do to make the land their own.

Violet was going to visit with the pastor's wife, and Angela was eager to do anything to keep from losing her mind.

She was in the middle of a home building project. It was days away from moving in and she needed to stop obsessing over the progress.

It had been several months ago, on her eighteenth birthday, that she had conspired with her dear mentor and grandfather stand-in, Clive Quackenbush, to own her own land. She had felt much trepidation over even trying for it, being a single woman and still so young. She was glad, though, that she eventually spoke up. The land committee in town had agreed to allow it, with certain conditions and Clive as a co-signer.

The normal conditions applied to men, to build a solid dwelling and break sod for a minimum of two acres in the first year. With the elegant farmhouse she was building, the previous owner's barn, a small cabin and the start of a promising apple orchard, she wasn't too concerned about all those stipulations. It was the other stipulations that had her a bit annoyed.

6

She was told she had to have a husband within a four-year period. 'To work the land', was their explanation. She had hired a land manager but they still insisted. She felt a twinge of independent rebellion over their ability to control her but she laid it aside. The fact that they allowed her this land was a step forward. Being told to marry within a timeframe ruffled her feathers, though.

She did want a husband, and indeed, had a candidate in mind for the job. Ted Greaves, a handsome and good-hearted young man, who was currently thousands of miles away in upstate New York, but he was a worthy choice. He had promised to come back to the West.

Lord willing, she prayed.

They had the start of a budding romance last year in San Francisco… but Ted had to return east to take care of his mother and sister. These actions showed his honor and duty to his loved ones. His promise to return to the West was ever-present on her mind.

"You could run errands in town. Clive is next door visiting with my Father. He would certainly give you a ride." Corinne suggested, "You need to think on something else besides your house building project. It is coming along beautifully and you need to let the workers work. If you watch over their shoulders so much they may stage a revolt." Corinne stifled a giggle.

Lucas patted Angela on the shoulder. He smiled showing his mirth as he stood up to fill a round of seconds for breakfast. "I have a few little things I could use. I could make a list. I would appreciate it." He gave his wife, Corinne, a wink before he sat down.

Angela agreed to the errands and made her way back to her rooms to change into something a little nicer for her visit to town. She rifled through her many dresses, most sewn by Marie next door and realized how many didn't fit the same as the year before. Angela sorted through the old and new ones that fit. Knowing somehow she needed to get things sorted out for packing purposes.

She was dressed and ready in a few minutes. She grabbed a simple bonnet and tied it around her chin.

Corinne and Lucas were putting on their coats when Angela made it back to the dining room table. Dolly had joined the party and it was announced that she was going to tag along with Angela. Angela was more than pleased.

Angela Fahey walked down Main Street in Oregon City with her friend Dolly at her side. Angela's mind was a jumble of thoughts, timetables and to-do lists.

They must have both been lost in thought because neither had said a word since they left the post office. Angela stepped around an impediment and warned her friend Dolly of the horse droppings that were threatening the path.

Angela and Dolly had decided early in their morning errands to buy some fresh fish near the waterfalls. Usually Saturday was a good day to check with the fishermen upstream, the local tribe was small but very skilled at catching the river fish.

Her friend Dolly was a good companion, a very quiet but wise girl. They were the same age and though Dolly was half- Hopi Indian they had several important things in common.

They were both orphans and they both had found a new start here in Oregon City with a circle of friends that were now considered family. They both rejoiced in belonging to people again. It was so much better than dwelling on how much they had lost. Dolly made a habit of surprising her friends by speaking profound words but staying silent, otherwise.

The two girls absorbed the day, peeking into the windows of shops, pointing at the things to be seen on Main Street.

They neared the courthouse and Millicent Quackenbush was seen in a burgundy dress and a long black coat. She had an average, motherly figure that was cinched tight with a corset. Her medium brown hair was curled stylishly. Angela assumed that Mrs. Q. had been to a church meeting. She was well known for her active service with every woman's club that the town church had. The town was a small one with only a few hundred people at the last count but since it was a more rural farm community the population of women was higher than other parts of the West. She wondered if the ladies of her own church, Spring Creek Fellowship, would be starting their own women's groups as the attendance grew.

Angela put on a polite smile as Millie came closer.

"Good morning, Mrs. Quackenbush." Angela said and Dolly repeated it.

"Good morning gals." Millie said and wore a smile that neither of the girls had seen. It seemed genuinely happy. They had seen her in many moods but this joyous expression had been held back.

"How is business in town, ma'am?" Dolly asked with a returning smile.

"Good for this time of year. People preparing for the winter snows. I am looking forward to the solitude that the snows bring. I have a lot of sewing to do this year. My grandson Silas is growing so big, I want to make him plenty of shirts and pants..." She sighed in her obvious delight.

Angela grinned as she had played a big role in the delivery of Silas Quackenbush the year before when she stayed with them in San Francisco. She had hopes for a visit to Portland in the spring to see Silas and his mother, Amber.

"How are they fairing in Portland, I only received word when they first arrived?" Angela sincerely wanted to know how the young couple was doing after their move from California to Portland.

Millie filled her in on the state of the fancy goods store and how fast Silas could run and all the little things a grandmother would be pleased with. "Amber is pushed to her limits trying to keep up with that boy. But he is a Quackenbush after all, trying to stop those young men from anything is nigh impossible."

Angela and Dolly both laughed and enjoyed hearing the funnier side of Millie Quackenbush.

After several minutes of sharing, Millie made her pardons and announced she had to get back to the store. Angela was happy to have a good visit under her belt with one of the town's more difficult members. Angela was working hard to become a solid member of this community and making friends would do a lot to help that.

Angela and Dolly made their way to the fish cart up the road. They both purchased a bag full of salmon and headed back toward the Hudson Bay store. Clive Quackenbush had promised them a ride back to Grant's Grove, a farm just outside of town.

Clive Quackenbush had the wagon ready and waiting in front of the store and he was reading a newspaper, sitting on the bench out front.

"Greetings Clive!" Angela said. "You should go upstream today and get the fresh salmon. They look wonderful." Angela saw his dark eyebrows perk up at the mention.

"You do know that I love some of that smoked salmon. Might have to make me a fresh smoker." Clive made a silly face to get the young women to laugh. It always worked.

"You be careful of going too far into the woods and smoking those fish, you will draw bears." Dolly said to tease. Clive folded the newspaper and sat it on the wagon seat.

"Oh, perhaps just a few black bears, they are no match for me. I am like young David from the bible and wrestle bears fer a hobby." Clive took on his best bear-wrestling stance.

John Pritchlan, a barrel chested man with a full brown beard, happened to walk by and laughed at Clive's wrestling pose.

"You meaning to attack those young ladies there, Clive? I thought your grandmother was a Quaker." John chuckled and stopped walking to join in the fun.

"Well, my grandmother went to a few meetings but she was too cantankerous to join." Clive's laughter rumbled in his chest. "I was just showing them how I wrestle with black bears. But only if they try to steal my salmon."

"There is a man across the river near Portland known for catching black bears and keeping them chained in front of his house. No lie." John Pritchlan shared.

"No kidding, hmmm. Makes ya wonder about folks. Oh yes… I never did get to congratulate you on your governorship. Should I bow, or just call you 'your majesty'?" Clive bowed and John smacked him with his hat across the top of his bowed shoulders.

"You knock that off. I have no intentions, like some around here, of making Oregon a country of its own. I will be getting papers off to the capitol to encourage the U.S. Congress and Senate to declare us a state." John tucked his hands into his pockets and he leaned back, seemingly proud of what he was trying to do.

"You keep up the good work, John, glad the folks got a good man for Oregon." Clive was sincere.

Clive gave a quick introduction of Angela and Dolly and they both shook his hand and congratulated him on his political win. People had been talking about him quite a bit in the last year and it was good to put a name with the face.

"You must be Miss Fahey." Mr. Pritchlan smiled and shook her hand. "My wife and I are members of the church in town and we heard about you being in San Francisco last year. We were praying for you and your brother."

Angela nodded and smiled. "I appreciate that sir, I mean Governor Pritchlan."

He waved off the formality. "I heard through the grapevine that you were able to reunite with your brother. What a blessing!" His smile was wide and sincere.

Angela pulled her smile out and hid all her true emotions about the family reunion with her brother. She had only told her dearest friends how the reunion had really gone. She was glad somehow that in town it was known as a pleasant event. It made it easier to her to pretend for now.

"Thank you so much." Angela smiled at the sentiment.

"I heard you have been building a fine house out on Spring Creek road."

"Yessir, I am anxious for it to be done. I came to town today to take my mind off the building. It only worked a little." Angela let some of her anxiety go about the mention of her brother and focused instead on her new home. It was a bright and shiny thought to ponder. "I do hope to be moving in soon. We shan't be able to paint the outside until the spring though."

"Do you know the colors yet?" Mr. Pritchlan was very friendly.

"I have seen many colors when I lived in Boston, I am still thinking on what would work best." Angela said with a twinkle in her eye.

"If you ever need a hand please do not hesitate. I do love house painting. There is something peaceful about it. I am sure my wife would be glad to drop by and plan for you a house warming party when you are settled in. Please be sure to send us notice. After praying for you so many months we feel we know ya."

"Yes sir, I will." Angela watched John tip his hat in farewell and head off on foot toward his destination. Clive chirped out a farewell and the new governor turned and gave a quick wave.

The two young women were scooted into the wagon and Clive grabbed the reins. He was concerned about a patch of rain that was threatening the peaceful fall day.

Grant's Grove was busy with late harvest activities. Lucas Grant was pulling dead logs off a wagon. Angela and Dolly went quickly inside to see if Corinne and Violet needed anything. Clive stayed behind to talk with Lucas.

———◆·◉·◆———◆———◆·◉·◆———

"Have you heard from Ted since the telegram?" Violet asked Angela when she joined the group at the dining table?

"No, but I expect to soon. It has been a few months and more steamships are coming every day. Bringing goods and news. I am filled with excitement. I sent him a few letters myself. But I must say I have been a coward." Angela looked down at her hands.

"Angela, you are never a coward. Truly you are being harsh upon yourself." Corinne said. She was a loyal friend who saw the best in Angela, always.

"Well, in this way I have been. I still have not shared that I got the deed for the land and that I am building a house. Ted may be very shocked by my actions. I hope he doesn't lose interest. I feel a bit selfish, by not telling him. What if my plans go against his own wishes for the future?" Angela's cheeks were pink from her own embarrassment.

"This has been bothering you a while hasn't it?" Violet asked.

"Yes, I feel like I have failed Ted. I made this life changing decision without him. We made no commitments but he did promise to come back for me." Angela was spilling all her fears out for her trusted friends to help her. She knew they would be honest and give her their true opinions. It would do nothing to fully ease her fears until Ted did indeed had come back.

"All you can do is wait and pray. You did nothing out of malice. I am sure he will see that." Corinne offered and took her hand as a comforting friend. "You will have time to pray on how to handle it. Would you change anything today if you could, give the land back and tear down the house?"

"No, I believe I would do it all over again." Angela said and nodded, knowing that she wanted her dream. She would just pray that Ted's dream could fit in with hers. "Thank you for letting me spill my thoughts. I will let it go for now. I have so much to do for the next few weeks. I will think on the future, and not buy trouble that is not here."

Angela ate lunch at Grant's Grove but wanted to leave before the afternoon was gone. She wanted to have a brief word with Dolly before she left though. A thought had been pressing on her for weeks and she wanted to talk to her quiet friend.

Their conversation was brief but meaningful. Angela left with a weight off of her shoulders. She had said what she felt led to say. It was in Dolly's hands now. She said a cheerful goodbye and headed on a walk to her home in progress. She knew the builders were putting in the floors and staircase today. She wanted to see her home take shape.

The new vicarage was a fine new cabin, settled a bit off the Spring Creek road. Spring Creek itself was near enough so to hear the water trickle by when the windows were open for the breeze. The farming community had worked hard this year to make the church and pastor's home a place to be proud of. Everyone knew that their church wasn't the fanciest but it was well-loved.

Violet made a habit of walking over and helping the pastor's wife whenever she could.

"Dear Violet, I appreciate the visit and the help on the children's clothing. You are such a blessing." Helen Whittlan was generous in every part of her life, especially in her gratitude.

Violet felt she owed this woman so much after taking her in when she was almost fifteen. She knew that they had been poor and struggling to make enough with their tiny congregation. Moneys in the offering plate had been small back then. Only a few farmers came every week. There was barely a usable road to get to the tiny cabin that served as the school and the church for the farm valley community.

"You know that I love coming and helping out and I'll be over again in a few days. I have a few new recipes to try this week." Violet said and was rewarded with a warm grin from Helen. Some women as they aged, they looked sour or mean. Helen had pretty cheeks and her smile was still as delightful as a baby's laugh. Violet secretly hoped that she could look so pretty and friendly as she got older.

"My darling Darrell and I will gobble up any recipe you wish us to try, my dear." Helen rinsed her small hands in the washbasin and wiped them off with her soft apron. "I have never seen anyone with a better natural gift for baking."

Violet's cheek warmed at the compliment and she wordlessly shrugged into her wool coat. Before she reached the door Helen stopped her.

"Eddie?" Helen asked the complicated question with just one word. Violet felt the start, the stop of all the pleasant and warm feelings and shook her head in the negative.

"Still on my knees praying every day." Helen said with a hint of moisture glinting in her dark eyes. She genuinely cared and Violet felt that caring deep within her. It helped her deal with the daily disappointment.

"I know you do. Thank you Helen." Violet was able to say before she left the parsonage. Violet pulled herself together in just those few seconds.

The air was brisk and Violet wanted to walk the half-mile back to Grant's Grove in record time. She kept her thoughts busy but the reminder of her husband snuck back in as she climbed over a rock and a small fallen tree to get to the footbridge over the creek. Eddie's huge smile was all she could see in her mind.

"He will come back to me." Violet said out loud as her heeled shoes clacked across the boards of the footbridge. It was only a few feet wide, built by Lucas and Russell Grant, so she tried to keep her eyes on her feet. A tumble into the cold creek was not on her agenda for the day.

"Lord, help me focus on doing your work, instead of my loneliness." Violet prayed sincerely. She had to admit to herself that a part of her ached for her husband, and another part of her was thrilled with her new life. She just knew that having Eddie back would make everything perfect. Some days she didn't handle her thoughts as well, her patience battle would be lost. She would cry and ask God why Eddie had left. But today her heart was peaceful. She felt a calm assurance that God had control of her life and she could wait.

The distraction came like a bolt of lightning, the thought of God's work in the prayer she muttered just a moment before bloomed into something. She had thought of it several times in the last few weeks, now she felt that inner knowing. She may be a simple girl, in some eyes, just a housekeeper or a bread baker, but suddenly she had some work to do and she knew the inspiration came from God.

The hooves of Clover pounded into the earth as Dolly rode. Her heartbeat matched the rhythm of the hooves as she cantered around the property. The Harpole's ranch house was behind her and the open fields lay ahead. Dolly could see the hint of yellow in the sky but the sun was hiding behind a western mountain ridge. She wore men's riding pants under her dress and her skirts were gathered around her saddle in a most unladylike manner. She did care how people thought of her, but she didn't want to ride sidesaddle. It was a waste of a ride in her opinion. She had never said it aloud, though. She was reserved in sharing her voice with anyone.

She would not call herself shy. But she rarely spoke unless she felt it was important. It was just her way. She had memories of her mother being quite talkative, so she knew that she did not get her quiet ways from her. *Perhaps my father was introverted.* She wondered.

She allowed the horse to slow to a walk and turned back toward Grant's Grove, she needed to get the horse back into the barn and then walk over to Chelsea Grant's home.

It was only a mile to the east from her workplace at the laboratory and greenhouse. She was becoming skilled at distilling medicinal oils from plants. She loved the work with the large copper alembic pots and the plants. It was fascinating to her, learning the science and then participating.

She had taken the ride to think. She had been invited to live with her friend, Angela Fahey, in her new house. She had said that she would gladly 'stay' with her. But she had not hinted at anything more permanent than the word 'stay' could suggest. She knew she was struggling with the idea of a home. Her new life in Oregon had allowed her to see a different way of living; a settled existence that grew roots and did not move about. In Dolly's mind it represented a solid lifestyle. Like an old tree that was rooted and part of the landscape. It was her favorite part about her new life. Yet, she, herself, did not join in. She was still anchored in her nomadic ways. Like her old tribe, who moved with the seasons, for food, water or harvesting the bounty of nature for the good of the Shoshone tribe.

Now here in the 'white-man's world' she still flitted from home to home. The Harpole Ranch with Marie and John and their young son, Cooper. He was an excellent young fisherman and adventurer.

She also stayed with her employer often, though Corinne Grant was much more than an employer, she was a dear friend and sister in Christ. A mile east of Grant's Grove was Russell, Lucas's brother, and his wife Chelsea. Dolly had a deep connection with Chelsea who had been the one to spend so much time teaching her English and sharing her faith with Dolly. It was never in a pushy way, but always there to answer questions, and Dolly always had many. Chelsea was the first to help her open up and talk. It was a rarity for Dolly and it always felt like she was imposing somehow. She knew that the way she had been treated by certain tribe members growing up, had been because her mother had married a white man.

She felt a sense of obligation to her former tribe. But now she felt a deeper sense of belonging with her new community. It was a hard situation to face. Many days she decided to push the thoughts of her old way of life to the deepest parts of her mind. Hoping to ignore it for as long as possible.

She would think more on what Angela had offered. It was a hard decision for her. She just didn't know why.

Chapter Two

November 1850
Dolly

"This blue muslin looks so lovely on you." Chelsea Grant stated to Dolly as she watched the young woman swirl around. They were in Chelsea Grant's roomy parlor. Chelsea had just finished sewing the final pieces on a dress for her friend. The fireplace was crackling with a cozy fire. It was still early in the morning, the sky just lighting up the windows with the yellow sunrise.

"I still wonder how people feel when they see me in white women's clothes." Dolly said with concern. "A young man called me a half-breed in town a few days ago." Dolly shared and grew quiet, examining her feelings about the encounter.

"Well, that's just foolish." Chelsea tried to downplay it but knew that some people were very sensitive about their skin color. Chelsea could never understand why some people just had to be hateful. "You may look a little different. But I know how beautiful and special you are." Chelsea saw Dolly smile. "It could be because of that hanging a few months ago in town. It was a big ruckus and the sheriff dealt a quick decision. Those three Comanche Indians were found guilty of killing that farmer, his wife and their child. It just doesn't settle right with me that the law in this town is one man. Sheriff Tudor is the law, the judge and jury. I know he is doing his best but I do miss a certain sense of civility of the justice system." Chelsea shook her head with determination not to think about the rumors that had been flying around during the weeks surrounding the arrest of those men. She would not even go into town while the hanged men were on display for days. "I know some people group everyone together. Some people may treat you badly and I am sorry for that." Chelsea said sincerely.

"My tribe in the mountains could be like that too. Clive was a trusted white man to the chief but many warriors of the tribe distrusted him and my father for their skin color. I think every culture may hold those feelings." Dolly said with a frown.

"You have seen so much for such a young lady, Dolly." Chelsea said.

"I know that I am lost between two worlds. I have settled into a new life that I love." Dolly's brown eyes lit up with some thought that Chelsea couldn't know. "If I could stay in Oregon forever, I would." Dolly nodded in confirmation of her statement.

"Isn't the choice yours?" Chelsea asked her. Her baby Sarah was in the other room beginning to wake up, by the murmuring sounds.

"It is complicated." Dolly said. "You go get Sarah. I need to go to work. Thank you for letting me stay. I will change into my warmer dress. This one will be lovely for church sometime." Dolly gave Chelsea a quick hug.

"We can talk more another day." Chelsea said as she was walking away.

Dolly gladly would discuss with her friend all that was on her heart. She was full of confusion and questions.

Dolly made her way to the spare bedroom where she sometimes stayed like the previous two nights. She changed into the green plaid flannel dress and pulled on the thick wool tights and warm ladies boots. The walk to her workplace would take her a little while. The wind was starting to have that smell of winter. Her black wool coat was pulled around her.

* * *

Dolly squinted at the sun as it came over the eastern mountains. Her thoughts settled lately on the tribe she left behind. They would be returning for her within the year, probably in the spring. She was seventeen summers old and according to the Shoshone tribe, she was of marriageable age. With her half-white status in the tribe she knew it would be difficult to find a good mate and she was certain within herself that she wanted none of that. Some people found her skills very valuable. It was the main reason why she had been sent to study under Corinne Grant in the first place. But her understanding of plants and skills were only one facet of how she saw herself.

Her hands knew so many things now too, such as, gathering berries, and spearing a fish. She could climb a tree, gather nuts and chase out game for the boys to shoot at with their hand-made bows. She could skin just about any creature set dead in front of her. Her aversion to the sticky blood and innards she had willed away when she little. She could gather

18

the reeds and weave a basket tight enough to hold water. Though she had always avoided using her teeth to pull. One of her favorite memories was her mother's laughter over basket and leather braiding, she had more pride in her straight teeth than her tight weaving.

Lately Dolly's drawing and beadwork had really improved. It was something she enjoyed and wanted to build upon.

She had her mother's eyes. But she had been told her face was different from the Hopi tribe from where her mother came. Her mother reminded her often when she was young that she had her father's face. He was a French trapper, who traded often with the Shoshone who had rescued her mother. They were allowed to marry as her mother had been held captive in an enemy camp and treated poorly. The men of the Shoshone tribe would take care of anyone in their tribe, but a damaged woman was not the ideal wife.

Dolly wondered now at her own dilemma. *Who were her people now?* When she left the tribe she had longed to branch out of her confines in the tribe. The roles of men and women set in seasons and their beliefs were non-shifting. There had been missionaries nearby that spoke of the one God and her mother had spoken about it too. She had passed on some of the stories her father shared with her. It had intrigued her as a child.

Since coming to Oregon and staying first with the Russell and Chelsea Grant and now Corinne and Lucas, she had learned and accepted the one God of the Bible. To her, the beliefs of her childhood and the ones that were just building inside her were confusing when put together. Her choices about where to stay and live would define who her people were. She had been accepted openly by this new family in Oregon. They taught her honestly and were always interested in what she had learned. It felt good to be accepted that way. But she had grown up with warnings about the white ways, their diseases and their guns. It seemed her reality was at odds with how she was taught.

How would she react when the chief sent for her? He would probably send her a husband. Should she go or send him and the Shoshone messengers back with a goodbye after they had raised her? Her mother and father both long gone, the tribe had fed, clothed and taught her like their own children. It was hard to think on. Her mind wanted to worry, her heart told her to try to pray, but the confusion over the one God was mixed up in all of these decisions. If she went back would she then also set aside this budding hope in something... more?

Who am I? Dolly asked herself. "Am I Bluebird of the Shoshone, or Dolly, a child of the one God?" She said out loud in a harsh whisper. No answers came but she sat in the quiet morning sitting on a stump, taking deep breaths and listening to the morning sounds.

She had been pondering something lately. A white tradition was to have a last name. To take on a father's surname. She remembered from her mother's stories that her father's name was Joseph Bouchard.

If she wanted, she could take on the name, Dolly Bluebird Bouchard. To honor her mother, and her father, even if she had never really known him. She had told her friend Angela, who also had lost her parents, about her contemplation of taken on her father's name. Angela had been very encouraging. She was near Angela's house and had thought of going to visit with her before she began her workday with her employer and mentor, Corinne Grant. The lab was busy after the harvest season. There was a barn full of harvested lavender flowers, it was Dolly and a few others who would do the work of boiling the flower in water to secrete the oil from it. Dolly loved her work with Corinne and they were talking of writing a book together about herbal remedies. There was so much here for her to cling to, Dolly thought. She was having a hard time thinking about any good reasons to return to the Wind River Mountains; where the Shoshone expected her back, sometime soon.

Chapter Three

November 1850
Angela Fahey

Her farmhouse was nearly completed. The house was bigger than she needed but it mattered little to her. The roof had been on for a few weeks and the wooden floors for the second level were put in just a few days ago. She had hired the local carpenter in town, Amos Drays, to build her staircase and two built-in corner cabinets. The cabinets had been an idea that sprung from a memory, of the house she had lived in with her family, such a short time in Boston. She could see in her mind's eye the cabinets, with decorated filigrees carved into the top and pretty dishes nestled within, they had glass doors on the lower portion, and the upper portion had pretty crystal stemware and a few pretty vases.

Two days ago while at the mercantile, Clive had pointed out a shipment that had come in. There were several bags of tulip bulbs that had arrived from the East. He said that most had gone to Portland for Amber and Gabe's new fancy goods store, but he had a few sent here. He knew of a few ladies who wouldn't mind some fancy tulips for their yards in the spring. She had snatched them up and written down the instructions on how to plant them properly. She set aside four of the tulip bulbs for a separate purpose. She would stop for that errand later in the day, but her morning plan was to plant these bulbs.

She wasn't fully moved into her home but she wanted to be soon. The fireplaces were the main issue. She had three of them and all three were not finished. She was promised that as soon as the order for more bricks was in the building of the fireplaces would resume.

As Angela dressed in her dark wool coat she wore for her outdoor duties, she realized the chill of the autumn day. She would not be able to be comfortable in her new home until she had heat. She knew Corinne had already left for the day to work in her lab. Her friend was busy keeping her oils brewing. However it worked Angela was always impressed. Corinne Grant inspired her every day. She was a woman who took pride in creating something that helped people.

Lucas and Russell were working on a project as Angela walked from the Grant property to her own. Last night, Lucas Grant had shown her and Corinne his plans. They had been reading about wind power and the ability to use it to gather water somehow. Lucas was always excited about irrigation and using his college agricultural knowledge to make things better not only for his farm but for a lot of farmers in the area.

She walked along Spring Creek, happy that the church she attended finally got its own building, next to the small farmhouse school and new parsonage cabin. Spring Creek Fellowship was on the sign.

On the other side of the valley there was Beaver Creek that fed into a small lake. With nearby Portland talking seriously about petitioning for statehood the county lines were being discussed in town. Angela felt proud to be part of this growing community. Her and her friends lived outside the city but close enough to get there if they needed supplies.

Angela waved to Russell and Lucas Grant and they waved back before they returned to their scheme. Angela smiled and blew on her hands to warm them as she walked. It was over a quarter mile from the Grant property to hers. On the west side of Spring Creek was Lucas and Corinne's land, on the east the property line split and all of Angela's land lay to the east. There was a nice hill were her farmhouse sat, safe from flooding, and gave her a nice view of the land. She could see Grant's Grove from her front porch. She could also see the large barn of the Harpole Ranch just beyond Corinne's large cabin. The greenhouse was closer to Angela's property and with its glass ceiling it gleamed whenever the sun shined.

There was an existing cabin on her property that was toward the eastern edge of the property, her land manager Earl had taken it on and cleaned it out from the previous landowner. It was closer to the road that ran along her property line. The Harpole ranch ran along the other side. John Harpole, Corinne's father, had built a tall white fence that looked fine along the road. He had some small growing pines that would make a lovely wind break someday. She had helped over the summer months with Cooper Harpole, now nine years old, with painting some of that fence. John Harpole was teaching his son the pride of taking care of the property. Cooper and Angela had a special bond, and a few secret fishing holes they shared together.

Once Angela finally reached her home she went inside and grabbed her work gloves and the bag of tulips, along with the spade and shovel she had purchased this week. The inside of her home was nothing to brag over yet. There were building materials everywhere. It was going to take a lot of work to make this place livable. Angela was trying to be patient, though. It would all come together in God's timing. She reminded herself of that often.

Once she was outside the door she saw Dolly walking up to her porch.

"Hello Angela." Dolly said. Her English was very good but she sounded rather formal. Angela knew the edges would wear off over time. Corinne informed her all the time that her Irish accent was nearly gone.

"Good morning, Dolly. You needing some company?" Angela asked. Knowing Dolly would sometimes come to her when she needed to talk.

"Yes, my mind is busy today. I need a friend to still my thoughts." Dolly said, her smile split her face when Angela gestured her to join her.

"You want to talk or do?" Angela asked. She could set aside her planting for Dolly, easily.

"Do, definitely, what are you planting?" Dolly asked. She grabbed the shovel away from Angela's full arms.

Angela explained her plan and Dolly began to dig in front of the porch.

"These are too-lips?" Dolly asked, not sure she knew exactly what she was saying.

"A spring bulb. You plant in the fall and they bloom in the spring. I doubt they have any medicinal purpose but they are beautiful and colorful. Clive had a shipment from New York." Angela said. At the mention of New York it made her think of Ted Greaves. Could she call him her beaux? His family was from upstate New York.

"I have heard of people having beautiful flower gardens, Chelsea told me how people took great pride in them." Dolly nodded and smiled. Her eyes grew wide as she took in the house and land around her. "Your house is so lovely."

"Have you decided if you want to stay with me?" Angela asked, hoping that Dolly indeed would come.

"Yes, I will." Dolly declared simply.

The two young women continued with their digging and Angela explained how Clive had told her to plant them. They had half the bulbs planted into the cold earth when Dolly finally started talking.

"I have decided to use my father's name." Dolly said, not looking up from the earth she was maneuvering around the bulb.

"That is good, so Dolly... Bouchard" Angela remembered.

"Dolly Bluebird Bouchard..." Dolly looked up with a radiant smile. Angela sat up and smiled back.

Dolly was not one that got emotional but Angela saw some misty tears in Dolly's eyes.

"My mother gave me the name Bluebird, and my father gave me the name Bouchard."

Angela reached over and patted her friend's shoulder. She didn't want to chase the girl away with too much affection but she wanted her to know she was there for her.

"I think that is beautiful." Angela finally shared through the emotions stuck in her own throat. Somehow knowing Dolly was accepting her father's name was profound to her. She knew she couldn't explain why.

They had the bulbs planted quickly and Dolly rushed off to get to her job before the watch-pin said nine a.m. Angela waved her off with a smile. She had a small bundle of bulbs she wanted to take over to the church. She would walk over to the Grant's and see if she could borrow the one-horse buggy. She pulled the small notebook from the pocket within her skirts along with the pencil.

She wrote out 'one horse and buggy'. Her list was growing but she knew that she could afford it. She had gone over and over her accounts and she knew that she would be fine for several years until she started making money off the trees, and her pet project with Clive in San Francisco. Her inheritance had made her feel independent. She knew such gratitude in her heart for what her friend Corinne had done, contacting that lawyer in Boston and getting not only the money from her family estate but also the treasured mementos in her family trunk. It was still tucked away safely at Corinne's house in the bedroom she had been living in. But soon, in her new home she would bring the treasures out. Her heart was full of hopes and dreams of a full house and lots of love.

Angela saw Corinne inside her glass greenhouse. Angela's closest friend was blurry through the steamy glass but Angela knew her dearest friend because of the dark blue dress she wore.

The door of the greenhouse let out a burst of warm and moist air.

"Angie, come here." Corinne stated and waved animatedly. "Today is a big day. Experimenting with a few trees for you. These almonds are from the Ukraine territory in Russia. The shell is thick and will hopefully withstand the harshest climate. Since you needed to be able to break ground first, Lucas and I thought to help you out, we would get started on some saplings for you. Next fall you can plant them if they can handle the weather. This will be an experiment of course. But we are so happy that you are joining in this adventure with us."

Angela saw the bag of seeds, the almonds all had a beige dimpled coating.

"We soaked twenty last night and have placed several in each pot. Not all of them will germinate. If more than one does we will keep an eye on them. We will be soaking more tonight. We hope to be able to have at least twenty trees for you to get started. If these are a good hardy batch then we will continue. It is a risk, some people said, that Oregon is too harsh for almonds. But one of my Boston greenhouse friends told me about a seed vendor in the Ukraine territory." Corinne was in good spirits and spoke lovingly about her plants. Her business had two parts; one part was about growing the plants themselves and the other about extracting the medicinal benefits. Angela loved the greenhouse with the brightness and warmth, but the lab was a little scarier. There were big caldrons and glass tubes and lots of contraptions. Corinne had herself a medicinal enterprise. Angela was so very proud of all her friend had accomplished.

Angela knew her farm was going to contribute. The almonds sprouts would grow and eventually bear almonds for Corinne to buy and produce almond oil.

Corinne dug into a pot with her leather-gloved hands and tended to another few almond seeds. These looked like they had been soaked. Corinne spoke lovingly to the little seeds, like talking to a child.

It reminded Angela about Corinne's lost pregnancy last spring. She was praying for her friend Cori and Lucas to have another chance. Seeing Corinne with a child was the next best thing to having a child of her own.

Someday… she reminded herself. *All in God's good timing.*

"I will need to know how much for the saplings next year. We will run this like a professional business." Angela said seriously once she had given it a moment's thought.

Corinne harrumphed.

"Not sure if that is a reasonable request my friend. This is an experiment to see if the trees can handle this environment." Corinne stated.

"Well, then let me cover the cost of the seeds." Angela said with a stubborn grin, enjoying the playful banter with her friend.

"Fine, give me one dollar, smarty pants." Corinne rolled her eyes.

"I will." Angela said with a laugh and satisfied tone.

"You are a little bit obnoxious." Corinne stated, she was smacking the dirt from her gloves.

"As are you, my sister-friend." Angela grabbed Corinne around the shoulders in a sideways hug.

"I need to borrow the small buggy if possible, and the horse." Angela asked.

"Of course, I have no need for it today." Corinne nodded. They took a walk to the barn together. Lucas and Russell were there as well as a stable hand, a new man Lucas had hired to care to the horses. Lucas wanted to focus more on the crops and breaking land than the maintenance of the barn. The stable hand was a lad of sixteen. Corinne thought his name was Barney, or something with a 'b'.

Corinne strode up to her husband and asked him a question in his ear. Lucas laughed and whispered back.

"Brandon," Corinne said with a secret smile then stepped away from her husband and waved to get the boy's attention away from mucking out the stall. "I would appreciate it greatly if you could get the buggy and Clover hitched up." Corinne smiled at herself for forgetting the lad's name again. "Thank you!" She called out as an after thought. Her brain was so busy with all the things she wanted to get done. She did not want to come across as rude to anyone. No one deserved that, even if she was distracted.

"Thanks Corinne, I am going to town after a quick trip to visit the church. I have some left over tulip bulbs I saved for Helen Whittlan." Angela smiled at the thought of being generous to that kind woman. The pastor and his wife of the Spring Creek Fellowship Church were the sweetest and most generous people. They had the habit of taking in orphan children and were such open and giving souls. Angela was feeling more and more a part of the church community and this was one way she could give something nice to someone who deserved it.

"That is a wonderful surprise." Corinne said sincerely. It gave her an idea to perhaps think of some other plants to help the church out come springtime.

"Also, since my barn isn't complete yet, would I be able to rent some space in your barn until mine is finished? I am promised to have my own barn space available within the week." Angela asked. Her head was bursting with ideas. There was so much to do.

"That isn't a problem. No rent necessary. Just put any funds you would into the offering plate." Corinne said and stuck her tongue out at her friend. They had a playful banter that made both of them feisty. Angela laughed and gave Corinne a pretend slug in the arm.

Corinne and Angela hugged each other and once the buggy was pulled around Angela gave a tip to the stable lad. She had heard that his father was away and his family was in need. He was the breadwinner of the family now. Brandon didn't look a day over fourteen.

"I will check for mail while I am in town. Going shopping for a horse and buggy myself today. As well as a few odds and ends." Angela waved to everyone and was off. Lucas had taken the time to teach her how to handle the reins and she had been out in it enough times by herself that she no longer felt nervous driving. She was glad for the warm bonnet as the cold wind whipped around her as she headed the mile to the church on the other side of the creek. It always made her nerves jump though when she had to roll through the water of the creek to cross it. In the creek the mud was sometimes thick. Russell and Lucas were planning a stone bridge to be built. All the farmers who lived on the road had agreed that it would make traveling to town a lot easier. This spring was going to be a busy one. Angela liked the idea of a quaint stone bridge. It would be near enough to her house she would be able to see it from her from porch.

Angela's nose was cold from her excursion but her heart was light. She felt so good doing something nice for the pastor's wife.

It was a short trip before she reached the freshly built church only a few miles up the very creek from her house. The winding dirt road was little more than a wagon track for trading routes started but Angela knew eventually with the church traffic the road would stand out more. The small cabin beside the church had smoke curling up from the chimney. She thought that at least one person was home. Angela parked the buggy in front of the church and tied the horse to the hitching post.

Helen Whittlan answered the door. She had flour on her apron and Angela grinned and smelled the remnants of breakfast wafting through the door.

"I just came to give you a small gift, I don't mean to interrupt anything." Angela said with a generous smile.

"Get yourself in, even for just a minute. No interruption, really. Just got the bread dough in a bowl, proofing on the countertop." Helen smacked her hands together sending flour dust spraying.

27

"Good plan, looking forward to having my own kitchen soon." Angela said, dreaming ahead to domestic bliss in her mind.

"You be sure to get together with Violet for bread starter. Her sourdough is better than anything I have ever come up with. Been teaching the youngins I have staying with us now about how to bake. One of these days I will have a proper lesson from Violet for them." Helen said emphatically. "They are both over at the schoolhouse. So glad we finally have a separate building for church services. But the schoolhouse was a good blessing for its time and place."

Helen was so practical. Angela enjoyed watching Helen move around her small kitchen with purpose. Angela offered to help but was shushed away with a big friendly smile from the pastor's wife.

"You are so good taking in orphans, you know that I am an orphan? I was sent off to a work orphanage before I had turned eight years old." Angela said, thinking back wasn't as painful now. She was just glad to see good people taking care of children out of the goodness of their hearts.

"Yes, I remember Corinne talking about it. She had struggled with waiting for you to travel the Oregon Trail and then again while you were off in California territory. We had many talks and prayers over you. Still keeping you in my prayers, child." Helen shared and gave a loving look to Angela, almost as a mother would. It warmed Angela's heart. This church family was such a blessing to her wounded heart.

"Knowing folks like you are taking in orphans, like you did for Violet, and now Diana and Lisa." Angela said.

For a moment Helen looked bewildered. "Violet isn't.." She stopped and paused. "Well, my husband and I try to do the Lord's bidding to the best of our abilities. He has always allowed for us to help those in need. I am always wishing to do more. Cannot help my heart." Helen finished.

Angela was curious about how Helen sounded at first but she didn't want to pry. Instead she asked about the pastor.

"Oh he is off felling timber with a parishioner. He works during the week. Our church is a bit small to have that be his only income. But with my egg money and his hard work we are setting aside money for the future. He is just past fifty and a hard worker. We just trust in the Lord to provide." Helen said with a grin. Her light brown hair held very little grey but the soft laugh lines around her smile showed her age a little.

"Well, he is an amazing preacher and will I pray you all will continue to be blessed, as you have blessed our community." Angela said sincerely.

28

"Speaking of blessings. I have brought you a small gift. It is nothing much really. But I hope you would enjoy it."

Angela handed over the bag of leftover bulbs of tulips.

"Clive said when he sold 'em to me that he doesn't know what color they will be but there is still time to get them into the ground. I planted mine this morning. The frost made getting them into the ground a little tricky but I finally got the bulbs planted."

Helen Whittlan made a fuss over the gift and Angela gave the woman a hug before she was off to town for her errands. She had lots to do today.

To get to town she had a few miles to travel and the road was bouncy in the buggy. She had a strap around her waist to keep her in the buggy seat. She was glad again for the warm bonnet. The wind was quite chilly when she got any kind of speed going. A few of the bumps along the wagon road bumped her right off the seat and she landed back down hard. She laughed at herself when she let out a gasp of surprise once or twice.

On the main road through town Angela weaved through the muddy areas. She had seen the roads worse but she did sometimes miss the pretty brick or cobblestone streets of Boston. It made for a fancier street when they were covered but she was part of a growing small town now. Her city girl ideas needed to settle back down into the realistic.

She stopped by the livery first. She asked a few questions about horses and buggies and got a few estimates. She would also be stopping by the Hudson Bay store to ask a few questions there. Either Clive or his son J.Q. would be able to tell her if the livery's offer for horse and buggy was a good one. Anyone related to Clive Quackenbush was trustworthy in her book. He was like a grandfather to her and had seen her through many trials in the last few years. His son Jedediah ran the store most days, but Clive took over sometimes. His office where he ran all his enterprises was located there. He had more than five Hudson Bay stores that Angela knew about, and now a fancy goods store in Portland. He was talking the other day about the town of Salem needing some trade goods. That man was always keeping his hands busy.

The post office was bustling with a line of several people waiting in the small space. There was a counter and the thin man at the counter was unknown to Angela. The newspaper had mentioned a new postmaster. She couldn't recall his name. He seemed out of place with a lot of men in this town. The thick shouldered rugged men of this town were plentiful, but she knew that as postmaster this man, even slight of build, would get his due respect.

We all want to communicate with the outside world. She thought to herself.

It was a few minutes wait. She politely conversed with the woman in front of her about the weather. 'When would the winter snows come?' Was on the minds of everyone.

It was finally her turn at the counter. She told her name, the Grants, the Harpoles and Violet Griffin to the postmaster. He shuffled through several boxes and was in the back room for a few minutes.

He came back with a bulging stack.

"My goodness!" Angela exclaimed with a smile. She signed the log the postmaster asked of her and she was out the door with a smile. Letters were worth their weight in gold!

Angela sat on the bench outside of the post office and sorted through the pile.

There were four envelopes addressed to her, one addressed to Violet, a stack of seven to Corinne and Lucas and another stack of six to Marie and John. Angela knew she didn't have time to read through all four addressed to her but she excitedly noted that there was two in Ted's handwriting. She would take the time now to read one and then if she could find the time later she would read the other, in essence to spread out the enjoyment of hearing from him.

She knew the immediate warmth of a blush was creeping across her face but she didn't care. She held the two letters from Ted and picked the thinner of the two. *Save the longer one for later.* She really did have a lot to do today. One letter would be a perfect pick-me-up for her to finish her to-do list.

Dear Angel,

I am missing you tremendously. Praying that I am not wandering around like a buffoon these last months as I have been preparing to come to Oregon.

The apartment we are sharing at the local boarding house is barely functional for all of us. My mother and Sophie share a bed, my Aunt Olivia is on a cot in a room small enough to be a pantry without a window. When I arrived there was no place but the floor in the parlor. The davenport was too small for me to stretch out on, though I did sincerely try. It was laughable. I finally gave up and now call the floor my bed.

The correspondence from Clive has been the convincing point for all the women of my family to agree to come with me to what my mother refers too as the 'wild country'. My sister Sophie, who will be fourteen in January, is delighted. She reads everything she can about the West. She made me tell her every detail about my own trip and experiences, both the good and the bad.

Clive sent a long telegram offering a business opportunity to the women of my family. I had told them about how my Mother and her sister Olivia were both lace makers. I was honest with him how much they were truly what sustained my father's poor attempt at farming. I believe that my father would have been a better man had not his brother Hank always been distracting him with schemes.

Now that I am home I see that my sister Sophie's lace making skills are expanding as well.

Clive wants to help them settle in, he has claimed to have rented a townhouse with a storefront attached within a block to his son Jedediah Quackenbush and the general store in Oregon City. In the letter we just received from Clive he detailed his thoughts. To sell lace from the storefront in Oregon City as well as Portland and perhaps even Salem to start. Depending on how well and fast they produce the lace products they may be able to provide goods to California territory and also Washington.

My Aunt Olivia is thrilled for the chance at adventure but also for the fresh start. I think her enthusiasm was the push my mother needed to accept the change. Though it may be a difficult change for all of the women at first. Please keep them in your prayers, sweet Angel.

I walked to what used to be my father's farm today. The abandoned state was a disappointment to the highest level. The barn is infested by rodents and spiders. The house is shut up tight - the front door boarded over. Seems the bank wanted to keep out the squatters.

I feel like everything here is lost, like everything that used to be vibrant has turned to gray ash.

I think of Oregon now as you said to me, back before I had seen it, you told me how it called to you, the people, the trees and the mountains. That is what Oregon is to me now.

Not only is it a land to begin again, but the place where you are.

I have been in correspondence with some contacts of Clive's and have a few decisions to make about when and how we will get to Oregon. My heart wants to leap into leaving now, but I want the safest passage for my family. They are precious cargo and I will abide by Clive's warning to check the reputation of any ship and Captain headed west.

Praying to see you soon, for now I am holding you in my heart. To see you again is my great desire, to gaze in your dazzling eyes and clasp hold of your sweet hand would be heavenly.

Sincerely yours,

Ted Greaves

Angela smiled as she read the words. She was still wearing the silver bracelet he had given her in the spring before he left. She didn't know what the future held for them but she missed his smile and sweetness. He was handsome, kind and a good man. She thought to herself. She had this hope that he would not arrive in Oregon and be upset with her because she made plans without him.

Angela wondered about the other letter but knew she must move forward with her day.

Chapter Four

Angela Fahey

Angela met with JQ at the mercantile and got a little advice about the horse and buggy situation. He was a lot like his father, Clive, and gave her sound advice. His wife was in the store and seemed a little put out with either JQ or perhaps she was in poor health. Either way the women's color was all washed out. Angela reminded herself after she thanked both JQ and his wife for the help that she should pray for Millie.

Lord, please bless Millie. Angela prayed in her head as she walked. God knew how to help her through whatever was ailing her, Angela was certain.

There had been a slight bit of a disappointment a few months before with his wife. She had made a rude comment to Corinne, but it had been forgiven and everyone had moved on.

After Angela's errands in town she headed back to her house in progress. She wanted to be sure the brick was being delivered as promised. When she drove by her house she saw several men at work and was pleased. She dropped the horse and buggy to Corinne's barn. She knew Violet and Clive were going out soon for an errand so she skipped any visiting and went straight to her house to see what the progress was going to be for the day.

She was thinking of Ted every few seconds on a loop through her head. All the questions of whether or not he was coming now gone. He had said his mother was convinced. Knowing he was really going to come let a weight off of her mind that she hadn't realized was there. When he left her, there had been a part of her that was sure he wouldn't be back. She had prepared her heart for that. She felt foolish now for doubting.

Now to just know when. Her thoughts said, to try and shake off the negative spin her mind had taken. She needed to learn that not everyone was going to disappoint her. She should learn to trust more. She put her mind on the future and she felt a peace enter her heart.

Would he be here by the summer? Would he like the house? Would he be upset that she had gone ahead and purchased land? Would he think her foolish for trying this on her own? The questions poured out and lay unanswered inside her heart but still she couldn't help but think all these things and more.

When she got to her property she was thrilled to see the brick had arrived. The men were busy working on a fireplace. Some men were constructing scaffolding to continue the building of the fireplace as it got taller. Angela was so happy to see the forward progress.

She went inside and put the parcels and mail on the table. She would have to make the happy deliveries to her friends later. Angela saw all the work that needed to be done inside but shook off the overwhelmed feelings. She would get things done, day-by-day, first things first.

She walked to the where the barn was going to be and was very pleased to see the outside walls were up. It was about one hundred feet from the road but Earl Burgess's cabin was nearby. He said he wanted to be close so he could hear if the animals were ever in distress.

She saw Earl talking to a few men that were standing near where the barn was going to be.

"There is my foreman." Angela waved when she saw that Earl was finished discussing something with the hired builders. With so many men gone to California Angela was paying top dollar for any hired help but it was worth it to her. She knew that all these men were going to work hard to get the bonus at the end, if they kept their good attitude and did quality work.

"Yes, Miss Fahey. Glad to finally have the materials for the barn. At last we can have a barn that we can be proud of." Earl had a square jaw and a happy smile. His growth of short beard was speckled with a few gray hairs but he seemed solid and strong. Losing his left hand in that accident a few years back hadn't slowed him down. Angela was glad to have his as her foreman. He was a positive and knowledgeable asset to her farm. He had a great sense of humor and a deep laugh that rolled through his stocky frame.

"I have my cabin cleared out, the man who owned it previously had left a lot behind. Guess he just wanted out of here. I had the kitchen stove workin' this morning and made some coffee. The smell of coffee made it mine." Earl said and gave a hearty chuckle.

"You are ahead of me, sir. My stove is in the kitchen but not hooked up yet. There is a hole in the wall for the piping to go through to the outside but they need to brick in the area to set the stove. I don't want to burn through the wood flooring. I had a dream a few nights ago that a bird flew through that very hole and built a nest on my countertop." Angela said in mock despair.

"Your house will be a beautiful sight Miss Angie. You will see. I promise I will help you chase out any creatures iffen they make it inside." Earl said with a grin. Angela gave him a friendly slug to his shoulder.

"How long before the barn is ready?" Angela asked.

"Should be just a few days. The men are motivated to get the bonus if they finish this week." Earl was excited and it showed in his voice.

"Well, we will have the barn's first occupant delivered soon. For this week the horse and buggy will be stored at the Grant's until the barn is ready. I made the purchase today. John Harpole has his horses for sale in town. I got a good family price." Angela grinned a little at the thought. "I don't want to always be borrowing the buggy from the neighbors anymore." Angela said with a proud grin. He told her the horse would be good for riding too. She would have to work on her trepidations. She would be praying about it. Her issues with horses could be overcome with time.

"I have told you about my friends, Edith and Henry Sparks. I got a letter back in the fall from them and they are coming west. I am considering building a home for them on the property. They were like parents to me when I was very hurt." Angela explained how she had been delayed on the Oregon Trail.

"I am so sad to hear about your struggle darlin'." Earl said and placed a hand on her shoulder.

Angela felt awkward about talking about that time in her life.

"God finds the people we need in our lives when we are at our lowest. I understand that very well myself." Earl said and looked to the stump left from his own accident.

"I call them Mama and Papa Sparks in my letters." Angela felt her emotions rise a little in memory of how much love they had given her. "I want them to live near me if possible. Maybe it may only be for a while but the thought makes me so happy... being here for them."

Earl nodded in understanding.

"Would you think on where you would put it? A cabin... I mean." Angela clarified. "I am leaning toward being near the creek. Perhaps it could be north of my house but far enough from the creek to prevent flooding in heavy rains. I would love your input. It would be a project for the spring. This would be a cabin, not a farmhouse. I know Edith loves the look of a cabin. She also would like to have a farm stand. She loves the growing garden and then blessing others with the harvest." Angela was nervous about this idea. Hoping he wouldn't think she was foolish.

"There is a nice spot about three hundred yards up from your house by the creek. There is an elevation for the house and a nice area for a large garden. The land there is ready for ground breaking without too much work. You have a good portion of your acreage like that. We have a while before we have to clear forestation to expand your orchards." Earl pulled out a piece of paper from his pocket. As he opened it she saw a rough drawing of her plot of land. He had marked where all the buildings were and any elevations were shaded and he had small x's marking trees or groups of trees. The circles were the apple trees that were already growing. Angela was very impressed by his work already.

For the next thirty minutes Angela and Earl were in deep discussion of future plans for the land. They were both happy to be finally be seeing the fruits of their visions.

November 19th, 1850
Violet Griffen

Violet was humming as she was working in the kitchen. She was thinking about how grateful she was for her job with Corinne and Lucas Grant. It was a common practice for her. She knew people didn't always understand her but she knew why she was always trying to stay upbeat and positive about every situation. She knew from personal experience that things could be worse, terribly worse. She would never explain herself when they asked 'Why was she so chipper?' She knew some would always consider her dim-witted for her happy shrug or spiritual excuse. Her favorite sayings for everyday trials usually involved a bible verse. "This is the day the Lord hath made, we should rejoice and be glad in it," from Psalm 118, or another she used often was, "Do not be grieved for the joy of the Lord is our strength." From Nehemiah 8.

She really wasn't bothered by those that questioned her, it had been a while since she had been cornered. The place she was in was a good one.

Corinne and Lucas had accepted her. They knew her beliefs and her character without asking of her past, and for that she was grateful.

Violet checked her bread proof and it was rising nicely. She had time to check the stew over the stove. The cast iron lid was hot and heavy. It took a heavy quilted pad and a good deal of arm strength to move the lid from the large pot to the counter. She was using the pot that she usually saved for the harvest meals, when she would be cooking for many mouths. Today she was planning a little do-goodin' as Clive liked to call it. It was the inspiration she had had when she was upset about her husband Eddie being gone for so long. She was thankful for the chance to do some good instead of focusing on her own troubles.

With Corinne and Lucas's permission she was going to spend her morning doing a few deliveries. There were some poor families around town that could use a good meal. Once the potatoes in the stew were soft enough she was going to serve out thirty portions in large glass jars. She had gathered enough baskets and lined them with rag towels. Clive Quackenbush was coming by in a buggy after lunchtime and he was going to help her make deliveries.

He was the owner of the local Hudson Bay store, part of the original town council, a town pioneer, an elder at the church and a government liaison for the natives and local and federal government. He was also an amazing man with boundless energy. Even at sixty he was a firecracker. He had been instrumental in her getting the housekeeping job with the Grants. The pay was good and the employers becoming more like family every day.

The morning was flying by and the biscuits she had cut out needed baking, and the bread she baked yesterday was loaded into a linen sack. There were fifteen loaves of bread to take along with the stew.

She knew she had ten minutes before she would need to check the biscuits. She had time to check her hair in the large mirror in her rooms. The Grants had not only provided her with a room but she had her own sitting room with a fireplace and a vanity. She felt utterly spoiled. With her neighbor Marie Harpole showing up with new clothes for her every few weeks she was feeling a bit decadent. She had never owned more than two dresses at once in her life until now. Violet saw the haphazard way her hair was laying down on the back of her head and swiftly pulled the pins out. She realized too late that she hadn't washed the flour from her hands. She ran swiftly to the nearby water basin and gave them a quick rinse. She grabbed the bristle brush quickly and got the snarls out of her blond hair swiftly, the hair crackling from her abuse. She did a very quick and simple braid and wrapped into a tidy bun at the nape of her neck. Nothing fancy was necessary, it would actually be inappropriate since she was visiting households that were struggling to survive. Her simple beige and blue housedress was adequate for the task and once several pins held her hair securely, Violet was done.

She ran back to the Dutch oven alongside the fireplace with a few minutes to spare. Her biscuits were not quite golden. Those were for the household today. Corinne, Lucas and Dolly would be by today for lunch, there was leftover roast beef from last night's supper and with the cheese and fresh biscuits they should all have plenty to eat. She heated up the gravy drippings and had it ready in the gravy boat on the table.

Lucas was in first, he was very dirty from head to toe. He apologized for his mess and walked outside and she could hear him smacking his legs and arms to get the dirt off him the best he could.

He came in laughing. "Well, I did the best I could. It's a bit chilly for a jump in the creek. I will try not to leave a trail." Lucas grinned and headed to the washbasin to see about the dirt on his hands and face.

Violet made a note that she would get water on to boil when she got back from her errand. After supper Lucas was certain to want a bath. In the back of the house was the washroom. It had a good-sized fireplace and she could get large quantities of water on to boil. The washtub for laundry was there as well as the household bathtub. It was luxurious to be able to bathe in, she had discovered. Something else she had never had before. The wooden tub was large and built well, with no leaks. She could submerge up to her chin!

The door from that room had two water barrels outside that were filled only when someone needed a bath or if it was laundry day. When she saw Cooper later today she would ask him to make sure those barrels were topped off. Violet always made sure Cooper was welled 'paid' for his water duties. She was always making him special treats. He was going to be a big brother soon. Him and his dog pepper should be around the place. She would keep her ears open.

Corinne and Dolly came by and lunch was friendly and everyone was talkative and in a good mood. After Violet ate quickly she went about her work. The stew, now with the lid off, had thickened and the potatoes were the perfect consistency. There were lots of chunky root vegetables, beef, barley, russet and red potato chunks. With a practiced hand she started ladling out the stew into the large jars. The stew was piping hot and the towel she was using to hold the jar was not quite thick enough to keep the heat away from her hand. With the first jar nearly full the heat was causing her pain. She got the jar to the counter in a wink but not before she squealed from the small bit of burning pain, it was involuntary but got everyone's attention.

A moment later she realized that the entire household was now in her kitchen. She calmed them.

"It got a bit hot, no harm done. Nearly dropped my first jar though. That would have broken my heart. One family would have only gotten one jar full." Violet pouted and tried to shoo them from 'her' kitchen.

"No way," Corinne said and Lucas wore a look just as determined.

The small team worked together and quickly got all thirty jars full of the hot stew. The lids were assembled and screwed on tightly by Lucas. He teased that he would try not to make them so tight no one could open them.

"Well, perhaps I am stronger than I look." Violet teased. "I pound out a lot of bread."

"You do indeed." Lucas said with a laugh.

"Some of the best bread I have ever tasted." Corinne added to praise Violet for her skills.

———◆•◎•◆━━◆•◎•◆———

At 12 o'clock Clive was there with his buggy, he stopped and sampled a biscuit loaded with a little beef and a few dips in the gravy. He declared her work to be fine. Violet shook her head at Clive and gathered her bagged bread.

The baskets were loaded with the stew, as many as could be squeezed in.

"You, Mrs. Griffin, are a good woman." Clive watched her tuck the letter inside her coat pocket and she buttoned it closed for safekeeping. "I hope your husband knows that he left behind a sweet and giving woman."

"I hope so too, Mr. Quackenbush." Violet said with a grin as Clive hopped aboard.

The buggy was light and they made good time back towards town. The outskirts of town had a pauper's camp, mostly women and children that Violet and Clive would be visiting. Some of the shacks were better than others. In total fifteen residences were there. As they delivered the two jars of stew and a loaf of bread to each place Clive and Violet got a small glimpse of how these folks were faring. Some had older children who did odd jobs around town for pennies, those families were usually better off. The young mother's were almost always destitute. Trying hard to scrape by. The 'gold-widow' stories got to Violet, though she tried hard not to let her emotions show too much. These men left their women behind for fortunes without thinking about the families' well being. Many women worried that their men would never return.

Clive had a small pad of paper and he wrote down any name of a child that was willing and old enough to do odd jobs for pay. He found out what they were willing to do and he promised to see if there was work for them. It was the least he could do.

The women were always willing to take on laundry or anything they could think of. The last residence was nothing more than a tent. Clive and Violet wordlessly assessed the situation and gave each a knowing look. Snow was a reality that could kill this family, and it could happen any day.

Violet and Clive announced themselves as visitors since there was nowhere to knock. A woman with dark eyes and hair peeked through the canvas that had been pushed aside.

"We have brought some food and bread. We are from the Spring Creek Fellowship Church." Violet had said these lines a few times before. Her voice sounded more certain after the first few homes.

"I am Magda, I thank you." The woman spoke with a thick Russian accent but she seemed to understand. "Galya, please come." Magda shuffled the red-cheeked baby on her hip and took a sideways step and moved the opening wider.

Violet saw the girl was young, early teens perhaps, with the same eyes and coloring as her mother. She would someday be a beauty.

"My daughter, Galina, this is my youngest Radimir. Miloslava and Pavel, my other two sons are in the woods hunting. They are good with their slingshots. They find rabbits and vermin sometimes." Magda spoke nervously as she had her daughter took the two large jars of stew. The loaf of bread Clive handed to Magda's free hand.

"Thank you very much." Galina spoke finally, holding the jars against her chest like treasure.

Clive took in the situation and realized the dire straights immediately. "May, I bother to ask where your husband is Mrs…"

"It's Varushkin." Magda answered his perusal to her surname. "My husband Slava is…what is word?" Magda paused.

"Gold hunting." Galina said with more anger than sadness in her tone.

"Ah…" Said Clive and Violet simultaneously. It was the tale of almost every woman they had spoken to.

"How old are you Galina? Is that your name?" Violet asked.

"I am thirteen this last September." Galina's eyes were dark and intelligent, she had wisdom behind them and Violet was drawn to her.

"You have the prettiest dark eyes, like your mother. " Violet said with a smile. "I work as a housekeeper over on Spring Creek, with the Grant family. I know they have wanted to hire on someone to help me with the washing. Would you be willing to take on a job a few days a week? I don't know the pay yet, but they are a good and generous people. They treat me very well."

"Yes ma'am, I would be glad for the work." Galina looked to her mother and the nod was the confirmation. Violet knew that anything to help this family was necessary. Their lives were in danger in this tent. The winter cold would do them in by January.

Violet wrote down the address and handed the note to Galina. "Can you read?" She asked.

"Yes, some, my brothers are better." Galina confessed. Violet smiled a half smile and dropped the conversation, she didn't want to make this girl uncomfortable.

"Do you need anything for the baby?" Clive asked Magda before they left.

"A few more nappies would be kind. With so few sometimes they are not dry when I need to change him… And some warm blankets. The nights are cold." Magda said, her voice swallowed up in the shame of asking for charity.

Violet and Clive left soon after, feeling heavy-hearted.

"It is not enough." Violet said as she rolled along in the buggy. "The laundry job is not enough."

"I know dear Violet. I am thinking." Clive said. His usual grin and light-heartedness replaced with a grim concentration.

Once they made it to town she bought a few supplies for the Grant household, just putting it on their account. She bought some yarn with her own money. She had a compulsion for yarn buying. She always needed a little bit more, just in case.

"I wonder Clive, if my old cabin has been repaired?" She asked as she made her purchases. JQ took her money wordlessly but Clive was loitering near Violet, still thoughtful on the situation outside of town.

"The town now owns that land." Clive said, knowing that the owner had skipped out with the gold fever crowd last year, not fulfilling the requirements for the land contract. "Let's stop by the land office and see what can be done. Even if it hasn't been repaired perhaps some church members would help out with it, I can see if the rent is cheap enough."

"I will gladly help with the rent. I have a little tucked away. I know if I hadn't gotten that job with the Grants my tent would have been next to theirs this year." Violet admitted.

She was still waiting to hear from her husband. Just one note had not been enough.

Violet shook away thoughts of Eddie and put her mind back on the problem at hand.

Chapter Five

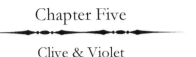

Clive & Violet

The visit to the land office had been fruitful. The land was owned by the town and the bank was eager to rent it with the acre of land to farm along with it. Clive gladly plunked down cash for a year's rent. It had been quite cheap to Clive's estimation. He knew the cabin must be in very poor condition for them to agree to such a low price.

Violet remained silent in the office but let out a gasp when they were outside, her breath let out a puff of frost. "Let the Lord be praised. Will you allow me to help with the cost of the rent?"

"No ma'am." Clive winked at her. Violet gave him a mischievous glare.

"Let's see what needs to be done to make the cabin livable." Clive said seriously. Violet jumped into the buggy wordlessly and they both rode silently, expecting the worst.

The cabin was a few miles outside of town, actually on the way to the Grant and Harpole's. The land here was broken into small parcels and several cabins peeked through the trees in the distance. When you looked further you could see a hill that Violet recognized now from the Grant land.

Violet saw the pitiful state of the cabin that had been the home she had shared with her husband, Eddie. It had a pathetic rubber tarpeline patch on the roof where a tree had taken out a section during a thunderstorm, a strange mixture of emotions rushed through her. Remembering the love she and Eddie had shared those precious months.

She thought with sadness that her husband had been away to California for longer than they had been together. The six months had been so sweet and loving, and they had hopes and dreams together. With him gone their marriage was beginning to look as pathetic as this leaky cabin.

"Let's peek inside. I am taking a few notes about what's going to be needed for the roof." Clive said. He could tell Violet was dealing with her own feelings about this rental cabin that she and her husband had shared.

The room smelled damp and musty. The roof had leaked and some of the floorboards were warped and ruined. But all the damage was contained in the main room.

"If we replaced the roof and the damaged floorboards we could get this place in working order pretty quickly. We will need a few men willing to do some heavy lifting." Clive said practically. Violet agreed.

"We will need to air it out a bit and take some soap and water to a few surfaces to get it freshened up. But the loft is untouched. There is room for two bedrooms up there. Not large but room for Galina on one side and the two boys on the other." Violet was making mental notes herself.

Clive handed her his list when she was done. She perused it.

"I think I want to replace the whole roof, now that I'm thinking on it. The logs are more prone to leaking. If we use flat boards and wood shingles it will keep the weather out better. "

Violet nodded. "I would like to add some kind of divide in the loft. And pegs for clothes and things." She had spent many hours envisioning children in that very loft.

"That's a grand scheme." Clive took the list back and scribbled down a few more things.

"I should get back to the Grant's. I will tell them about it and the Harpole's later. I have some work to get done today." Violet wanted away from the moldy air. She was remembering her days of fear hovering under that leaky roof and wondering how she would survive. It had only been just a few months past but her new life made her feel so safe now.

"I will tell the Harpole's and swing by a few others from Spring Creek Church. I have a feeling that folks will want to get involved." Clive said.

"This is a good thing, Clive." Violet said and took a deep breath once she was outside.

"Yes ma'am, it is. God is always showing up and teaching us all to remember our harder days. I remember in my young days having to accept help when my Pa was struggling to get a good crop in. I never did lean toward farming because of a few bad years. Too much rain, too little rain. The delicate balance of weather was always warring with my Pa. That is why I focused on business." Clive shared as they got into the buggy.

With a click of the tongue the horses pulled them forward toward Violet's new home. A place she felt blessed and safe.

Chapter Six

Angela Fahey

Angela saw that Clive's buggy was just outside the Grant's home, she smiled to herself at the happy thought of seeing Clive and knowing she had letters for Violet. There was something about delivering good news.

The door was opened for her and Violet was there, her smile bright and welcoming.

"Greetings all." Angela said, she saw Lucas and Clive discussing something heatedly while eating their lunch.

"Violet." Angela grabbed the blond woman's arm gently.

Violet had turned her head to the kitchen to get a bowl of hot stew for her friend.

"I have something for you." Angela smiled. Knowing this would make her friend's day better.

She handed over the letter addressed to Violet Griffin.

Violet squeaked over seeing the handwriting and gave Angela the biggest hug.

"Oh, bless you Angela." Violet said and escaped the room to read it.

Angela knew her way around the kitchen and got a bowl of stew and a few warm biscuits.

She sat at the table and got caught up on the news of the day.

Once she heard about the Varushkin family she wanted to get involved.

Violet Griffen

Violet could feel tears behind her eyes before she even opened the letter. She needed to hear from her husband. It had been too long and the time apart had been more than their time together. She was starting to have that nagging fear that he was gone for good. Every woman had heard those stories about the man that just thought he wanted to settle down and get married but then one day they took off and never returned.

Violet shook off her fear and sat down in her small private sitting room. Her rocking chair had a soft cushion and she sunk in and gingerly opened her husband's letter, with a prayer for good news.

Darlin wife,

The trip to Callaforni has been full of trubble and trials. The groop I was wit fought so much about ware to fine the gold we ended up goin our seprate ways. I end up in a small tent town cald nuggit springs, I haz been panning fer gold and found sum dust alredy.
I am sory it tuk so long to write but I had so liddell good nuws I didnt want to say.
I luv you my Violet.

Eddie

Violet cried and cherished every word, no matter his spelling. He had been learning from her how to write better before he left. But he still had a ways to go. Having something in her hands made her heart so much lighter. It had taken months to reach her with the misspelled address but it had found a way to her. She said a prayer of thanks and read it through several more times before she joined everyone out in the big parlor.

Violet had a thought as she was walking through the large cabin about the timing of the letter. Just today she had done something good, just because God had put it in her heart. Now she knew she was no saint, and she tried the best she could to live a good life and be good to others but not everyday was like today had been. She felt strongly about what she and Clive had started. Helping the families in need in their community felt so good and right, that it swelled inside her with that good feeling of giving. Now she had a reward she wasn't expecting in the pocket of her dress. She felt the inner feeling of God's presence, knowing He was with her, she was not alone and in despair without her husband. He had watched out for her. She had a song of thanks on her heart as she joined with the others. Today was a day for blessings.

Grant's Grove

"I must be allowed to help as well." Angela said firmly.

"I will be pitching in too." Lucas declared.

"I think we will have lots of folks from the church willing to help out this family." Clive said. He had his pencil and notepad out again, going over all the details of what needed accomplishing.

"I will head over to my brother's place and get him to bring his tools. Since the land is paid for we could start taking out any rotten boards today or tomorrow even. I say we leave the roof on until we are ready to tear it off and replace it but the inside can be worked on and get the rotten boards out and clear out the damage and any mold that may be there." Lucas said and took a long swig of coffee.

"I agree. The inside needs a lot of work but thankfully only the floor and ceiling were damaged. The walls are solid and with the floorboards and roof replaced the house will be safe and sound." Clive nibbled on his pencil for a minute, thinking.

"I want to talk with Marie about how we can add more than just a safe home but also some essentials. If us womenfolk all work together we could get the family some warm clothes and blankets they need too." Violet said.

"I think we could head over and see if she if free to plan with us." Corinne said.

Angela and Violet both nodded.

"I will drive over to the church and talk with Pastor Whittlann and his wife. See what they think." Clive swigged down his last swallow of coffee from his mug and grabbed his hat from the back of his chair.

Everyone said a hearty goodbye and Clive swung himself into his warm flannel coat and was gone.

Corinne, Angela and Violet plotted things out for a minute and were all ready to leave within a few minutes themselves.

They all felt pulled in by this good deed and wanted to see it bloom into something they could all be proud of.

Corinne Grant

Corinne's heart was light as she was walking along the pathway from her father's home. The breeze held a chill in the air. It was November after all. Marie, Violet, Angela and Corinne had all shared ideas on how to get some warmer clothes for the Varushkin family. It made her think of the verse that she had read many times.

Mark 12:30-31

And thou shalt love the Lord thy God with all thy heart, and with all thy soul, and with all thy mind, and with all thy strength: this is the first commandment. And the second is like, namely this, Thou shalt love thy neighbor as thyself. There is none other commandment greater than these.

The small church would be setting a good example to everyone in town to set their hearts to helping the poor instead of ignoring them the way many larger cities do. Just because people had fallen on hard times does not make them any less worthy of compassion.

Corinne knew that she had been born blessed with a family that was wealthy. Her time on the Oregon Trail had been the hardest of her life. The daily challenges had been good for her, Corinne reasoned. It had been a terrible and beautiful struggle. It showed her how much she needed to rely on God. Back in the Spring she had been challenged again when she lost her child to miscarriage. Her heart was still healing, though every month it got a little easier. Her worries were calmer in her heart now. She still had the negative thoughts creep in sometimes. Wondering if she would ever be able to get pregnant again, or if she did, would she have another miscarriage? It was more difficult than she could have ever imagined. Watching Marie blooming with pregnancy wasn't easy on her heart but she was leaning on God for strength.

Her husband, Lucas, was an amazing and patient man, a gentle guide that kept her calm. He always seemed to know when she needed encouraging. Perhaps she showed her emotions too easily across her face. She had been accused of that a few times in her life.

Corinne smiled and took in the view of the mountains around her. A few peaks had white caps. But snow hadn't touched her cabin roof yet this year. Angela and Violet had stayed with Marie so Corinne had a slow peaceful walk back to her green house. She knew that she would be doubling its size next year. The frame had already been ordered and a glass company in Sacramento wrote back that they could provide her with thick enough glass. The West was growing and it made her heart proud knowing that she was part of expanding this great country.

Corinne saw her father alongside his barn talking to a familiar face. Corinne took a moment to look, with wonder at a young man she hadn't seen since her last day on the Oregon Trail.

Reggie Gardner, looking taller and thicker through the chest was standing nearby, Corinne picked up her step and let out a holler when she got closer.

"Reggie! What has happened to you?" Corinne said once she could see that Reggie was happy to see her. His same smile and dark hair brought back so many memories. This young man had been a big part of her survival on the trail.

"Well, Corinne, you are looking pretty as a postcard. I just heard that you and Lucas got hitched." Reggie grinned and accepted the bear hug from Corinne.

"Yes, it did seem meant to be. You are looking so good." Corinne patted his arm and watched him blush.

John Harpole, Corinne's father, chimed in. "He nearly doubled in size."

"Well, I guess the good Lord decided I wasn't going to be skinny as a bean pole any more. My family always was full of late bloomers. I followed tradition." Reggie said with a laugh.

"You staying in these parts or just visiting?" Corinne asked with a sincere hope that he would stay. It had been a mystery to her when he had disappeared from town right after they all had arrived in Oregon.

"I am hoping to stay. Was just discussing some opportunities with yer Pa. Hoping we can work out an agreement." Reggie said and tapped his cowboy hat against his leg nervously.

"Well, Pa, you be good to Reggie here." Corinne gave her father a smile and a wink. Then turned back to Reggie. "Dinner at my house up the path at seven. I insist. Angela will want a chance to see you and catch up. We will all want to know where you disappeared to these last two years." Corinne let the men get back to their talk and headed up the path herself. She knew that the roast beef that Violet was cooking would feed everyone. Even Dolly would be joining their dinner table.

Reggie will sure be shocked to hear her speaking English. Corinne thought. The last he had seen Dolly, she was still barely older than a child and couldn't speak a lick of English. Now she was almost a woman and helping Corinne run a thriving business. Corinne was amazed how the last two years had brought about so many blessings.

Angela was home from San Francisco, building her dream home on the property next to hers and Lucas's. It was really a miracle.

Corinne checked on the roast when she got home and saw Lucas working hard on a drawing at the table.

"You working on your new project?" Corinne asked as she puttered around the kitchen. Violet had everything in order and Corinne was just making sure there wasn't any thing she could do to help. With another mouth to feed she wanted to be kind to Violet and wash up anything that needed it. As usual Violet had everything tidy and orderly. A few mugs from earlier were dry on a towel. Corinne put them away and hung the towel on the bar nearby.

She sat at the table to visit and pester her husband a little bit.

"I am." Lucas answered. "Something I read about in an article. Been studying the windmills they have been using back East. Going to talk to the blacksmith in town and see if we can talk out a few ideas I have." Lucas looked up from his paper and gave his wife a handsome smile.

"You inspire me everyday, Lucas Grant." Corinne said. She was admiring the boyish gleam in his eye and the way he always looked at her.

"Just trying to keep up with you, dear wife." Lucas grabbed her hand from her lap and pulled her over to him. He stood and forgot about his project for a moment as he kissed his wife properly.

Corinne enjoyed his spontaneous romantic moment, and thanked the Lord again for her many blessings. After a few moments of an embrace Lucas let her go with a promise of many more kisses in her future buried in the twinkle in his eye.

"I saw Reggie Gardner just now on the way home from our meeting with Marie." Corinne said.

"Glad to hear he is back in town. He was a smart lad, hope he can get his own place around here." Lucas said sincerely. He had gotten along with Reggie on the trail and recognized a young man with a good head on his young shoulders.

"He is a lad no longer. Reggie has filled out, must of been something in the water he's been drinking. The skinny lad looks like a man now." Corinne said matter-of-factly.

Lucas raised his eyebrow.

"What?" Corinne said innocently. Then threw her hands up in surrender. "Just wait until you see for yourself. You have no worries of me being wooed away from your many, many charms. He just looks very different. It was shocking, is all." Corinne laughed and her eyes grew wide at her husband's glare.

"I may have to kiss you again to remind you of my many…many…charms." Lucas said with that look in his eye again.

"Angela and Violet are due back any minute. You can save your kisses for later, darling husband." Corinne stood up and stepped away from the table. Knowing much more romantic banter would distract them both.

"The girls were going over patterns to make clothes for the Varushkin children." She said and scooted out of reach playfully.

"I spoke with Russell and we are going out first thing in the morning tomorrow to pull up the floorboards. Also anything that smells of mold or mildew will be pulled out." He had his far off look of thinking. Corinne thought he looked handsome, even when serious. He turned and gave her a smile, seeing she was staring and admiring his face. He gave her a wink to let her know he noticed.

"I think this is a great opportunity to do good in the community. This is after all, what God calls us to do. To love our neighbors." Lucas said enthusiastically before burying his head back into his plans.

Chapter Seven

November 1850
Angela Fahey

Angela had delivered her letters to everyone and spent a long visit with Marie. She wanted to get back to Corinne's before dinner to clean up and have a moment to read the other letter. Her heart was still so happy from the words from earlier in the day from Ted. She felt double blessed that she still had another letter to cherish. She was glad that she had waited, for the anticipation all day had been wonderful. Doing a good deed while waiting for it was also part of the blessing.

Angela and Violet walked along the path from the Harpole ranch to the Grant's home. Smoke curled up from the several fireplaces and Angela and Violet spoke of the day's events and letters as they walked.

Corinne was in the kitchen and Lucas still at the table.

"Your roast is looking wonderful Violet. I just peeked at it. The smell is making my mouth water. We have extra guests coming tonight so I wanted to get a start on helping you get ready." Corinne was holding napkins and cutlery and settled them on the large countertop, the silverware jingled as they settled.

"Oh, thank you Corinne, who all is coming?" Violet shrugged out of her coat and joined her in the kitchen.

"Well Angela is already here, Dolly will be over shortly but the guest will be a stranger to you but not to Angela." Corinne said with mischief in her eye.

Angela laughed at her friend's mysterious look and stood on the other side of the counter trying to think of who it could be.

"I can't guess, so you are just going to have to say it outright, Cori." Angela declared.

"Reggie Gardner is back in town!" Corinne said and watched the surprise come over her friend's face.

"Well, honestly, that is a surprise." Angela had not seen him since she was left behind in Fort Kearney over two years before. He had been a servant working alongside her on the Oregon Trail with Corinne's first husband. They had become comrades. She would be glad to see him again. The night he left he promised to pray for her as she healed from her horrible accident. She knew he had felt guilt over what had happened, Angela would love a chance to ease his mind. He had seemed to be quite burdened by her being so hurt. Reggie had a good heart, Angela remembered. "I do hope he is in good health." Angela said sincerely.

"Yes, very much so, he has grown taller and wider in the last few years." Corinne said and smiled.

"That will be interesting to see." Angela grinned then she looked distracted. "Ladies, I need a few minutes, this letter is burning a hole in my pocket. I will be back to help with dinner after I freshen up and read it." Angela blushed, she couldn't help it. Ted's words were precious.

"We have dinner handled, you take your time." Violet said and with both hands shooed her away.

Angela was in her own room and plopped on her bed. The crisp paper and Ted's bold lettering on the front had her heart jumping already.

Dearest Angel,

The words are pouring through my brain yet I pause with my pen. We had set about to ship out a trunk to Oregon to Clive for him to sell through the store in Portland. My mother, aunt and sister have been making lace non-stop, doilies, collars and several fancy lace shawls. We had the shipment ready with a captain I had made enquiries with about getting to the West. The shipment was planned for the trunk only. But a telegram came this morning. The ship had been full but for cargo. We had scheduled a trip aboard as passengers in late February, but a family who had rented a room had canceled for this currently scheduled trip. The room is ours, and since we are friends of Clive, (his reputation is an excellent one) we will dine with the Captain every night. We are leaving for Panama in three days. We have only a few trunks of personal luggage for my mother and aunt sold nearly everything before I came back.

The Captain has informed me that the land crossing should only take a day with the donkeys. The other ship will be with the Captain's respected friend. I was told we should arrive in Sacramento by early November. We will get a ferry soon as we can to Oregon City. I will send a telegram once we arrive.

I truly had no hope to see you before next year. My prayers were answered this morning and I will see you within just a few months. I do hope this letter arrives before I do. But the pleasure of surprising you would have its rewards.

It is a one-day trip to get to Long Island by carriage so we are packing away. We will stay in a hotel near the docks. I am so thoroughly excited and overjoyed at the thought that I am only a few months away from seeing you. I know I am speaking redundantly. My brain is a shambles. My sister Sophia has declared me a lovesick puppy and I can only agree that she is right.

We all get a fresh start. Aunt Olivia has declared she is going to marry a rugged mountain man. We all laugh but she is determined and her seriousness on the subject just makes us laugh even more. My mother is still mourning my father but we all hope the change of scenery and circumstances will begin to cheer her. We will continue to pray for her, I know you will join us in that.

I am off to pack my things with lifted spirits. I cannot thank God enough for this surprise blessing. I am sending you all my devotion.

Sincerely,

Thaddeus Greaves

Angela blinked a few times and caught the breath she had been holding. The words 'early November' kept leaping in her mind. It is mid November! He could come any week now. Ted could be here anytime.

Her heart and cheeks were aglow. She took a minute to pause and think about Ted, she had somehow set it aside in her brain that he was really trying to come back to see her. She didn't know what to do or think but she would let him have a spot in her head tonight. She wanted to know what her heart was doing but she could not put rational thought together yet. All she knew was that he was coming.

"Oh Lord, please give them safe passage. Thank you Lord." She prayed aloud.

Angela spent some time on her hair, the wind and bonnet had mussed it today and she pulled her red locks out of its pins and brushed it thoroughly before re-pinning it up. She left a portion down in the back and was pleased with the waves. She was getting better at doing her own hair. She had spent so many years with the maids cap on she had grown accustomed to the simple style. Wearing it down and fussed with was the way a lady wore her hair. She didn't really feel the part of fashionable lady but she was still trying. She had a good support group around her that reminded her often that she was accepted as she was.

She changed into a nicer dress and wondered how it would feel to see Ted again. Angela smiled to herself remembering his eyes and his sincerity. She took the bracelet out from under the sleeve of her dress and rubbed her fingers over the engraving.

Hope was written on the flattened silver oval. She may have not have clung to the hope as he had encouraged her before he left San Francisco last spring. She was being honest with herself for a moment and realized that she had put Ted into the back of her mind as a beautiful memory and had very little hope of ever seeing him again. The thought gave her pain realizing why she had tried to set aside her feelings for him. She knew she had been abandoned by so many, her parents by dying, her stepfather and brother by choice. She felt her emotions rising and tried to stuff them back where they belonged. This was not the time to pull out the heavy feelings and get herself all worked up.

Angela took a few deep breaths and thought about her house. It was a happy thought that made her think of the future. Now she had a pleasant vision to add to it. She could be proud to show her home to Ted. She prayed for the Lord to calm her heart. She would have time to deal with her emotions but she didn't want to do it now.

Chapter Eight

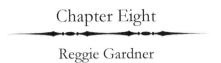

Reggie Gardner

Reggie was happy to be settled into his new home. The cabin was a good one, only a few cobwebs and dust from the months it had sat empty. He was told in town that it had been built two years previously. It had two acres and a well near the house. Reggie had tasted the water earlier and it was fresh and cold. He had a lot to do to make the home functional. He needed a new water barrel. The previous owners must have taken theirs with them. Right now he had a bucket of water on the counter.

He had unpacked one mug to use for drinking. The cold water had been brisk when he had tidied himself up. He planned to ride over to Corinne and Lucas's home and have dinner. He knew that Angela Fahey and Dolly would be there this evening. He was uncertain what to think about seeing Angela. She had been the main reason he hadn't stayed in Oregon after he had finished the trail. He had so many things to work out in his mind about how guilty he had felt about Angela's accident.

Could he even call it that? His boss at the time had sent her out into the dangerous dark night. It had been done maliciously and Reggie had known. He knew his employer's disdain for his wife Corinne and her maid. Reggie had just wanted the chance for a fresh start out west. Being Andrew Temple's assistant had started as a well-paid job that he enjoyed. Doing Andrew's personal shopping before they left for the trip had been a pleasure. Making arrangements and even handling Andrew's accounts had been a good challenge. Reggie prided himself on being the one member of his family that had gone all the way through school. He had done so many jobs and gleaned his knowledge from every business owner he worked for.

His parents were back in New Jersey. His father worked as a bricklayer. He was good at his job but could not read more than a few words. His mother could not read at all, she had been washing laundry for money her whole life. Reggie knew he needed to send them a letter. He would make it short and kind. They would certainly need to find someone to read it to them.

He would send them money as well. He had been paid well by the captain he worked for. At first he had been a paid deckhand but then the captain found out about his math skills and put him on the books. Soon Reggie began going inland to ports and the captain used him in negotiating at a few vendors. Reggie enjoyed the travel but he still felt that nagging feeling that he had been running away from some of the horrors on land. At sea he found a lot of time to think and to pray. He sensed the huge scope of the sea and felt small.

He had found God on the open sea. He had been raised to believe in God. But never before in his life had he talked to God like he did that year aboard the *Emerald Eye*. The merchant captain always had claimed his great grandfather had been a Spanish pirate who had started their families' fortune with emeralds he had stolen from an African ship loaded with the precious stones. Reggie laughed and always went along with the captain's stories but knew that they were pretty far fetched. The captain was also one to exclaim over the faith his mother had taught him as a child.

"God is not a respecter of persons." Captain Castillo said. "My mother reminded me often enough. Being a third son, I needed to hear it. I felt like I had no respect from my father because I was not the tallest or fastest among my brothers. But my mother reminded me to remember that God cares for everyone equally. Better than us humans could ever do. We always tend to pick favorites when it comes to people." The captain was always giving Reggie good things to think about.

"One day when I was young, we lived in South Carolina, on the coast and we had been in the country for only a few years." Captain Castillo had lost track of his sentence in a memory, then remembered what he was going to say. "When I was on the shore I noticed all the clammers out early gathering clams for the day. Some were being lazy in the summer heat and there I was, when I felt God was showing me how the lazy people were. Suddenly it was clear to me, that if I worked hard I could earn my own way. In this new country, it did not matter if I was the third son. If I worked hard and kept up with my studies I could be what I wanted to be." Reggie remembered the Captain's words and the story rang true in his heart.

That kind captain had a great influence over Reggie, helping him forget the painful and dark situations that had burrowed deep in his heart.

Reggie made it through the door at the Grant's home and was bombarded by women. Corinne, Angela and Dolly all were eagerly waiting with big smiles. Every one of them looking radiant and healthier than the last he had seen of them over two years before.

"Reggie!" Corinne, the hostess gave the young man a hug and got a handshake from her husband, Lucas.

"So glad you came back to Oregon." Lucas said sincerely and backed away with a laugh as Angela pushed her way through to get her hug in.

"Me too." Reggie said and laughed. Angela looked healthy and had a pink glow to her cheeks that did his heart good. The old guilt fell away like a heavy weight as he realized his endless prayers for her had all come to fruition.

"Angela Fahey, you are looking better than I ever saw ya." Reggie said. He had hoped it hadn't sounded like a flirtation but as a friend. "I was more worried for you than I could have ever said."

Angela shook his hand hard after the brief hug. "I know Reggie, I know you did. I am glad to finally put your heart at peace. God took good care of me." Angela smiled sincerely. Seeing his face smile had been good for her too. It closed that old chapter, all the pain from that trip was now be a distance memory. No one was left to hold any more guilt or shame, just a freshly healed wound. She prayed a prayer of thankfulness in her heart. "Come see Dolly. She is the most changed from all of us."

Reggie could see the young Indian woman was indeed different from the last he had seen her. She had grown nearly a foot and no longer had her little braids and beaded dress, instead she was dressed in a pretty maroon dress with white lace around her collar. He had never noticed her soft brown eyes being so wise or intense before.

"Hello Reggie, it is good to see you again." Dolly said in perfect English, taking him back a bit.

Reggie raised his eyebrows in surprise. "Your English has really come along. I know people that spend their whole life speaking English and don't sound as good as that." Reggie laughed. He liked seeing that Dolly had a little blush to her cheeks.

"I have been learning to read from the Bible. Chelsea and Clive spent so much time teaching me, I would not want to dishonor all their hard work by being a bad student." Dolly said with all seriousness.

"Even before you spoke English, I could tell from your actions that you would always work hard at whatever task you had before you. That is something you cannot teach. That is just a part of you, Dolly. It will be very good to be able to speak with you now. I hope you will be in the area for more time." Reggie said, meaning it. Somehow he remembered how the tribe she was from, wanted her to learn from Corinne about plants and herbs. How long would they allow her to stay and learn?

"I am here now, they have not yet come back for me." Dolly said with a smile. "I am thankful for everyday God gives me here in Oregon. I feel very blessed." Dolly hinted at her new faith and felt bold.

Reggie felt himself grinning and hoped that he didn't look like a fool. He looked around and noticed everyone else was busy getting dinner ready. Reggie and Dolly had been talking alone for the last minute.

"I am glad to meet you again Dolly." Reggie said lamely, meaning to say more but feeling tongue-tied. He was always this ways around girls, well, girls he was attracted too. His thoughts leapt to the *attracted* part of his thinking and realized that Dolly had indeed grown into a beautiful young woman. In his past he would just avoid the girls he found attractive, because his shyness would become overwhelming. Perhaps, knowing he could have no future with Dolly, as she was promised to go back to her tribe, he could push away his nerves and just be her friend.

Reggie smiled and watched Dolly join the women at the table and she folded napkins and placed them around the table. Her movements were deliberate and graceful. She fit into this world better than he expected. He would enjoy getting to know her better. But he would keep it limited to friendship, and keep his attraction pushed back. There was no room for that here.

Grant's Grove

"Ted is coming this month if his letter proves true!" Angela shared her good news at the dinner table. Everyone joined in her celebrating. Reggie teased and begged to hear her story of how they met.

"It was in God's hands. We first met at this dirty tent church in San Francisco and he began working for Clive's grandson Gabriel Quackenbush at the Hudson Bay store there. It was not the place to fall in love but somehow we did." Angela smiled and got a little misty thinking that he could be sailing close to the California coast any day. In her mind she could see the ships gliding through the mist of the bay. "I am still not sure I believe it." Angie said with a shaky voice.

"You will when you get the telegram. I think you will be anxious until you do." Corinne said.

"I will keep you distracted, Angie. We will be busy getting your house ready, perhaps also for a wedding this year." Dolly said with a teasing grin.

Angela blushed to a near purple color and she gave a glare to her friend across the table. "It is too soon for that. I have yet to meet his mother. I do hope she likes me." Angela said and held her pink cheeks until they went back to normal.

Lucas piped in with his own teasing. "Well, we have to approve of him too, ya know, Angie. Can't have some fool living next door."

This brought Angie's color back up to a glowing pink. Angie had no words and just huffed before she could stop the laugh that everyone else had started.

"Lucas, you know a fool for a neighbor makes for good entertainment. It might work out just fine." Corinne winked at her husband.

The night continued on with great conversation. After dinner Lucas played the violin and Violet sang a hymn. Reggie and Dolly played checkers by the fire. Angela and Corinne talked of the house, Ted and the Varushkin family.

Reggie left after ten o'clock excited for his new job starting the next day at the Harpole Ranch as the new bookkeeper. He was promised some fresh baked bread from Violet to help his empty kitchen and Corinne asked for him to come by her greenhouse when he could spare a minute. She wanted to show off her growing things.

Dolly waved shyly from the back of the room but she did notice that he gave her a nod before leaving. His dark eyes and quiet ways were a pleasant mystery to her. Somehow she was just very happy to see him back.

Chapter Nine

November 23rd, 1850
Varushkin Cabin

The next day was a flurry of activity. Lucas and Russell pulled up all the rotten floorboards from the rental cabin for the Varushkin family. Clive set about getting papers from the land office setting the contract through Slava Varushkin and getting it set up to be the same low cost for the future rentals. Clive was worried that the rent would go up once the church and local farmers put all the work and money into the place. The land office obliged at giving the rent as the same rate for the next ten years. Clive had signed in Slava's place until he was home from California. He tried to be as truthful as he could when asked if he was given power of attorney.

"Well, I am taking care of things for them while Slava's gone to Cali…" Clive said hoping the clerk would accept that as an answer.

"Sounds good Clive, awfully nice of ya. Just have Slava come in and sign the rental form when he gets back." The clerk said wit a friendly nod.

"I will. " Clive signed above the line making it a legal contract. Leaving enough space for Slava Varushkin to leave his signature or mark when he could." Clive sent up a prayer for the man, wherever he may be, for his safety.

The Varushkin family had a home. He wanted to ride over and tell them but something held him back. He wanted to make sure that it was all done in God's timing. Today wasn't the right day. *Tonight is the church meeting, perhaps after that.* Clive thought to himself.

The church meeting had gone well. Almost everyone was there that lived nearby. The meeting started with Pastor Whittlan telling what he had heard about the Varushkin family, they were hard on their luck, he shared the story about the husband Slava, how he had been injured and his promised wages were denied. Once the situation was explained the agreed upon solution was offered by Clive, the men all agreed to meet up on Saturday to help. Several people had donated money for materials to replace the roof and some of the flooring. One person suggested that instead of just having a curtain in the loft to actually build a wall for privacy. The mention was seconded and immediately that person offered to pay into the pot for supplies.

Angela and Violet sat next to each other. They kept looking at each other as the men were getting the details worked out. Wordlessly they knew this was the right thing. Sometimes it just felt good to be part of something that would help someone else.

The details were all laid out and even some women spoke up, offering their help in getting warm clothes and blankets together for the family. Some practical women discussed how the family would survive with no winter stores. People began talking about going through their own root cellars, extras could be shared. Men offered firewood and a few household supplies to get them started.

After the meeting Corinne and Lucas invited their own close family and friends over for some pie. Violet and Marie had been doing some baking.

"I am just so proud of all of us!" Violet said as she was slicing up the pie next to Marie at the kitchen counter. "I love seeing how a community can really come together. This just makes everything I was raised to believe come true in my heart. *How to truly love your neighbor*, Violet thought for a moment that she was prattling but Marie smiled and gave her shoulder a conspiratorial bump with her own shoulder.

"You are right to feel that way, I am so glad you found it in your heart to help those families. You have shown us all how to be good Christians this week." Marie said and plopped a piece of apple pie on a plate.

The chatter from the parlor was working its way into a pleasant party-like roar but Violet and Marie were having their own little sharing time in the kitchen. To both of them it was the heart of the home, their favorite place.

"I just saw the tents one day a few weeks ago and it bothered me; so much that little-by-little, the idea formed and I just couldn't shake it off any more. I just pray that the Lord will be blessed by all of this. I know it was God prompting me to be good to these people. Because I know that I could be there with them. Had God not stepped in and found me this great home to work and live in I would be starving in a shack outside of town too." Violet let a tear slip down her cheek and swiped it away with her shoulder, for her hands were busy.

"Tomorrow you and I can make a trip into town and tell them." Marie said.

"No, I think not Marie, it's getting too close to your delivery time to be jostling around in a wagon to town. Down by the creek it nearly shook me out of my seat the other day. I can go with Angela or someone else. I want you to be safe and sound. That little one is counting on you." Violet stood her ground, something she rarely did. But she cared deeply for the family around her. Her neighbors were more to her than just the family she worked with, they were dear to her.

"I see your point and concede. But I will make sure you have company." Marie was stacking small plates loaded down with pie up her arms, like a fancy waiter in a restaurant. Violet did the same. They both knew how to serve folks. It was built into them, like a calling from the Lord.

November 24th, 1850
Violet & Angela

Marie had followed through. Angela and Violet were together in Angela's new buggy. Angela had gotten up early and headed out to the barn while everyone was still eating. She had grabbed a piece of toast as Violet ran it to her by the door.

"You need to eat something. I will be out in a few minutes. Gotta feed the troops and I will be ready." Violet said.

"Thanks, I will be back in a few minutes, I want to make sure I have learned how to hook it up properly myself safely, just in case Earl isn't around to help me. I am trying to be as self-sufficient as I can be until my situation changes." Angela said.

Violet wiggled her eyebrows in an unspoken tease. They both knew what she was teasing her about.

The barn was warmer than the outside air. There were several horses eating contentedly, the animals were jostling around in their own morning routines. Angela perked up with excitement that soon her barn would be ready.

Her brown horse, she had not picked a name yet, was waiting, and looking pretty in the last stall. The stable hand, Brandon, was behind her and helped her get the door open and the horse out safely.

"You still are a little skittish and the horses can sense it. If you trust them they will trust you more." He said wisely.

"Thank you." Angela said sincerely, she wanted to learn. "Should I help you get the horse hooked up?"

"I will walk you through the steps. But if I say to back up you do it quick. I don't want you getting hurt. This boy seems a gentle soul but we don't want to spook him if he is still needs a strong hand to guide him. He might take advantage of you yet." He said.

Angela nodded, realizing she had a lot to learn. House, barn, farm and life had thrown lots of new things her way. She suddenly realized how young she was to go off on her own.

Getting the buggy set up only took a few minutes and she again tipped the stable boy. He had taught her a lot. She needed to spend some time with the horse, she would get Corinne out here with her and teach her how to brush and groom the animal. He said it helped with the bonding too.

Her buggy had room for three people and a side door that closed. It had a collapsible roof for sunny days but today it was up. It helped block a little wind, but the cold air smelled of snow as Angela showed up in front of Grant's Grove to pick up Violet. Violet was rushing to jump into the buggy as she was still buttoning her coat. Her long dark blue scarf dangled around her arm. She wrapped it around her neck when she got into her seat. Angela thought the scarf made Violet's blue eyes stand out, with the stunning cornflower blue and her pink cheeks, from Angela's perception, her friend was darling.

"Oh Violet, you look pretty as a painted postcard." Angela said sincerely.

"Why thank you, I was just thinking of my Eddie. I had a dream of him last night. I pray he will be home soon." Violet smiled and reached into her pocket for the gloves that matched the scarf she had crocheted herself.

"So how many times have you read the letter since the other day?" Angela asked with more than a little teasing in her voice.

"I am pretty sure I have it memorized. It is so silly but I miss the most foolish things about him." Violet blushed a deeper red than the winter pink. "His smell, and the way he always loved my cooking." Violet sighed.

"I know what you mean." Angela said, thinking of Ted just then. "Knowing Ted could be here anytime has been driving me slowly into insanity. I can barely sleep."

"I can tell you, I woke up early. I am so excited to the bearer of good news." Violet said.

"Me too, Vie, me too." Angela gave a sideways hug to her friend and they were off into the brisk morning.

<hr />

Galina Varushkin

Galina Varushkin stirred the stubborn coals of the fire outside the tent. She had gotten the fire up to a roar not even an hour ago and the cold wind was trying to steal the warmth away. She grabbed some of the shaved wood from her pocket and a few dry sticks and tried to coax a new blaze from the embers. She could not afford more matches. They had three left when she started that morning and no money. The water she had gone for last night had been frozen with a thin layer of ice in the bucket this morning. The water had been bone chilling as she had washed her hands. The tent was so dirty. The dirt floor just made everything impossible to clean. Her mother was always a tidy person, she had always kept their small cabin extremely clean, she had been raised in a strict household with many siblings and they all worked to keep the place clean, as that would honor the Lord.

Galya could see the dirt under her own fingernails and tried to push away the concern. She had to stop caring or she would cry. Tears were no use here. She remembered the stories of starvation from her mother about her home country. Galya was not certain this new land was treating them any better. The last two weeks had been the worst of her life, Galina reasoned. Everyone was cold and hungry. The boys had found little food and their fishing had come up with little to nothing in days. They had set traps but were told by the land owner to take them down.

The stew they had received from the nice young woman had been the only decent food they had had this month. Galina said her morning prayers this morning as she rose in a desperate tone.

"Please Lord, I need hope today. We need You here. " Her words had cut off when she had to fight back a sob. She did not want to wake her mother and baby brother. She took her tattered blanket and covered them with it. She hoped that they would sleep a bit longer. Sleep was the only good thing left. You weren't hungry while you slept.

Galina got the blaze going again and warmed up the water from the river. The tripod over the fire seemed sturdy enough for a brisk wind and then she grabbed a few buckets to retrieve more water. She wanted to wash a few clothes today so she and the boys could work. That girl, Violet, Galina remembered her name finally, had said she could work for extra money doing laundry. She knew her clothes were not clean and they all probably smelled as bad as everyone else on Pauper Row. But she would not bring shame on her mother. She would wash one dress and a shirt and pants for each of the boys. There was a little soap left. Perhaps with the laundry job they would have enough to get enough wood scraps to build four walls and a roof like the others on the 'row'. They were shanty houses but they would survive better. Right now she knew the odds of the baby dying of exposure was a good one. The fear licked at the back of her mind. The seasonal clock in her head reminded her of the time. How much time do they have left?

Lord help us. Galina prayed again. She got to the Willamette River and filled the buckets full of river water, it was moving pretty fast and it did have a little sedimentary dirt in it. It wasn't as clean as the flowing creeks and springs but it would work for laundry purposes well enough. She didn't care for the taste of it when it was muddier but sometimes it was all they had.

As she carried the buckets back slowly she sang an old song her mother had taught her. It had been in Russian first but her mother changed it to English when they were little.

> The Lord gives us food,
> The Lord gives us love,
> The Lord hears our prayers from up above,
> Our God is so good,
> He sent his own Son,
> He came to bless everyone.

It was a children's song and her mother had taught all the children these words. Galina had tried to learn to read and could read a few words, but her mother had always spoken longingly about having a child of hers that could read the Bible. Galina had wanted to be the first in her family that could read. Her brothers, she admitted to herself, did read better than her. Her days of schooling were always cut short. The teacher in the lumber camp was a man who did not like girls in his class. He was always sending the girls home to help their families. Galya had been friends with another lumberjack's daughter, Heidi. They both were eager to learn but somehow the teacher at the small school there in the small village near Salem had not wanted to teach her or Heidi, saying often that a girl's place was helping her mother.

The lumber camp ended up moving Heidi's parents to a different location. Galya's father was moved closer to Oregon City and Heidi was not heard from anymore. That was only a year ago, she thought. Since neither one could read nor write well they could not compose letters, even if they could afford the paper.

She hummed and sang a bit then stopped. Galina thought of the words to the song and nearly wept.

She sang the song again aloud, as a prayer for the words to bring truth.

> The Lord gives us food,
> The Lord gives us love,
> The Lord hears our prayers from up above,

Galina had tears coursing down her dirty cheeks but with her hands full she could not wipe them away. She felt the tears turn cold as they escaped down her chin. She prayed again. Within a single moment she felt a calming Peace. The sound of the water splashing over the buckets was all she heard in the still of the morning but somehow she knew God heard her prayer.

She took a big breath in and let it out, making a frosty cloud in front of her face. She had always loved the winter, the frost and snow being the most fun part of the year. This year was her first year of dread concerning the cold and snow.

She felt calm now, and smiled at her frosty breaths. God would provide, she thought to herself. He heard her prayers. She just knew it.

The water buckets were still close to full when she got back to the fire. Her mother was up and poking the fire with a long stick. The baby was invisible under all the blankets.

"You boiling water for laundry, Galya?" Her mother asked using her pet name.

"Yes Mama," Galina said. "I want to go to the house where Violet works and see if that job is available. I need a clean dress. I will wash some clothes for the boys too." Galina poured the water into the black pot hanging on the tripod.

"That is good." Magda said to her daughter, she nodded. Her own clothes could use a washing but the work would be hard enough in the cold without adding more to the day's workload.

The sound of a horse and buggy interrupted the thoughts of Galina and she had a wishful hope that perhaps the Violet woman had brought more stew. That would be a good answer to her prayers.

"Mrs. Varushkin?" The voice asked after the horse and buggy had stopped.

Galina and her mother walked around the backside of the tent to see the Violet and another woman with her. Violet carried no stew, Galina noticed. Galya tried not to let her heart drop.

"Mrs. Varushkin, this is my friend Angela Fahey. She is a friend and neighbor." Violet and the young woman with red hair shared a glance and a laugh.

"I am Magdalena, please feel free to call me that." Magda said.

Galina heard her mother speaking. Galya was wondering about the peaceful moment she had had with God just a few minutes before. She was so disappointed by the lack of jars in the woman's hands that she barely heard Violet speaking.

"We have come with good tidings. Our church has come together for your family to provide you with safe lodging for the year. We know your husband is away, like my own husband." Violet said and grabbed Magdalena's free hand.

"Lodging?" Galina asked, wondering what they meant.

"Yes, we have a home that is rented for you. My old home was available for rent. The church has rented the property under your name and will repair the roof and prepare it for you within the next few days. We were worried that you all were suffering in the cold and we invite you to come stay with the Grant's and the Harpole family while the house is being prepared for you. Your new home has some acreage and a well set up already." Violet smiled.

Magdalena looked at Galya and they both seemed confused. The baby let out a small simper that brought them out of their stupor.

"I am understanding…" Magdalena's accent seemed thicker than earlier. "You rented a house for us, and the church is fixing it for us to live in."

"Yes, it is paid for the next year. In your husband's name so you have no worries this winter. We may have a few jobs lined up so you will be independent soon as well." Angela said with some excitement in her own voice.

"We have not been to your church." Magdalena stated.

"You are welcome if you wish. But there is no obligation for you to come. We just are doing God's work. We saw your family's need in this hard time and God led us to help you." Violet said softly. "God helped me just this last year when I was hungry and cold. He heard my prayers and answered." Violet said. Galya nearly gasped as it fully sunk in. God was looking out for her family.

<hr />

It took Galina an hour of calling along the Willamette River to find her brothers. Her mother was packing their meager belongings in the wagon that had come with the nice man named Clive. She was eager to get out of that tent and in between prayers of thanks to God she panted in the cold wind. Her brothers were far out in their hunting or mischief making, she was certain it was a mixture.

Once they answered her call she caught them up on the happenings. They dropped the gathered sticks they had been carrying and all ran together back to the tent. The boys were excited for the new adventure.

The boys, Milo and Pavel, would be staying in the home of Chelsea and Russell Grant, and Magda, Galina and baby Radimir would be staying with Corinne and Lucas Grant.

The wagon dropped off all the clothes and belongings to the respective cabins. Milo and Pavel were happy to meet Brody. Pavel was only a year older that Brody and they all seemed ready for a new friendship. Magda gave firm instructions to her boys to behave and had a talk with Chelsea expressing her gratitude.

"I am glad to help." Chelsea said generously. "It will be wonderful for Brody to have some playmates."

"You must understand how truly I wish to thank you." Magda was overwhelmed by the day's events and the generosity of people she had never met.

Chelsea gave Magda a loving pat on the shoulder.

"I will be praying for your family." Chelsea shared. "We have all had the times when we needed a fresh start."

Grant's Grove was the next stop and Magda and Galina were happily shown where they would be sleeping. Clive took over with explanations of all that would be happening over the next few days.

Marie volunteered to take baby Radi while Clive took Magda and Galina to the cabin.

Clive clarified several times not to worry about the sad state of the roof. The men of the church had supplies and plans for the home to make it safe and warm.

The visit was brief but profound for the mother and her daughter. They could see the cabin needed repairs but the structure of the rest of the building had promise. It would be the largest home they had lived in. Galina had never slept in a room alone in her life. When she was told about the walled loft plans she was overwhelmed.

Her prayers from the morning had been for food and warmth. She had dreamt of thin flimsy walls to make their tent into a shack. Knowing God had led these people to help her family was something so much more powerful than she could have known.

She was thanking God with every breath for the rest of the night.

Grant's Grove

Corinne awoke early, wanting to help Violet with the breakfast preparations. Having a full house was a reminder to her that someday she wanted to fill the home with children and life. She was trusting God everyday to lay aside the doubts about her ability to be a mother.

The wagon was brimming with bodies as they pulled onto the property that was now rented for the Varushkins. The children climbed out and the boys whooped over something they saw to their liking. It turned out to be a tree they thought was a perfect climbing tree. Corinne and Violet laughed at the fun of seeing these children finding joy in such a strange and child-like way.

Angela stayed behind and was watching the baby Radimir, and Chelsea's daughter Sarah. So Galina and her mother were able to help on the rebuild project.

The floorboards had been pulled and the place had been aired out and smelled fresh. Lucas and Russell were inside laying new boards and there was a group of men gathered around Clive and Pastor Whittlan.

Once Corinne got closer to the group she realized that they were the roof committee. The round wood beams were removed within an hour, they were set-aside for the family to use for any projects. Straight boards were unloaded off a wagon and settled on a dry, flat patch of the yard. The roof went on faster than anyone could imagine. The hardest part was working around the chimney cut out. The men were pretty experienced at hard work and figuring how to build just about anything. Once the roof was well underway the women set about getting the inside ready for inhabitants. Lucas and Russell were available to lend some muscle to any ideas that sprang from the fertile minds of the women.

While Corinne was throwing out some scraps from the floor she saw the young boys were busy at work. It seemed Clive was overseeing more than the roof build. But also the troops of young boys were put to task.

A wagonload full of firewood had arrived to give the family a healthy supply of heat for the winter months. The boys were instructed carefully about what Clive wanted and where. Clive took no nonsense from the boys at first, but once he saw the good work he was full of compliments and friendly banter.

The first stack of firewood was high and the boys were working on a second by the time Corinne made a second visit outside the cabin.

Corinne smiled to herself seeing the boys together, Cooper, Brody, Milo and Pavel. Somehow she knew they would all grow up to be hard working men like their fathers.

The Varushkin's new neighbor, a plump farmer named Darryl made his way over. Corinne had never met him, but Violet seemed to know him and introduced him to Magdalena. He seemed friendly enough.

Corinne was back in the house and checking over what was going to be needed for the Varushkin family. The fireplace was clean, and she got a fire going easily. Everyone was happy as the room filled with warmth. The roof boards were on and now the crew was applying wooden shingles to it. Clive had been talking to the men how the shingles were made of a dense wood, Corinne just knew the men were doing everything they could to make they home safe and warm.

Angela Fahey

Angela had her hands full with baby Radimir, and Sarah. Little Sarah Grant wanted to run around and explore everything. Her brown shiny hair was in a loose braid and she was adorable, but that girl had some spunk. Angela was betting that Chelsea often had her hands full. It made her think that once she was set up in her own house she would ask to take Sarah more often, she knew it would give Chelsea a chance to get work done and perhaps enjoy a little down time too. Angela smiled with her plan.

She knew that the home for the Varushkin family would be nearly complete today. Tomorrow they would be moving in.

She had hopes to help the Varushkin family out with any necessities. She would pray that they would be open for the charity. She knew from experience that she hadn't always been open to it herself. But if she had little ones the situation would be different.

Radimir started getting cranky close to lunchtime. He was only a few months old and Angela was guessing that he was getting hungry. She had changed a nappy and he was clean and dry, he seemed a little tired and started to grab out with his tiny fingers. It only took Angela a few seconds to realize what he wanted.

"Sorry, big fella, I cannot help you with that." Angela chuckled and smoothed her hand over Radimir's head. He didn't have much hair but the fuzz of brown starting to make an appearance, was soft to the touch.

Sarah had settled finally with a few wooden blocks and one of Angela's handkerchiefs. You never knew what would amuse a child. Sometimes you just had to let them play with whatever they found, as long as it is safe.

Radimir fussed and cried more as the hour passed closer to noon.

Angela was relieved to see Magdalena Varushkin cross the front window toward the door.

Madgalena was inside and the baby boy responded immediately. She barely had her coat off before Radimir tried to squirm out of Angela's arms.

"I think he is hungry." Angela said lamely.

"Yes, I will be relieved myself. I should have come back an hour ago. I was making an arrangement with my neighbor. It took longer than I expected." Magdalena took her son and sat on the soft chair. "I will need to change my dress, would you mind watching Radi for a few minutes after I feed him?"

Angela nodded and sat with Sarah, giving Magdalena some privacy to feed her son. She had noticed that Magdalena's dress was damp across the front. She had forgotten about that, Edith Sparks had talked about breastfeeding with her but that was pushed back in her memory far enough that she hadn't thought about it.

Once the feeding was over Magdalena handed a sleepy Radi to Angela, Magdalena was back within a few minutes with a fresh dress and a cloth sling for Radi to rest in.

"I think I can take him along. The dangerous work is done and Corinne has heat in the fireplace in the cabin. Mostly I am just there to observe. He will sleep now for a while. He likes the sling." Magdalena smiled and her dark eyes lit up warmly. "Thank you so much Angela, it is really a pleasure to meet you. Corinne told me that house on the hill to the north a ways is yours. I am glad we shall be close neighbors. Your kindness…" She paused, her throat getting thick with emotions. "You and your friends are good people of God."

Angela felt moved enough to lean forward to embrace the woman. It was a wordless moment, a connection that was immediately felt.

"I have been on the receiving end of charity before. It is bigger than we can explain. Being saved from something we were trapped in." Angela said once she pulled away from the embrace.

Magdalena nodded with tear-filled eyes. She held Radimir with one arm and her free hand grasped Angela by the shoulder. With a small smile of understanding from both of them they resumed their duties.

John Harpole was waiting with a carriage outside. Angela assumed he had checked in on his wife. Angela picked up Sarah and watched through the window as John helped Magdalena into the back seat of the carriage. It was smart looking carriage, with shiny black wood and a leather canopy over the top, to keep off any rain or wind, the wheels rims were painted a bright cherry red.

Once John, Magdalena and baby were off safely Angela bundled up Sarah and herself, snatched a few blocks and the fun handkerchief, and they walked over to the Harpole's Ranch.

The wind was brisk and Angela sheltered Sarah from the wind with her warm scarf. Sarah's body was warm and snuggled in as Angela carried her. It definitely triggered motherly feelings and Angela thought again of her home, and all those rooms she built.

Marie was in pleasant spirits in her kitchen. She was baking and cooking away. Angela and Sarah removed all the layers and coats and joined Marie at the countertop. Sarah held her hands up to be picked up. Angela heaved the young girl up and was rewarded with a sweet smile.

"I bet your arms are getting tired." Marie teased.

"Surprisingly yes. Once or twice to pick them up is fine but the repeated action is what gets to ya." Angela said, and placed a kiss on the top of Sarah's head.

The counter top was laden with food. Several bread loaves, a few quart jars of soup and two-dozen biscuits cooling on the other counter.

"You planning a feast?" Angela asked.

"Just getting enough food together for the Varushkins. I know that they will need a few days to get settled in. Having a few meals ready to warm up will go a long way to make Magda's job easier." Marie went through all the food with Angela, also sharing her ideas about the next few days.

"I know they have no money. Magda told Violet as much yesterday. I was wondering how they would have enough food stocks. I know I will be having to purchase my food stocks this year and possibly next." Angela knew that the winters were unforgiving for those with little money.

"I do believe almost all of the families at the church will be delivering foodstuffs in the next few days. Violet said the root cellar was sound, so John said he would help me go through things tomorrow. I know we have plenty. This way we will actually have more room for my canning jars. I am always running out of room." Marie said with a grin.

"I know they will have needs that will come up, I am praying how I can be of help." Angela said with concern. She was new at being on the other side of helping. She didn't want to push her way in where it wasn't wanted, but she knows what it meant to have nothing.

"I do know that Corinne has hired on Galina for a day or two a week to help Violet keep up with the laundry." Marie said.

"I had hopes of doing the same. I will be doing a lot of work to get my house set up and ready. Having a helping hand would bless me, and I know the funds will bless her household. I will talk to Galina and her mother tonight. We can work out a schedule." Angela's mind was in a whirl about all that she had to do. Today was good for her. To focus on something besides herself and the house build.

The afternoon passed quickly with the pleasant visit. Angela kept Sarah entertained and got to talk and visit with Marie. Angela heard the sounds of carriages and wagons and knew that Chelsea would be coming for her daughter.

Angela said a quick farewell and bundled herself and Sarah up for the short walk back to the Grant's cabin.

Chelsea was indeed glad to see her baby girl and thanked Angela profusely. Chelsea wanted to get home and get dinner started and see if Sarah would take a nap. Some of the men stayed behind to get a few more things done on the Varushkin's cabin before they called it a night.

Chapter Ten

Grant's Grove

The Grant cabin was full, with the Grant's, Violet, Angela, Magdalena, Galina and Radi. Dolly had decided to stay with Chelsea to help her manage all the rowdy boys and Sarah. Once dinner was served and cleaned up, the adults started to feel the effects of a long and hard working day.

Violet and Magdalena were the first to call the evening done and went to their rooms. Angela shared her room with Galina and she had an extra cot that was brought in. Angela had volunteered to use the cot every night, but Galina would only agree to split the time. The night before Galina had slept on the bed so Angela knew Galina wasn't about to accept anything but the cot that evening.

Corinne and Lucas were at the table planning out something, it was the time of night they liked to make plans and lists. Angela found their habits amusing. The two of them had so many ideas between them.

Angela and Galina talked of little things; just chitchat and then Galina started sharing her experiences.

"When you and Violet came a few days ago, it was already a tough day. I was going to try and get some work here at the Grant's house. I was trying so hard to stop thinking the worst." Galina said with emotion lodged in her throat.

Angela saw a few desperate days herself and knew those feelings.

"The cold was coming." Angela stated. She had seen the state of that tent out on the edge of town. She had seen what cold and exposure could do to a young child. "I was sent to a work orphanage when I was almost eight years old. The room I stayed in had no heat for years. Winters were cold, so very cold. The floor was dirt and flat stone in some areas. I remember we girls would pile into our cots as many as could fit and share our flimsy threadbare blankets. I remember waking up one morning to girls screaming in the next bunk. A three-year-old girl had died. She had been suffering with first a cold and then it got worse progressively. The two girls in bed with girl were traumatized. After that the people that ran the orphanage brought in a wood stove. It wasn't run all winter but they did give us wood a few days a week. We would ration it and save it for the coldest days." Angela shook her head at the memories of that dark and dirty place.

"You must have been so afraid." Galina said.

"I was, that was why I knew you would understand." Angela placed a hand over Galina's hand.

"But I feel so guilty now. It's two days since we have been in the cold. We have been saved and I have thanked God many times but I still am so selfish in my thoughts." Galina confessed and looked down at her lap.

"You have been working so hard, and being so helpful. I have seen no selfish actions on your part." Angela wanted to defend Galina but she could see the stress written across the girl's face.

"In my heart all I have been thinking about is how everyone must think we are so disgusting. That day you and Violet came to us I was attempting to wash some clothes for us. It was so very difficult. I used the last of the matches to get the fire started to get the pot boiling. The wind was whipping and trying to steal the fire. I had spoken to God that day like I never had before. Trusting in Him…" Galina's voice caught. Angela patted her hand in support.

"He heard your prayers." Angela said.

"Yes, and all I keep thinking is that our clothes and bodies are so dirty. Everyone will think we are disgusting people." Galina finally confessed it all. "I should be thankful that we are all safe and warm, and I am overwhelmed with shame over such matters."

"Oh sweet girl, I wish I would have known, we should have thought of helping you with a bath and laundry." Angela felt her own emotions well up within her. She had known shame in front of people. Going into the fancy houses to work, half-starved and dirty.

"I shall remedy this immediately. I cannot get a bath drawn without waking the house. But I can get your hair washed. Then in the morning we can get up a little earlier and fill the tub for everyone to get a bath before moving day. Starting fresh." Angela suggested. She saw that Galina liked the idea.

Angela sent Galina to the kitchen to start a kettle. Angela went to get a deep basin to wash the girl's hair in. Corinne came from the other room curious about the activity.

"Oh, Cori, my heart in nearly broke in two. This poor girl has been ashamed these last days because she hasn't been able to clean herself or their clothes since the weather turned." Angela said in a hushed tone. She didn't want the girl to hear them talking.

"Oh, I should have thought of that. Here we are doing all the good things for the outside and not thinking of them as people." Corinne said and she felt for the girl. She was at a loss on how to make it up to them.

"I was thinking to help her wash her hair tonight, her hair can dry by the fire. I will leave her the soap and basin for her to wash simply. But I am also thinking about the clothes. What can we do tonight?" Corinne pondered. Clothes took so long to dry indoors this time of year.

"It is just after 8:30, do you think the Harpole's will be up still?" Angela asked.

"Yes, Maria likes to stay up and crochet most nights past 10. Cooper will be fighting his bedtime right about now." Corinne laughed. "What did you have in mind?"

Angela and Corinne talked for a minute and they had a plan. There wasn't much they could do with the boy's clothes on short notice but the women had a thought about how to help their new neighbors in a small way.

Angela took the large basin and had found her favorite lavender hair rinse that Corinne had made for her. She was honored to share it with Galina.

Angela poured the bowl nearly half full of the water with room temperature water that had been carried in a few hours before. After dinner Lucas always topped off the indoor water jar.

Galina joined her at the counter and they waited for the water to boil. Together Angela and Cori brought out a folding wall to give the girl some privacy. It was lightweight. They placed a towel on the floor because the girl was worried about dripping water.

An hour later Galina was settled in a rocking chair by the fire in a terrycloth dressing gown, clean and smelling of lavender and a hint of vanilla. She was brushing out her long brown hair.

Angela enjoyed seeing the smile on the young girl's face as they set about their other tasks. Lucas claimed to have an early morning so he headed off to bed. Corinne came back from her visit to her father's house.

Angela and Corinne headed off to the back bedroom and came out a few minutes later with two dresses.

They sat on the davenport next to Galina and saw the question in her eyes.

"I was just packing and realized that I may have a dress or two that I have grown out of still lingering in my closet." Angela held up a simple dark green cotton dress. "I know tomorrow is moving day so you will need something practical for everyday. But I have a potential Sunday dress and a nicer dress in case you need something for a barn dance. I know that people are talking about having one near Michaelmas." Angela grinned as she saw the gratitude in Galina's face.

"Oh that is lovely. May I try it on?" She said and first then paused. "Are ya sure it no longer fits ya?" She looked a little suspicious about the gift.

"Ya, pretty sure. In the last few years I grew a bit more up top and through the hips. Just enough to make that dress tighter on me than is decent." Angela said, trying to sound a bit like Clive. Corinne started giggling and for a minute they both joined in.

"Ok, that does sound reasonable. We have accepted so much charity, I hate to take more from your families." Galina said and looked to the bundle in Corinne's arms.

"It's from Marie, she claims to have outgrown this dress too. She said it's been hanging there for a year untouched. She needs more room in her closet. And it's true, that woman loves to sew. When she runs out of room in her closets she makes clothes for other people. You should see her room full of fabric. I think it was supposed to be an extra pantry for harvest season but she turned it into a fabric room." Corinne said and Angela confirmed with a nod. "We were thinking that it may fit your ma. It may need a belt or a little stitching here or there, but both you women could have clean clothes to start your new life. We tried to find something for the boys but it is too short a notice. The drying time this time of year would have the boys' clothes wet still. But I have found that boys care less about the cleanliness."

"You both are so very kind." Galina said sincerely and ran off to try on her dress in the room she was sharing with Angela.

After a few minutes Galina came out and declared it to be a great fit. It was a little longer than necessary, young girls could wear dresses to a few inches below the knee. This dress came to her ankles and made her look a bit older. It was a dark blue with a cream lace trim on the collar and the sleeves. The print on the fabric was beige and black pinstripe. Galina had never owned anything so nice.

"Well, it does look lovely on you, even for an everyday dress this coloring really suits your dark eyes." Corinne said.

Galina glowed with the praise.

"Oh I have a cream colored apron that goes with that perfectly. You are really saving me some time and energy. I will be moving myself in a few days, Lord willing, and I want to only move things I need. I will be rummaging through the closet and trunks to see what fits and what doesn't." Angela said and a yawn came out without her permission. "I think that young Sarah plumb wore me out today. That girl has some energy."

"I will get changed quickly and let you go to bed. May I hang this on a hanger for tonight?" Galina asked, looking so young and vulnerable.

"Of course. You take as long as you need. I will chat with Corinne until you are ready." Angela said.

"Also, I know you and Violet have worked out days to do laundry. If you want to bring your laundry here and do it all together it will save time and water for you and your house. We have plenty of space in the mud room for both our households clothes to dry inside, and then outside come spring." Corinne said with confidence, she was getting more comfortable with her role in the household. She knew this young girl was glad for the work and she knew her family needed the funds.

With Galina off to change into her nightgown, Corinne and Angela had a nice chat by the warm fire. Enjoying the feeling of helping others and also remembering being thirteen years old and how the turbulent emotions take over often.

The lights were out soon and the Grant cabin was all in slumber. The next day would be a full one.

Varushkin Cabin

Galina heaved the trunk from the back of the wagon. Clive was next to her, doing the same. She knew that the kitchen items were stored in this trunk. They had been using it mostly as a seat in the tent. She was glad to get the pans, kettles, and plates out and put them away. Galina knew her mother was beside herself with joy. She had even heard her mother singing an old Polish song as she was helping the boys get the fire started in the fireplace when they first arrived. It had been a few months since she had heard her mother singing. It was good for all of them to get this fresh start.

The trunk was heavy but Galina got it settled on the wooden table that was near the kitchen. It was a good place to unload and then she and her mother could find a resting place for everything. The countertop was loaded down with food from Marie Harpole. The food would last them several days. It was just a blessing. It would give them time to get settled. There was so much work to do and meal preparation would be a few days away.

Galina was looking forward to Sunday service in a few days. She had a new dress to wear. Her mother was going to hem up the dresses that Angela had given her. Galina liked them long but her mother declared that she could lower her hem when she was fifteen and no sooner. Her mother had been smiling so much the last few days. It really was good to see.

Galina knew her younger brothers would be going back to school soon. Since they were still young enough. There was a part of her that was envious. She wanted to go too. Her reading was still so terrible. She would just have to persuade the boys to teach her.

The cabin was cozy and warm once all the trunks were brought in. Galina saw more people arriving as she gathered some wood to put in the firewood box inside. She saw people with baskets full of things. Galina said her hundredth prayer of thanks as she quickly went inside. The dark clouds were rolling in and threatened rain. They were lucky to have had a break in the rain this week. Looks like that would soon end.

"Thank you Lord for the roof, the warm fire, and the food." Galina whispered her prayer.

The neighbors gave them plenty of food to last them several months. Stewed tomatoes and onions, strawberry preserves, honey, pickles, sauerkraut, all canned by Helen Whittlan, the preacher's wife. She and Galina's mother seemed to strike an immediate friendship over the sauerkraut. Helen's father had been from the old country.

Marie, John Harpole, Corinne and Lucas shared baskets of root vegetables, potatoes, radishes and carrots. They also brought a pumpkin which would be indoors. They figured it wouldn't keep too much longer. The stem was looking a bit dry. It looked to have a week or two before it would turn.

Galina thought about pumpkin bread and cookies. She once had a pumpkin pie. It was like pudding and the spice was delicious.

Some other neighbors brought a few practical things, candles, lanterns, and some fresh butter. Chelsea brought a big stack of freshly sewn nappies for the baby. She had crocheted hats and scarves for every one in the family.

The new neighbor Darryl came by with fresh milk and the boys promised to help him muck stalls in the barn for fresh milk every week.

Reggie Gardner, who lived a few acres away, brought some grocery staples, a large sack of flour, sugar, and a side of smoked bacon. The main room was overflowing with items and people.

Pastor Whittlan got the crowd to quiet down. "I would like to give these folks some space to get settled but I thought we should say a prayer first before we leave them to their new home."

The crowd murmured its approval.

"Dear Lord, we pray a blessing over this house and family. Let Your peace and love reign in this home. May the children grow in their love of You. Please bless the father of these children and bring him home safely. In the name of Jesus we pray."

Everyone said "Amen" together. The group disbanded soon after, Magdalena was sure to thank everyone over and over as they left.

Once the house was quiet Galina and Magda worked together to make a plan for the house. Pavel who was seven was put in charge of watching Radi while everyone else unpacked.

As Galina and Magdalena worked together quickly to make the kitchen serviceable, the rain began to pour outside. The wind howled for the remainder of the day.

A few hours later Galina put her mattress on the rope bed. The soft feather ticking was nicer than any bed she had ever slept on. She put fresh linen on everyone's beds. The boys' side of the loft had a high bed built into the edge. Milo was nine and Mother had declared that he would have the top bed. Pavel would take the lower one. They had pegs on the wall and Galina put out clothes for them to wear for the next day. Knowing her first chore in the morning was going to be washing their clothes. She knew the blessing of fresh clean clothes and wanted her brothers to feel it too, whether they wanted it or not. Galina smirked at the idea. She knew they would be forced to take a bath tomorrow too. She had noticed that Chelsea Grant had washed their faces down pretty thoroughly as they had been very dirty. But she was sure not even the sweet nature of Chelsea Grant could urge them into a water tub.

After Milo and Pavel went to bed, Galina sat in the main room downstairs. There was a love seat and two rocking chairs by the fire. Only one of the rocking chairs had been theirs. The others had just been in the cabin that morning. It hadn't been there the day before. Someone had probably come by late last night or very early in the morning to deliver them. Galina was overwhelmed with gratitude.

"I hear the rain slowing down." Her mother spoke softly. Radi was asleep in her arms.

"I keep feeling the cold in my bones from just a few days ago." Galina said.

Magda nodded silently but tears slipped down her cheeks. Galina took Radi from her and took him to the crib in the bedroom behind the kitchen. She came back and sat next to her mother on the loveseat.

"I feel the cold too Galya." Her mother said with a tight throat.

"I spoke to God the day they came to tell us. It was the first time I truly had faith of my own." Galina said.

"You have such wisdom in you, my child. God will do amazing work through you." Her mother said simply. They held each other for a little while until they could no longer stay awake. It had been a good day.

Chapter Eleven

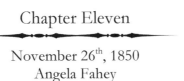

November 26th, 1850
Angela Fahey

The morning had been cold but the clouds broke early enough for the bricklayers to finish the last chimney. Two men had been putting plaster on the upstairs walls. They were making a racket with their singing but it made Angela laugh. The men were brothers and singing Spanish songs made them happy workers. They had done a beautiful job of plastering the downstairs the week before. The sanding had left dust everywhere, a fine white powder covering every surface. Angela knew the same would happen upstairs but she worked hard at cleaning to stay on top of it.

Angela had a fire going in the kitchen stove. The temperature was cold outside and having any heat was a blessing while Angela tried to get any work done in her new house. She had so many things to do and she was at a loss to where to start.

The fireplace that was in the parlor that shared wall with her bedroom would be done today. She could officially move in if she wanted to. The thought excited and scared her at the same time.

Earl Burgess knocked on her front door.

She ran to the door and let him in. She was holding a hand towel in her hand.

"May I?" Earl asked. His eyes glanced at what she was holding.

"Of course." She handed him the towel.

Earl wiped some moisture off his head and stomped his feet on the rug before he came in.

"Did it start raining again?" Angela asked with a bit of worry in her voice. The bricklayers would not be able to work in the rain.

"Just a sprinkle, but the bricklayers are done. They put a rubber tarpeline over the last bit of work to keep it dry while it sets. No fire for you today for that fireplace unless the rain stops soon. But if there is no rain tomorrow they may light it for you and the heat might set it faster." Earl explained.

Angela nodded and invited him to sit at the table with her.

"I don't want to get anything dirty." Earl said in protest.

"Earl Burgess, what harm are you going to do to a wooden chair? This entire place is covered in plaster dust, saw dust, dirt and probably things I don't even know about. Sit yerself a spell." Angela pointed to the chair. Earl chuckled and did as he was told.

"I think I am in over my head Earl." Angela confessed. Her green eyes lit up with mirth mixed with a little fear. Her exaggerated grin was comical.

"Well, we all do that at least once in our lives Miss Fahey." Earl chuckled again and the rumble of it made Angela smile.

"I am going to smack your arm next time you call me Miss Fahey." She smiled.

"Angela…" He corrected quickly. "You will do alright. It is a big house but you will make your way in it." He said with certainty. "You will have me nearby, your friends are near enough to ring a bell and they would come a runnin'." His right hand was work roughened. His left hand was missing from an accident years before.

"You got your place all cozy?" Angela asked, taking the focus off of her.

"Yes'm, I do. The fireplace had a lot of ash in it, but after a few cleanings it was good as gold. I was going to give your horse a ride later to give him some exercise. You asked the other day if we needed another hand. I was thinking on it. There is a young lad of fifteen looking for live-in work. The lad, Warren, is well known for being raised on a farm. He could bunk in my spare room. I could buy that milk cow from the neighbor. He could take care of the animals, exercise your horse and milk the cow. I know I will need a spare hand now and then. We will be felling a lot of trees over the winter months, as weather allows. Gotta clear some space for your new trees." Earl smiled wistfully. He could see the future of the land in his head as much as she could.

"You hire him, just make sure he knows that I will be paying him. Some men don't wanna work for a woman." Angela said. "Oh… I look forward to having my own jersey cow." She sighed distractedly. Her brain was going a thousand directions. She was eager to move in. She was thinking about how many days it would be before she could.

"I will call on the lad later today, umm Warren Martin, to see if he would like the job and the spare room. There is plenty of work to be done for you as well, I see." Earl looked around at the house. "At least you have some heat in the kitchen now."

The wood stove was burning and the crackle and pop of the fresh wood she had just put in there was a comforting sound. Angela nodded and looked to the wood stove. It was the center of her kitchen and she loved the look of it, shiny black and cast iron, with floral patterns on the covers and edges.

"I love my stove, isn't it a beautiful sight." Angela gushed. "I have lots to do but I will have plenty of long winter days to do it. Dolly has agreed to stay with me a lot over the winter." Angela smiled at the thought, her own home, and a houseguest. Even with all the work that needed doing she was determined to think about the future.

Earl stood and stretched, ready to leave. A knock at the door startled them both.

Angela could see through the side window that Clive was at the door.

She opened the door and let him in. "You braving the rain?" She asked with a smile. She handed him a kitchen towel to dry himself off.

"Yes indeed, glad to see you have some heat now." Clive shook Earl's hand. "You liking the new job, Earl?"

Earl laughed and patted Clive on the shoulder. "You know I love being back on the land."

They chatted amicably for a minute and Angela went back to her kitchen. She was trying to get the dishes unpacked and put them into the cabinet next to the dining room table.

"Talk to you tomorrow, Miss Fahey, umm Angela." Earl called out and waved as he was headed out the door.

"See you in the morning, by the barn." Angela called out as he left. She really enjoyed the walk over every morning to meet with Earl. She was going to have new morning habits soon, she realized. She looked forward to the challenge.

Clive took a moment and shook off his boots. He was wearing thick wool socks that looked ready for an Oregon winter.

"That stove looks mighty fine in here, Red." Clive stood next to the wood stove a minute later and was bending over, checking it out from all sides. His hands were hovering over the top to get some warmth.

"Thank you! You helped pick it." Angela pulled a burner cover off and the heat poured through it and the bright orange logs could be seen. "I haven't tried to bake with it yet but it is very similar to the stove at the Grants' place." She covered the burner hole with a sliding metal sound. The cast iron was heavy and would take a little time getting used to. She pulled the hook out of the cover and hung the device back on the peg she had placed behind the stove.

"You will learn the ways of it quickly, you are a smart gal." Clive said with his usual mirth. He was always such pleasant company. Nothing could ever impair his mood.

She explained how she would have to wait another day or two to move in.

"That was the only part I was worried about." He admitted about the fireplaces and the finicky nature with rain. "But the rain doesn't look like it will stick around. The clouds are clearing up and to the north there is some sunshine peeking through the clouds."

"I do hope so. The masons are helping Earl with a fire pit by the barn. It was dug out but there was a load of leftover bricks, he thought that would put them to good use. The rest will be stored in the barn, for something else down the road." Angela felt her hope returning of being able to light the fireplace that day.

"Well, I will let you get back to your projects. I brought a few crates of things that you might be needing and housewarming gift from me to you. Also, I brought a small token from someone else." Clive lifted his eyebrows as he saw the curiosity rise in her face.

He pulled an envelope out of the inside jacket pocket. Angela was helpless against the squeal that escaped. He handed her the note and she gave him a kiss on the cheek.

"Let me grab those crates for you." Clive said as he pulled on his boots, but he heard the rip of the envelope and she was going to be busy for another minute or two. He chuckled over young people in general and went to retrieve his offering.

Angela opened the envelope with shaky hands. It was only one page and was a short note but she treasured every word.

Darling Angel,

We arrived in Sacramento five days ago. I sent a telegram to you and to Clive but have heard that the telegraph service is inconsistent. I sent forward a few belongings on a steamship that had cargo room. I wish we all could be aboard it. We have passage on a steam ship leaving soon and should be in Oregon within a week or two, depending on the weather.

It has been such a long wait to see your green eyes again but the memory keeps me going on the hard journey.

The women of my family all send a greeting. I pray you stay safe and warm.

Yours,

Ted Greaves

Angela set the letter down with joy in her heart. She would read it again later, for now she could relax and know that Ted was safe. She had been waiting for word. Now she had it. The journey wasn't finished for him, but the longest wait was over.

Angela turned her focus to Clive who was unloading crates in her dining room. He brought a tarp over and was holding a crow bar.

"You want the honors?" He handed her the crow bar and she wordlessly began to pry up the top boards.

The first crate had several wrapped items. Angela pulled up two chairs and she began unwrapping the treasures. First was a wall clock, stained a dark burgundy, with a fancy number plate and a brass pendulum. Angela gasped and held it up to get the full view. It was about three feet tall and a little heavy. It had a glass door and a brass coated chain hanging next to the pendulum in the back.

"You should be able to pull the chains once a week to keep it going. I have one that is similar." Clive said.

"Clive, this is beautiful. Thank you so much." Angela grabbed his hand and gave it a squeeze.

"O hush, yer welcome." Clive said with a smirk.

Next in the large crate was a set of brass candlesticks. Together whey could hold six candles. Wrapped in linen was a large selection of candles, creamy white and tapered. There were two cast iron pans in the bottom. They clunked together as Angela pulled one from the box.

"You will need to season those with lots of butter and lard for a while to get them to their peak performance. Wash them with as little water as possible. They will lean toward rustin' if you douse them. Dry 'em up good." Clive accepted the hugs and thank yous from her with a lot of laughs and affection.

"I will take good care of them. I made such a huge list, but I didn't think of cast iron pans. I do have a copper stock pot, though." Angela grinned sheepishly. "I am sure I have forgotten so many little things. I feel excited and foolish for stepping out on my own. But somehow I just felt it was time."

"We all learn so much the first time we do step out, child. It's part of the growing pains. The first winter I was on my own, I nearly froze to death. I was so short on firewood that I had to burn my chairs and bedposts during a blizzard. Did that only one time. Fear was a mighty good motivator." Clive chuckled, remembering the cold wind sneaking through his tiny cabin. "I was seventeen and doing my first round of trapping on my own. That was over forty years ago. I believe I was in Michigan, had been near the great lake Michigan."

"I just love your stories, Clive, I do hope you will be coming by to visit often. I promise to always have a warm fire and coffee at the ready." Angela couldn't help but love Clive. He was so very good to her. She was feeling emotional and overwhelmed by the gifts. She held a hand to her heart and wished for the lump in her throat to go away.

"Oh the next box is full of more practical items, go ahead and pop off one of the boards but not all. Just for you to see, no need to pull anything out until later. I daresay I am adding to your workload for the day." Clive watched Angela pull up the first board with a squeak of wood. The box was sectioned, linen bags were showing.

"Potatoes, white and red, carrots, cabbages, radishes, onions, I have a cart still in the wagon to bring in, but I wasn't sure if you wanted the glass jars inside or in the root cellar. I labeled everything with the help of Millie, you will want to get the root vegetables in the root cellar in a day or so, I can load the box for you when you would like it." He pointed to the cast iron hand truck he had next to him.

"You are a dear, I hope that Millie did not mind helping. I do not want to put anyone out." Angela was a little concerned when she heard Millicent Quackenbush mentioned. Her relationship with JQ's wife was a little strained at times.

"No worries, Red, she was well rewarded for helping me, and canning jars are her joy. I bet if you asked her for a lesson in canning you could win her over for good." Clive gave her a wink. "I bribed her with a new stove, a match for yours, a few days before asking her this favor. She was happy as a clam."

"We can take the vegetables down anytime you like, the jars can go in my pantry inside. Come see. I had the shelves put up yesterday." Angela pulled Clive along, excited to show off her large pantry. "I know it is big, too big for me now, but I hope to have a full house someday. I built a pantry big enough for the family I want. Is that silly?"

"Not at all, you have a generous heart. I believe there is a lot of love for you to share with others." Clive said sincerely.

The pantry had a swinging door, a hook for a lantern and a small pained window in the back to let in natural light. The two-sided pantry was tall. Under the right side was a folded stepladder.

"It was Earl's idea." Angela confessed.

"Good thinkin', the pantry is a handsome one. One can never have too much storage space." Clive said. "I shall bring in the jars directly and then you may unload at your leisure. I will come by tomorrow and help you with the root cellar." Clive ran one hand along the smooth wood of a shelf and nodded in approval.

"Clive, can I say thank you for all your gifts one more time?" Angela asked with a sweet and thankful look.

"Only once more, just imagine that it was your ma and pa, sending a few gifts from heaven. They would be so very, very proud of you." Clive said, all humor gone from his voice and if Angela could have guessed it would have sounded a tiniest bit husky from emotion.

Angela gave Clive a hug around his middle and let her head rest on a shoulder. She let a tear or two fall. She muttered a 'thank you' against his chest and he pecked a fatherly kiss on the top of her head.

***

Angela was walking back to Grant's Grove after her full day at her house. The bricklayers came back and removed the tarp from the chimney top. They started a fire in her fireplace while she worked with Clive on the vegetables and pantry loading. Her arms were sore from the many chores she had been doing but it was a good reminder that she was still alive and working hard toward her goals. Her old injury made her leg ache sometimes but she chose to ignore it.

Angela passed the road and looked to the creek that crossed it. The rains from the week before had swollen the creek and made the passage more difficult. Her property was on both sides of the creek and there was a large pretty willow tree that was near the road. Its branches hung down over the water. Her heart swelled at the ownership of such a beautiful tree. She imagined sitting under it next to Ted, talking as the water trickled by. The wind against her cheek reminded her to keep walking. She could daydream about Ted later, in the warmth of the Grant cabin. She laughed at herself.

Corinne's laboratory was a hundred yards off the road. It was a simple square structure that had two tall pines in the front. The chimney along the north side was still smoking, proof that work was still being done. Angela stopped in to chat with Dolly.

Dolly was easy to find. She was organizing small bottles into a crate. Angela said hello and wove her way around the equipment to find her.

"More lavender oil?" Angela asked.

"Yes, this small crate is going to the apothecary. We have so many orders. We will be shipping some out to California next week. Some of those boxes will move on to New York and Boston. We have had a good harvest this year." Dolly was smiling, as her hands worked.

"You and Corinne make a great partnership." Angela said sincerely, she enjoyed hearing about all that they did, even if she didn't fully understand it.

"I am looking forward to learning more and trying out new oils too. Corinne has been writing letters to doctors and apothecaries from all over, she wants to know about any oils that have been used for medicinal purposes. I have an idea to meet with other native tribes, north of here. There are many healers found amongst the native people. We want to learn their healing remedies too." Dolly said smiling then the smile faded for a moment. Angela patted her arm to get her attention.

"That is a great idea, why does it sadden you?" Angela asked. Noticing the tiny emotional changes in her friends face as she spoke. Dolly was hard to read sometimes, but Angela was learning to notice the little things.

"I am just thinking of the timing. I fear I am running out of time here." Dolly said soberly.

"You do not have to go back, do you? You are free to stay where you wish?" Angela asked, hoping the answer was an easy one, but somehow knowing that it wasn't.

"I am praying about the right course for me. The answers will come." Dolly said as a way to finish that topic. Angela could tell that Dolly was torn, but she respected her and let the matter drop.

"On another note, I believe my home will be ready to move into tomorrow. Are you still planning to come?" Angela asked.

Dolly was smiling again. "Yes! I am thrilled to be staying with you. I also want to come with you in the morning tomorrow as it is your Friday visit with the school children. I will not work tomorrow, instead I will be moving into your house. I think I am ready to stop moving from house to house so often. If your offer still holds I think I would like to consider your house my home. At least until your plans change, or your last name." Dolly teased, and was rewarded with a pink blush on Angela's cheeks.

"I am glad you are willing to live with me. I think it is a safer plan, I think I could live alone without fear but I know that people will talk. I try not to care but knowing we will be together makes me happy. You will be very close to your work with Corinne as well." Angela patted her friend's shoulder. The crate was now full of the dark brown bottles. She lifted it and placed it in a shelf along the east-facing wall next to the door.

"I am done for the day. Let's find Corinne and tell her our good news." Dolly led Angela to the door and found her long coat and scarf on a peg.

They walked to the greenhouse nearby. The steamy glass distorted the shapes inside. The warm rush of air felt wonderful on their faces.

Corinne was near the front door with Reggie Gardner. Reggie was holding a notepad and scribbling as Corinne was talking animatedly.

Angela said hello first, and gave a silly look to Dolly who had suddenly turned shy and was staring at her feet.

"Greetings," Reggie said. He was smiling and set the notepad down to extend a hand to Angela and then to Dolly. Dolly only looked up to nod and shook his hand and then she looked back to her feet.

"Reggie has agreed to work for both myself and my father, I need a bookkeeper and he is willing. I am so thrilled." Corinne patted him on the back and grinned.

"Yes, well I am glad for the work. I am staying in a small cabin close to town but I have some goals I am working toward." Reggie smiled shyly and then cleared his throat.

"I just came by to let you know Cori, that Dolly and I are moving into the house tomorrow. She is coming with me in the morning to the school. We will come back here first with your treasures." Angela said, she turned to Dolly but she wasn't looking up at all.

"That is wonderful. You need any more money for the children?" Corinne asked.

"No, I have plenty left." Angela said. "My penny pouch is full. You gave me enough for months last time."

"Are you still the 'plant lady'?" Reggie asked then chuckled.

"Of course. It was a good way to get lots of good samples, and it certainly blesses on both sides." Corinne said.

They all chatted about the fun finds they had had since they started it back up in the late spring. For every student that brought in usable plants the child got a penny for that week and the school also received a penny. The schoolteacher was glad for the help. He was adding books and supplies to the school with the additional funds.

Angela and Dolly left a few minutes later.

"You were so quiet in there." Angela stated, looking to Dolly for some sign of a problem.

"Yes," Dolly said simply.

"Does Reggie make you nervous?" Angela was guessing and giggled when Dolly looked perplexed.

Dolly didn't say anything but her embarrassment was showing across her cheekbones.

"I will not tease you anymore… today." Angela said and laughed again. Dolly looked relieved but Angela was already plotting.

Once Angela and Dolly reached the Grant's cabin they both saw Violet and Galina standing out front.

"Galya!" Angela called out, adopting the girl's nickname. They had become closer over the last few weeks. Angela usually did her own laundry with Violet and Galina to socialize through the task.

"Hello Angela, I am glad to see you." Galina pulled on her mittens and knit hat. Her brown hair was wispy and escaping her braid.

"I am glad too, you saved me the walk. I was hoping to hire your help tomorrow and Saturday if possible. Dolly and I are moving into my house. I was hoping for an extra set of hands to help with all the little things I have to do." Angela was hoping the girl would be happy with the extra work. She was rewarded with a smile from Galina.

"I would be happy too. I will make sure it is okay for Saturday with my mother. I can let you know tomorrow." Galina said, she was very relieved to have extra work. Her family needed any extra funds they could get.

"You can meet us at the school at seven tomorrow morning if you wish as I know it is on your route. Both Dolly and I will be collecting the plants the school children gather. Then we can walk back together." Angela suggested and she saw Galina nod.

Galina waved and took off on a brisk walk toward the footbridge that Lucas and Russell had built over the creek behind the Grant's house. It was a two-mile walk but she made good time.

Violet Griffen

Violet stirred the stew contentedly, enjoying the way the herbs and vegetables combined into the aroma. She thought of her pleasant day with Galina. She was finding the young girl a pleasant working companion. Galina had shared that day about how hard she was working to forgive her father for leaving. It had been a building point for them. She had told Galina that her husband had gone to California for gold too, that had been tipping point and Galina cried and shared her disappointments too.

She had wiped away a few of her own tears over a washtub this past year. "Sometimes you could get your best thinking done over such tasks." She had shared. She missed her husband, more than she could say. Every month that went by made her marriage vows seem further and further away.

Angela and Dolly were busy packing up the last of their property. Violet was excited for them, knowing how Angela was feeling about starting her life.

Violet felt content where she was, wishing Eddie was with her. Knowing they could continue living here with the Grants once he returned. She had discussed it with Lucas and Corinne, and they had agreed that with her own wing of the cabin they could all live there easily. Lucas and Corinne were very easygoing and Violet could see it working out well. She just wished that Eddie knew, somehow. She could try and write letters but she had no idea where exactly he was.

Corinne and Lucas were due home soon and Violet set the table for dinner. She filled the water in the pitcher with some hot water so everyone could wash up when it was time to eat. She poured the cold water into the basin she used to wash the dishes. She would add boiling water to it later when dishes were ready for washing. Waste not, want not.

She slid the small tin of rolls into the brick oven over the hearth. She had raspberry tarts cooling on the counter top for everyone to enjoy after dinner. Her raspberry preserves had turned out well. She had written down the recipe and would be using it again. It was just the perfect amount of sweetness, a hint of rosemary and then lemon juice to add a little tartness. Violet was enjoying herself in the big kitchen. The canning had been hard work but she felt a huge sense of well-being seeing the full pantry at the end of it.

Once Corinne and Lucas were home, Violet announced the time of dinner and told everyone to wash up. Everyone gladly obliged. Violet felt the importance of this last meal with Angela living there. Dolly was always moving from place to place, but this was a big move for Angela.

Lucas said the prayer over the meal and then Violet served. Everyone was chatting excitedly over the day's events. Violet was praised for her efforts and then praised again with the raspberry tarts devoured.

Angela went to bed first, claiming exhaustion after the busy day. She knew she would be getting up early to get her new life started. Lucas promised to have the wagon ready for when she and Dolly would be returning from the schoolhouse.

Lucas and Corinne sat by the fire. Violet headed to her rooms before she went to bed, she got her fire going and sat in her rocking chair and crocheted by herself until she was tired. She was thinking of Eddie, trying to remember every little thing about him. Time was trying to chase away her few memories, but she was determined to hold on to them.

Chapter 12

November 29th, 1850
Angela Fahey

Angela settled her weary body into a chair at the noon hour. She had risen early to get a good start on her move. Violet already had fresh coffee on and once a cup was shared, the day flew by. Clothes, trunks and crates were heaved and loaded into John Harpole's largest wagon. Angela was grateful for the break in the rainy weather to get her life moved with the least amount of hassle.

Corinne convinced Angela not do the school activity, Corinne herself went to the schoolhouse and then walked back with Galina, then everyone joined into the sorting, and unloading.

Violet brought lunch ingredients in with a loaded picnic basket. Violet tackled the kitchen with gusto and got the sawdust and building materials out of sight. The dining room table was set and food would be bubbling on the new stove in a few hours.

Angela could feel the muscles in her shoulders burning from all the trips in and out of the house. She was ready for a lunch break. Clive, Corinne and Dolly all were eager for a break too.

Earl stopped in a few times, making sure his extra hands weren't needed but his mind was occupied often with the finishing of the barn. The outside of the barn was finished. It was beautiful and more than big enough, the men had painted it a dark brick red. The inside stalls were still in progress.

The lunch was quiet at first with everyone focused on eating the delicious creamy potato soup and ham sandwiches. After a few minutes though, the moving party woke up from their work stupor and conversation began to flow. Everyone had a favorite part of the house to talk about. Corinne loved the front porch that wrapped around the house. Every angle offered a beautiful view. Clive and Violet both loved the kitchen. They felt it was the heart of the home. Dolly in her quiet way exclaimed over a certain window seat that overlooked the valley. The southwestern sky was her preferred view in the evening. The twilight hour was her favorite time of day.

After lunch the day got busier, Clive and Angela got to work putting her bed together. The brass bed was a special purchase that Clive had found in Sacramento, it never did make it to the store in Portland. The mattress was made by a craftsman in town. The gossip in town spread quickly about the bed and mattress. Several prominent families contacted Clive to seek bed frames and mattresses for themselves. Angela laughed at herself often, wondering how she became a trendsetter here in the West. Rope beds worked well and were more comfortable than laying in a cot, but the luxury of the brass beds with a real mattress was the buzz around the townsfolk who could afford it.

She had a lovely patchwork quilt and soft pillows to add to the bed when it was all put together. Violet and Corinne were busy putting the curtains up on the windows around the house. Angela had two crates of linens, from curtains to dish towels to bed sheets; some for beds she did not even own yet.

Galina felt privileged to help Angela unpack and hang up all of her clothing. Once they finished that job, the parlor needed to be arranged from the cluttered heap of boxes into a place to relax. Rugs and tables were put into place, a cozy fire started, and a few lamp wicks were trimmed and prepared, to be lit when necessary.

Dolly's room was settled soon after, with her own single brass bed and mattress.

"It is too soft, I do not think I could sleep in such comfort." Dolly smiled during her false protest. She loved the dark green quilt that was on her bed. She was on the second floor and felt special to have her own woodstove and a soft chair by the window. Angela had surprised her by having a selection of a few books in a bookcase in her room. Angela promised to have the walls painted in the spring. Dolly did not mind the wooden walls but would agree to any wishes that Angela made for the house. Dolly thought back a few years and remembered the tent walls and lying on the damp earth with a blanket between the ground and her body. *How could I go back to that life Lord, unless you will it for me?*

By five at night the move was declared a success. The wagon was empty and enough rooms were done to make the home livable. There were a hundred other projects to do but Angela felt she was ready to tackle them another day.

Corinne and Violet walked back to Grant's Grove after a few congratulations and hugs. Violet left a pot of stew and loaf of bread in Angela's clean kitchen.

Clive left soon after only popping back in to deposit a large pot of burgundy mums by the front door.

"Might brighten up your new home." Clive gave Angela and Dolly a wave before he escaped. Angela knew he didn't want another thank you, it was just his way.

"I cannot believe how much was done in one day." Dolly said with her eyes wide. "I feel so special that you let me stay with you. It feels like such an adventure." Her grin was infectious and Angela grabbed Dolly sideways by the shoulders.

"I am so glad that you are here with me."

The sky was darkening within an hour of everyone leaving and Angela was glad to be in her kitchen warming up the food left by Violet. She poked at her wood stove and lit the fireplace in the parlor. Then she lit the small round wood stove in her room on the other side of the wall where the master bedroom of the house was. The window faced west and Angela took a moment to watch the last bit of light fade over the hills.

Dolly was busy unpacking and Angela climbed the stairs to see her progress.

Dolly was surrounded by the contents of a crate. Angela was curious about all the interesting belongings. Obviously Dolly had brought some of her old life with her.

"I am not sure what to do with everything. I have moved around so much that I haven't looked at these things in more than a year." Dolly said softly, her voice was full of emotion, which was unusual for her.

"If you like, we can find a way to put them on display. There is plenty of room for shelves in here. I want to have plenty of shelves in all the bedrooms." Angela offered. She wanted Dolly to be happy here.

"That would be..." Dolly faltered a moment. She said nothing more but nodded her approval of the idea.

Angela decided to leave the young woman to her thoughts. She changed the subject. "Don't forget to light your wood stove. It will make it nice and cozy in here by bedtime. I can tell the temperature is dropping outside." Angela gave Dolly a friendly pat on the shoulder and left her alone.

Angie slid her hand along the banister rail as she walked down the stairs, taking pride in the home she owned. She had a lot of work to make it perfect, but it was hers. She lit a few candles and kerosene lamps around the house and enjoyed how the light glowed off her new shiny wood floors. It reminded her that she had rugs to make, and so many other little things. But she was content. The first part of her dream was coming true, the home was hers. Now she needed to make a family to fill it.

A knock at the front door startled Angela but she recovered quickly. She walked to the door briskly, her feet clicking and echoing across the hardwood. Reggie Gardner was at the door. Angela smiled and let Dolly know they had a guest with a loud yell. "We have a visitor!" She heard a scuffling upstairs as a sign that Dolly heard. She opened the door and Reggie stood nervously on the porch. His hands were moving restlessly with some wrapped gifts.

"Oh Reggie, you are my first official guest." Angela gave him a brief hug when he came in and took his coat and hat.

"I am pleased to be the first." He smiled genuinely and then his eyes shot to the staircase.

Angela turned and saw Dolly coming down the stairs. She turned back to see Reggie but she could tell all his attention was on her friend. Angela tried to hide her smile, but she failed. She couldn't help but notice that Dolly's blush was deep even with her tan complexion; the dark pink in her cheeks was unmistakable.

"You must stay to supper, Violet left stew and sourdough bread as a housewarming gift. We can make use of my new table," Angela said with mirth in her voice. Reggie returned his attention to Angela and nodded wordlessly. When Dolly had gotten closer she shook his hand quietly and mumbled a few words of welcome.

"I brought the ladies of the house a gift and the house itself a gift, so no one is left out." Reggie finally found his words.

"Thank you Reggie." Angela said with sincerity.

He fumbled with the packages in his arms and set one down on the nearby table. He peaked inside one and handed it to Dolly and the other object to Angela.

"These first." He said nervously.

Angela opened her oddly shaped gift to see three yellow roses wrapped with baby's breath.

"Oh my!" Angela gasped. And she looked over to see Dolly's equally beautiful pink rosebuds.

"These are so lovely. These smell like summer!" Dolly exclaimed surprising Angela immensely. She was always so quiet.

"And this one is for the house." Reggie's face had a little extra color that Angela was trying to ignore. He handed the wrapped gift to Angela.

100

She didn't fail to notice that Reggie snuck in a glance at Dolly every chance he could.

Angela ripped off the tan parchment paper and twine. It was a frame with an embroidered floral design with a decorative oval and dark green letters perfectly stitched with Home Sweet Home.

"This is the perfect gift!" Angela blinked away a misty tear, when she realized that this place was indeed hers. She gave Reggie another hug. "I am so very glad you are back Reggie. You are the very best kind of friend."

Reggie couldn't stop grinning. "I did hope you would like it. I saw it in a shop in town. The wife of the owner made it herself. The flowers I bought from Corinne. We have discussed the roses all week. I saw them when I was doing the books for her. I am amazed that she can keep the summer blooms alive this far into the fall."

Dolly nodded enthusiastically. "I love the greenhouse." She stated simply. Angela was proud of her friend, she knew her quiet nature and seeing how hard she was trying to communicate with Reggie, it made Angela wonder how she was really feeling about their visitor.

"Would you like a quick tour before we eat?" Angela offered.

"I wouldn't mind showing him around." Dolly spoke out with forcefulness that shocked Angela a little.

"That would be wonderful." Reggie said and offered Dolly his arm.

"That works just fine. I will get the table set." Angela shut her mouth and got to work, fighting a laugh that wanted to bubble out. She glanced over her shoulder when she got to the bubbling pot of stew. She could hear Dolly's soft voice talking about the parlor. The warm glow from the lamps and candles was a perfect setting for any couple to find romance. Her heart skipped a bit thinking of giving a similar tour with Ted.

The dinner went extremely well and Angela was proud of herself after all was done. Reggie had been a friendly houseguest and though he seemed to have a special interest in her friend Dolly, he was friendly to both women. Even with crates and boxes scattered around the place, her home felt cozy and welcoming.

Reggie said goodbye near ten o'clock. Angela could hear the rain falling harder than the soft drizzle of the last week. Within the hour the rumble of thunder rolled through the house. Dolly and Angela sat in the parlor going over a list of things that were needed in town. Angela had hopes of going to town in a day or so. They looked at each other when the thunder rolled again, even louder.

Dolly laughed.

"We are ninnies." Angela declared and laughed herself.

"Perhaps." Dolly said simply and laughed again.

"All we need now is a spider to crawl through here and we will go screaming back to Grant's Grove looking to Lucas to keep us protected." Angela rolled her eyes at the trickle of dread or fear that coursed through her. It wasn't strong enough to be a real fear. She had felt worse in emergency situations, falling into ravines and fires raging through cities. Now it was a dull fear, like knowing she couldn't handle what lay ahead. That she had jumped into independence too early and she would pay for it dearly.

"We will learn to be on our own. Until change comes again." Dolly said with the laughter still hiding in the corners of her lips.

"I just hope I haven't been a fool." Angela said seriously.

"If we all knew how everything would turn out there would be no anticipation or a need for hope." Dolly said and stood up, stretching her arms over her head.

"As always Dolly, you are so wise." Angela said with a shake of her head.

Dolly shrugged and gave a wave and said a goodnight.

Angela crawled into her own bed a few minutes later. She had a new nightgown that was warm flannel. Her room was also warm and cozy. The bed was bigger than she needed and she wondered if she needed a cat or a dog to keep her company at night.

Or a husband?

The thought crept up on her without warning and she shook it away for now.

I have time for that, Lord willing. It was a mixture of hope and a prayer.

For now she watched lightning flash through the window, it was far off and not scary. She hoped it would stay far away. Her hopes drifted as she lost the battle to exhaustion after a full day.

The thunder rolled through Willamette Valley all night but the two tired young women slept.

Chapter Thirteen

November 30th, 1850
Angela Fahey

Angela had flour all over herself. She had basket full of warm rolls and two more trays to bake. She had an hour before Violet would arrive.

The stable lad from Grant's Grove had delivered a message while Angela ate her breakfast, a few hours earlier. Dolly left early to work at the lab. Angela had the house to herself and for a few minutes had no idea what she was going to do. Her to do list was enormous but she felt at a loss to know where to start.

She was eating her toast with strawberries preserves she had received from Clive, probably made by Millie Quackenbush, and she begrudgingly admitted that the preserves were indeed delicious. The knock at the door startled her tremendously. Her house was very quiet.

She saw Brandon, the stable lad from Grant's Grove, at the door. She smiled and welcomed him in, letting him know in the future to use the back door. It was less formal and had a mudroom. He nodded and handed her the note when he was inside.

"From Mrs. Violet!" He said quickly.

"Thank you. One moment please." Angela opened the note.

Angela,

Perhaps on this fine wet day you might be up for more do-gooding before the roads make buggy travel impossible. I have a plan, and you have a stove. Would you be willing to bake enough warm rolls to feed four families on the outskirts of town?

I have the dough made. I can send it back with Brandon if you agree. Do you need a baking pan… if yes?

Violet G.

Angela smiled and walked to her parlor where paper and a pencil were found. Her response was quick. She grabbed a tip for Brandon from a jar she kept on the desk. Just a few pennies in there for now but she hoped to fill it will egg money someday when she had chickens again.

Violet,

Yes, do-gooding is the perfect activity for today. I have the necessary pans. Send over the dough. I will begin warming the oven now. What time do I need to be ready?

Angela F.

With a tip and a smile she sent off Brandon on his quest back to Violet, who most certainly tipped him well in her own way.

A few minutes later young Brandon was back, his brown slouchy hat damp from the morning rain. He had a large basket covered in a towel. Inside was a bowl of risen dough and a small note with Violet's instructions for the rolls. A smaller bowl of butter was next to the dough.

Brandon scooted back to his work at the stables with two tips jangling happily together in his pocket.

Angela set out all the fixins' and read through the instructions.

Three hours later she was happily covered in flour, her hands and fingernails a bit sticky from working and cutting the dough. She started a large kettle of water to boil and got a washbasin full of water. Once the water was hot she added it to the pitcher and the warm water was ready. With the last two sheets of rolls baking she washed the countertop off, scrubbing at the sticky bits trying to dry into glue to the side of the counter. She was satisfied after it was all put to right. The dough bowl was clean waiting to be returned and the butter dish still sitting on the stove, the butter melted and a basting brush sat on a small plate nearby ready for the next batch of fresh rolls.

Angela carried the pitcher of warm water and the basin bowl to the nightstand in her room. Knowing she had a few minutes before the rolls were done. She changed out of her housedress and then washed her hands and arms thoroughly. She didn't feel like wearing a fashionable full-skirted dress, but she was trying harder to dress like a lady. She had been pressured more than once by Corinne and Marie to remember her place in the community now. She was now even more aware of it, she was a landowner.

Marie Harpole's words returned to her. 'If we want the West to be civilized we have to do our part.'

With her sweet voice in her head Angela pulled out the pile of petticoats and her corset. It was harder and harder to put the thing on after the comfort of going without it. Without a maid, Angela had settled on an easier corset that fastened in the front. She had a whale bone corset that she had bought on a whim last year but without the pulling and tying from the back it was useless to her now.

The brick red dress with the full round bell was on and Angela was buttoning the last of the buttons when the smell of the baked rolls reminded her to bolt to the kitchen. Ten steps from her bedroom door to the kitchen and the rolls were pulled out, perfectly browned. With a careful drizzle of butter she basted both pans and with a thick towel in hand she flipped the rolls into the basket, filling it to the top. The towel was draped back over it and with very careful hands she washed again, trying desperately not to get any of the melted butter or water on her dress.

She quickly braided two sections of her hair and pulled them up and around to the back of her head and with a few pins made a ladylike style. The waves in the back draped down to the middle of her back, she admired the image from the looking glass in the hallway. She tried on two bonnets and decided on the dark brown one with the pleats. She took a moment and pinned a dark red ribbon around just so, and it matched her dress. No one could complain about her not being civilized. Her lace up boots she was wearing would do well, especially if there was mud. These were her easiest shoes to clean.

Violet arrived in the Grant's buggy and she had a basket tucked in behind her. Violet exclaimed over Angela's new dress and once the basket was tucked away safely the young girls were off. The sun came out as the rolled through Spring Creek. The winter snows were fought off for another day.

Chapter Fourteen

Ted Greaves

The steamship pulled around another bend in the rushing river. The chugging of the wheel was pushing hard against the water. The men in the engine room were yelling and working hard with bulging muscles to keep the engine fires lit.

The morning mist was still lingering and the passengers stayed away from the outer decks as ordered from the Captain earlier. The ride inland was harder than the trip out, it was a dangerous current and if the vessel wasn't steered well they would all be in danger of a crash.

The ship took several hours of slow progress until it made it past a few narrow spaces. There was a man walking the decks yelling out news whenever possible. He hollered, "just passing Portland. Prepare yourselves for landing."

Ted had learned the waterfall near the downtown area of Oregon City made it dangerous to go any closer. That and stray logs from the logging operation had the way clogged for any sailing vessel. Even a rowboat would be hard pressed to battle it out with the enormous logs that the logging companies floated downstream to the mills along the riverfront. So they would land at a dock just outside of town, only a few miles.

The passengers were all happy to hear that the time to disembark had finally arrived. Bags and belongings were kept close, loved ones closer.

Ted and his sister Sophia Greaves were off the ship first. Their mother and his Aunt lagged behind. Sophia enjoyed the view as the morning mist cleared. The mountain splendor had her mesmerized. Ted grinned with a looked that said, "*I told ya!*"

"That there is Mount Hood." Ted pointed at the highest peak. It was hiding in a shroud of clouds but still a sight to see.

"I think you were right all along, brother. I love the mountains already." Sophia smiled brightly. Her age was only fourteen but she was a young beauty with blond curls and bright pink cheeks. Ted had promised that he would keep her safe and not allow anyone to snatch her away until she was old enough to be snatched. She found his jokes funny but sometimes she chose not to laugh to keep him on edge. One cannot give your older brother too much of an advantage.

They watched as their Mother and Aunt Olivia made their way to the gangplank. They both had large bags and had paid the porter handsomely to carry them all down for them once the passengers were unloaded.

Sophia and Ted discussed amongst themselves why exactly it was taking so long for them to get off the vessel.

They had no decent theories so they had to let it go and remain patient while staying out of the way of the other passengers.

Ted could hear the jangling of harnesses and looked about to see if anyone from town was coming to check on the unloading. He had sent a telegram ahead but he wasn't sure if anyone would guess what day they would arrive.

He was hoping to hire a wagon so they would not have to carry all of their belongings to town. That would make for a very long and uncomfortable day. He tried to stay focused on task, but he knew that within a few hours he could see Angela again and his usually patient nature was being tested.

His mother had complained so much on the steamship he had been slightly tempted to move to a different room, because all her complaints could be heard through the walls. There was no helping it, though, all the rooms were full.

After thirty minutes of waiting, the two sisters showed up.

Amelia Greaves, Ted's mother, sighed in an exasperated way and her sister, Olivia, gave her a nudge with her elbow.

"Ted, this place is lovely." Olivia said with a wink.

"I am so glad you agree. It would be a long trip to take you back if you didn't like it." Ted laughed good-naturedly, though only half his heart was in it.

"I am exhausted, is it far to town?" His mother asked with another sigh.

"It is close, two miles or less. I will see to getting a conveyance for our trunks and things." Ted was glad for an excuse to walk away. He gave his sister and Aunt a knowing look to hold on for a little while longer.

"Go then, Thaddeus dear. We shall stay here." His mother shooed him off.

Ted wandered through the crowd. He saw a road that he vaguely remembered that headed toward town.

He wondered for a moment if he should just walk toward town and try to hire a wagon, or wait for people in town to send wagons as they customarily did when they heard the steam ship whistle.

Impatience won out and after taking a look around and seeing no one he knew he started down the road on foot toward Oregon City.

It wasn't three minutes before he finally saw a familiar face. Clive and his son JQ were atop a wagon not 100 feet away making their way down the road.

<hr />

Clive waved at Ted and stood up halfway, to make sure he could be seen. JQ had the reins.

They picked up Ted as soon as they reached him and Clive clapped the young man on the back a few times.

"Well, Ted, it is good to see ya. I had high hopes that you would make it back." Clive declared before the wagon started moving again. "You just missed the rain, you may have brought the sun with you from California."

Ted just grinned then gave JQ instructions of where to find his family.

"I am not sure I could have stayed there for too long, had the womenfolk been dead set on staying east I would have spent my savings making sure they were set up safe and sound. But I am glad they agreed to come with me." Ted said. He sat on a bench in the back and Clive was half-turned in the front seat to chat with his friend.

"I am too. I am happy they are willing to continue their work here too. The women of the west will be glad of their fine skills. I got one trunk in on the steamboat yesterday. They do excellent work." Clive said sincerely. "I knew you would not be far behind the trunks. I have not yet delivered the note to Angela." He stretched his face into a regretful look.

"It must have been delayed, I sent it off several weeks ago. I guess I can deliver her notice of my arrival in person." Ted smiled at the thought. "I wished we could have been on that ship for so many days, to hear it was delayed eases my mind a bit. That boat had only cargo room. We had to wait for a steamship with passenger room. This one we came on was full, we were lucky to get on at all." Ted realized he was chatting nervously but he knew Clive wouldn't mind so much. He would understand any nerves... probably better than anyone else. He had been a witness to his and Angela's relationship. His own family still probably did not know how he truly felt about Angela. He had never known anyone like her.

The wagon reached the unloading area for the luggage and passengers. Clive and Ted left JQ behind to watch the rig.

The women were very happy to see Ted again and they could tell from the description that his friend Clive was with him.

"I am so glad to meet you finally!" Sophia blurted before they were all introduced.

Clive laughed heartily and shook her hand.

"I declare you are even prettier than your brother." Clive said with another laugh. "I do have myself a weakness for blondes and strawberry blondes especially." Clive gave a gracious bow and was introduced to Ted's mother, Aunt and sister properly. Clive gave the women a wink that was just on the right side of proper but bordering on the edge of flirtatious.

All three women couldn't help but smile. Clive had his ways. Each hand was shaken and proper 'how-do-ya-does' were said. Ted beamed at each one. He was so very happy to finally be here.

"Your chariot, or should I say wagon, awaits." Clive led the women to the wagon and Ted lined up the trunks. He asked a porter to watch the unattended bags while he carried the first heavy trunk to the wagon. Clive was getting the women settled into the benches and went back with Ted to finish the packing. Three trips and everything was loaded. Ted noticed that Clive carried just as many as he did. The man was a human dynamo.

The ride to town was quick. JQ was introduced but Clive took over with the town information. He gave them little tidbits about town life and where they would be staying.

"I hope you like the place. It is two doors down from the Hudson Bay store. It is a two story townhouse. It has an area in front for the selling of your wares and a lovely parlor for you to work in. I tried to furnish it as nicely as I could with what is available. There is a kitchen and dining room downstairs as well. All the bedrooms are upstairs and furnished also. I do hope ya like it." Clive said, he was using his best charm on his friend's family members and it seemed to be working.

"Is there any saloons nearby? I do hate the noise and ruckus." Amelia asked with a frown.

"No ma'am. There is a drinking establishment, an inn that serves ale but mostly it is a place to get warm and eat a hearty stew. It is a few streets over but the law in this town does not take to a loud kind of establishment as it is a quiet town. This is a family friendly community. We may not have as much culture as some of the bigger towns in the west but we have a lovely community that prides itself on family values." Clive was sincere in his speech and it calmed Ted's mother immediately.

She nodded as he described the community. Seemingly glad to know that her family was safe.

"Mr. Quackenbush, you did mention that there would be a need for our goods out here. Is there enough business in town to keep us going?" Olivia spoke up finally.

"In our town that may not be the case but I have store owners in five towns in Oregon and also Sacramento and San Francisco have sent enquiries." Clive said. That had all the women satisfied.

They were riding through town and Sophia and Ted were excited to see all the different businesses.

"Oh, a newspaper and an apothecary?" Sophia said with a surprise.

"The Oregon Gazette has just received its printing press. They are hoping to have their first issue come out in the next few weeks." JQ piped in.

"That is wonderful!" Olivia stated and clapped her hands together excitedly.

The wagon rolled up to the townhouse and everyone poured out of the wagon in his or her turn. Most seemed pleased with the fine appearance of the place. It had a lovely bit of a lawn out front, which Olivia declared would make a wonderful garden. Sophia loved the front porch with the front door gleaming; the panes of glass would be an elegant entrance for their customers.

Amelia Greaves kept her thoughts to herself but a mild sour expression barely left her face that day.

Chapter Fifteen

Violet & Angela

The sun had warmed up the day tremendously and Violet and Angela arrived at the shacks of Pauper Row in good spirits. The cold rain of the morning was gone and their mood was light.

With bulging baskets in hand they arrived to the first shack, Violet and Angela shared a look and a smile before they knocked. It felt good to both of them to share their blessings.

The shack was quiet and there was no answer. Angela knocked again, rapping louder on the wooden plank door. Still no answer came.

"Perhaps they are gone for the day." Violet wondered but doubted within herself.

Angela shrugged and in a moment of boldness she pushed the door open a little bit to peek in. When she saw the empty room she opened it further. The place was empty.

"Oh Angela, they are gone." Violet said with a smile.

"Oh… I do hope they have found better circumstances. This is a blessing indeed." Angela smiled and sighed, envisioning a family escaping the poverty of this poor shack.

"Well, it means the other families will have extra." Violet said with a relieved smile.

Angela and Violet walked down the dirt path to the next shack further down, closer to the woods. Angela heaved the awkward basket up her arm a few times while walking to keep the basket from dropping.

Violet knocked on the second shack's door. There was no answer again. Both Violet and Angela turned to look at each other and then wordlessly turned to look through the nearby area and woods. When they had been here before the place had been busy with family life, children playing outside, more than one fire burning, and supper cooking in pots. There was nary a soul in site, just the two women carrying baskets. The do-gooders were standing there, with no good to do.

"Where have they all gone?" Angela asked in dread, knowing in her heart that all the souls here could not possibly have changed their fortunes in a week's time.

"Perhaps the news of the Varushkin family has urged the church in town to be charitable. Ya know they wouldn't want to be outdone by us country bumpkins, especially in a charity project." Violet said hopefully. It did ease Angela's mind a little.

"I could go to town to find out." Angela said.

"I cannot stay, I need to return to work. I am helping Marie tonight. She is having a hard time on her feet. She is due to deliver that baby any day now." Violet frowned.

"Do not fret. I can easily hire a ride back to my house. The livery in town belongs to John Harpole's ranch and they have always been good to me, I have gotten a ride from them before when I had no buggy. They treat me like family, as they would for you too. You go back, I will go to town and ask Clive or JQ if they know about what has happened here. I will come by and let you know what I find out. I need to know what has happened to these poor families. I must know if they are safe."

Violet nodded, agreeing with Angela, then her face brightened with an idea. "I will take the food to the Varushkin cabin. At least it will do some good anyway. It is on the way and will be a blessing. I will see if Galya will also help at Marie's. I'm sure Marie wouldn't mind an extra hand to help out."

"That is a grand plan, Vie. I will see you later, wish everyone well for me. I will be back by the afternoon, Lord willing." Angela set the basket into the buggy after they walked back to the road.

"I will dear friend, you be safe by yourself." Violet said with concern.

"It is but a half mile to town." Angela waved off her friend's worry and starting walking. Angela waved as Violet as the buggy pulled away.

The smell of rain from earlier lingered in the air but Angela stayed away from any mud as she walked. The grass was damp but the sun was doing a good job of drying it. Angela took in the scenery as she walked along, thinking and praying as she went.

She noticed that a lot of the trees had lost all but just the last bit of leaves. The fall colors were fading to the drab brown that preceded the winter snows. She dreaded thinking of how these families would survive with no homes, or winter stores. She laid the negative thought aside and instead focused on praying for their safety.

She made it to town with a peaceful heart, knowing God would take care of these people, like He had taken care of her.

112

Clive Quackenbush & The Greaves Family

The front room of the townhouse was spacious and lovely, with shining wood floors and a curving staircase that led upstairs to the living quarters.

"I took the liberty of hiring you a cook and housekeeper for the next few months. To make sure your stay is comfortable. Her name is Beatrice Glasner and I do hope you will get along well. She is staying in the maid's room beyond the kitchen. If you all get on, I am sure she would be open to staying." Clive stated, seeing at least Olivia and Sophia were paying attention. Ted was carrying luggage up the stairs and Amelia was seated in the front parlor. She had found an elegant love seat that Clive had purchased in Portland a few weeks before.

At least that pleases her. He thought to himself. He forced himself not to chuckle, not even softly.

"A cook, oh that will make our jobs so much easier." Olivia stated with an abundance of gratitude. "We can focus on our lace as much as we can. How delightful is that?" Olivia grabbed her niece, Sophia's, hand and they smiled together. Clive could see the resemblance of all the women in the room. He was glad for Ted and his sister, that their Aunt had a cheerful disposition. It would make the change easier.

"I was hoping that you would see it that way. Your lacework is exquisite ladies." He turned to include Amelia in the speech but she didn't turn her eyes away from looking out the window. He turned back to his captive audience. "I know the West will be better dressed because of your work."

Both Olivia and Sophia blushed over his praise prettily. He smiled his best charming smile and led the two women to the back of the townhouse.

"The back yard has a tall fence around and has a new well. I see plenty of potential for an elegant flower garden, perhaps a table and chairs for tea time, weather permitting of course." Clive had done a lot of work to make sure his new employees would be happy. Though they would be able to sell their wares to townsfolk, he planned on purchasing a lot of goods from them and making a good profit in other towns. If he was correct in his assumptions they would all make a very comfortable living. He wanted to see them be successful. He also looked forward to the happy ladies in town when they realized how easy it would be to get quality lace. He had an appointment with the milliner tomorrow to sell them lace that he had received from the steamship yesterday.

He looked forward to the gasps of delight from the owners.

Clive finished the tour of the townhouse with a stroll through the kitchen, Amelia had joined them to meet Beatrice, and Clive was pleased to see the scowl was less noticeable now.

Beatrice was a pleasant and plump woman in her late forties. She had rosy cheeks and light brown hair that hinted at turning white with a few curls that were showing underneath the cotton mop hat.

"I do hope we all can work well together. My boys have farms outside of town but with my husband gone I wanted to return to what I love best, which is cooking and keeping house. I only ask that every other Saturday I can take time off to see my children and grand babies. I will always have dinner made ahead for ya. Also I would like to go to church every Sunday morning after breakfast is served but I leave the moment the service is done to be about me work." Beatrice gave the meekest little bow of respect to both Amelia and Olivia, as they were the new masters of the house.

Olivia looked to Amelia and they both nodded.

"Ms. Glasner, that is agreed. Every other Saturday is acceptable, but I would like to add in a day off once a month to attend to any business you need during the week. It was an arrangement I had with an employer myself once and it worked well when situations arose." Olivia said diplomatically.

Clive thought the situation was handled well. Ted arrived for a quick introduction while wiping his brow with a handkerchief. He was done with all the unloading and he was ready to get things settled.

Ted and Clive made their way through the house. Ted brought in the firewood from the large box on the side of the house. He got the fireplace ready with kindling and a neat stack of extra wood for when it was needed. The day wasn't chilly yet so he didn't light any fires. He repeated his chore for the wood stoves that were upstairs. They each had a large bedroom of their own with a small wood stove in each. Ted knew he would be kept busy this winter obtaining enough wood to keep everyone warm.

Clive pointed Sophia to the storage room, where tables, kerosene lamps and candles were stored. "Supplies are kept in the pantry across the hall from Beatrice's room. She will be able to help you find anything, she helped me get the place in order."

Sophia was pleased to know everything was so well settled. Her mind had imagined a harder beginning for them. She knew that Ted's friend and mentor, Clive, was the reason for the ease of the situation.

"I cannot thank you enough for all you have done. We needed a fresh start. Thank you for helping us achieve that." Sophia's light blue eyes were sincere. Clive was won over.

"You are most welcome child. We all deserve a fresh start, don't we?" Clive clipped her on the chin conspiratorially and joined Ted back in the parlor.

"I need to be heading back to the store. I suppose you all will need a late lunch? I think Beatrice has something ready for you whenever you feel ready. I have taken the liberty of filling the water barrels for you today. Beatrice could perhaps draw a bath in the kitchen later for those who would want it. Otherwise the bathhouse is a street over on the right... a very nice and respectable establishment. On my honor." Clive winked and gave the household a wave.

The Greaves family took a moment to collectively sigh before Ted made his announcement.

"I do believe a late lunch would be perfect. Then I plan on hiring a horse. I would like to see Angela today if possible. Let her know I am here." Ted said and smiled when his sister made kissy faces at him.

"A grand scheme, Thaddeus." Olivia laughed. "I will see if Beatrice is ready for us. Ted, you better find a clean shirt and slacks." Olivia snapped her fingers in jest at her nephew and laughed heartily.

Amelia sat in her chair, and tried not to scowl.

Angela had spoken to JQ and learned nothing about the families at the edge of town. He recommended waiting for Clive. Since Clive had promised to return by two.

Angela sat on the bench outside the store and waited. Wondering how so many families could have vanished without the town knowing about it. It was indeed a mystery. Angela pulled her bonnet off and let the sun warm her face. She usually avoided the risk of freckles but knowing the sun would be spare over the winter months she soaked up any last little bit of warmth she could. It felt heavenly after a cold wet few days.

Clive poked her on the shoulder to rouse her from her sunbathing.

"You are going freckle up, Red." He jested.

"I know, but I couldn't resist the last bit of autumn. If I was pretending, I could almost imagine that was a summer sun warming my face. Then Father Winter would be a long ways off." Angela smiled and stood to her feet, she grabbed her unneeded coat and then fluffed out her full round skirts.

"You look like a fashion plate today!" Clive whistled and gave the fair maiden a turn.

"I am trying so very hard to be appropriate, especially now that I am a landowner." Angela said with a furrowed brow.

"You need not worry Red, you are doing a grand job." Clive patted her shoulder. "What brings you all the way to town. I figured you would be lost in boxes and rug making." He smiled at the picture she made in his mind.

"I need to ask you about the families outside of town." Angela said.

Clive claimed ignorance, so Angela and Clive sat on the bench while she told him about what she had found.

Ted was done with eating and changed into clean clothes. He looked over the paper that Clive had left for them. A neat drawing of the streets in town with all the businesses labeled. He could easily find the general store and the livery; they were only a few doors down.

Ted said 'goodbye' to the women of the house, getting a few sly smiles but he was glad the teasing had simmered down. He didn't mind a little bit of razzing about Angela but the trip had been a long one, and not everyone had a pleasant attitude about the move or his romance. He was starting to suspect that his mother resented it. He was hoping that he was wrong and that she was just tense from the long hard journey.

Ted stood on the front porch surveying the street around him. This was his new home. He took a minute to pray. He knew that he should have with his whole family, but the mood had been off. He would recommend it later with everyone, in the quiet before bedtime. Maybe even a little Bible reading, if he could even find his Bible in the chaos.

Lord God, please bless my family in this new place. Lord I ask for your guidance with my relationship with Angela, and also Lord I need your help to talk to my mother. She seems inconsolable most days. I do not know how to reach her Lord. Please comfort her in her loss and help her to find her happiness again.

Ted whispered 'amen' while leaning on the front porch railing. He had many more words to pray but knew he needed to focus on his task. He knew he would be spending plenty of prayer time over the next weeks as they all adjusted to their new life. For now he wanted to focus on the best part of this whole trip. He was desperate to know that Angela had not forgotten him.

He stepped off the porch and turned to the left, he had a plan, to visit the general store, get directions to where Angela was staying, then hire a horse or buggy. Anything to get to her!

He only took five steps when he saw Clive. Clive was standing up from a bench in front of what Ted thought was his store. He was talking to a lady in a dark red dress, its silhouette was elegant and fashionable. Ted was surprised to see that kind of fashion this far in the West. He had seen many in simpler styles more suited to the pioneer life, or harlots in scandalous clothes that he would quickly turn his eyes away from.

Ted kept walking but was ready to catch Clive's attention when he was finished with visiting.

When he got closer he heard Clive speaking.

"Red, I will certainly look into that. We should find out how those families have faired. You can trust me to find out." Clive turned away and he must have sensed Ted walking near him. He smiled and gasped a bit. "Oh, yes, I plumb forgot!"

He took a step away from the lady and she was finally revealed to Ted.

Ted stopped and brought a hand to his chest in surprise. "Oh, my Angel!" He said in a rough whisper, just loud enough for Angela to hear and turn herself.

Chapter Sixteen

Oregon City

Angela's mind registered his voice before she really believed that the man just a few feet in front of her was indeed her Ted.

'My Angel' he had stated quietly. And to her he was her Ted. *He looked so good*, she thought instantly. His curly blond hair was a little longer. His eyes the same blue. He had grown, maybe through the shoulders but his jaw was still as determined and his face still the picture of sincerity.

Within a moment she stepped closer. Not saying a word. She may have gasped but she couldn't be sure.

"May I?" Ted asked, confusing her. Then she realized he was asking to come closer.

She nodded frantically. *Yes, you fool come closer!* She wanted to yell but she said nothing.

He stepped nearer to her and the warm scent of him sparked a memory. Of a first kiss and a last kiss.

He placed a hand on her cheek and she closed her eyes, enjoying the warmth of his hand more than a thousand sunny summer days.

"You are more beautiful than I remember." He sighed and rubbed his thumb over her cheekbone. "How is that possible? You are taller too."

Angela opened her eyes and smiled warmly.

"I missed you." She said, feeling foolish for saying something so obvious. She remembered crying her heart out on that bench in San Francisco, she had known he was being honorable by leaving to go back to take care of his family, but it still had hurt so very much.

"And I you, Angel." Ted kissed her on the cheek. He wanted to give her time and respect. Mauling her with a thousand kisses is what he wanted to do, but they were in the street. She deserved to be courted and wooed properly. He owed that to her. But he was so very tempted.

Angela flushed a deep red and wanted to be kissed again. She thought about kissing him herself. She took stock of the moment and knew he was being honorable again.

Blast! She thought. *I will be a respectable lady and not kiss him in the middle of the street.* Surely everyone living on this street including Millicent Quackenbush was watching.

Angela searched her brain for something to say... *anything*.

"Thank you for coming." She said lamely. She had spent the last year reading poetry and imagining seeing his face again so often and here she was, having a romantic reunion and they both were quiet as church mice.

Ted opened his mouth, perhaps trying to say something more thrilling than 'thank you for coming' when a shriek scared them both out of their wits. Ted grabbed her arm protectively and turned to see the danger.

It was his sister, two doors down, leaning over the porch railing, then giggling and running towards them.

Angela saw the young woman looked a lot like her brother, her hair blonder and her cheekbones a little higher. The young woman had a smile that was infectious and Angela couldn't help but smile in return.

"You must be Angela!" Sophia stopped just a few feet from colliding into the reunited couple. She was a little out of breath. "I shouldn't run while wearing a corset!" Her cheeks were red from that small amount of exercise. She bent at the waist a little and was gasping.

Angela laughed. "It is a perilous venture to do anything in a corset except for perhaps needlework."

Sophia put out her hand in a modern way to greet Angela. Angela shook her hand and they both laughed a little more, already feeling comfortable around each other.

"This is my sister, Sophia." Ted said unnecessarily.

"I cannot express how happy I am to finally meet you. I have read about your whole family in Ted's letters." Angela blushed realizing that she had used Ted's given name. It was very informal considering the last few minutes of awkwardness.

"Ted has told me all about you. He was right about a few things. Your red hair is divine, and you have a sweetness that shows through your eyes." Sophia looked from Angela to Ted. She enjoyed making them both blush.

Angela paused on the compliment, letting it sink in. "Those are kind words." She said meekly, not trusting her voice.

Ted clasped her hand and squeezed it, sending a thrill through her fingers that raced to her heart.

"I would love a chance to introduce you to my whole family. If you could take a moment." Ted asked.

"I would be glad too."

"Such a pleasure to meet you Miss Fahey." Olivia said warmly. Angie liked her immediately.

"Please, you may all call me Angela. I insist." Angela looked around the room and was torn.

Ted's mother had been introduced but had said nothing. She had nodded but her expression had been flat.

Angela worked harder to make her smile as friendly as possible.

"I am so happy to know you made the journey safely. I went overland and it was very brutal. I am glad to never have to make the trip again. Lord willing." She smiled nervously.

"The quarters on both ships were very comfortable. I'd say the worst of it was the land crossing in Panama… I hopefully have ridden my last donkey." Olivia laughed aloud and Angela couldn't help but join in. She was happy to see that Ted's mother smiled briefly over her sister's comment.

"I am sure you all are tired from your journey. I do need to get back home. A dear friend is expecting to give birth any day. I do want to check on her before the dinner hour. It was such a pleasure to finally meet you all." Angela hoped that she had made a decent impression.

"I would love to escort Angela home. I shall be back for dinner." Ted announced then took Angela's arm.

Angela felt heat fill her cheeks at the way he had taken her arm. In many circles this would be a declaration to the family of his intentions. Angela tried not to let her mind wander too fast in the direction it wanted to go. She knew that she had a few things to talk over with him. She did not want to assume that he was her beau until she confessed to a few things.

A minute later they were at the livery.

"I was going to hire a buggy to get home. I rode into town with a friend, our plans were changed, I have a buggy at home but…" She knew she was prattling on.

"I need to secure a conveyance for my family anyhow. This just gives me a lovely excuse to see you home. Are you still staying at the Grant's place?" Ted was feeling more comfortable.

"Well, no. But I wanted to tell you about some recent changes." Angela said with a nervous smile.

"Oh, that is no problem. Let me talk to the livery manager and we can talk as much as we like on the way."

Angela agreed and stayed on the bench out front and planned out her words carefully for the ride they would share home.

It was a few minutes later that Ted came out of the large building and summoned her to walk with him to the back where there was a large black topped surrey waiting. It was painted a shiny black with a hard topped roof and it had two benches for seating and an area behind the benches for storage.

"It is handsome. It was available to rent and board here. This will do the job of getting my family from here to there." Ted said with a grin. Angela enjoyed seeing him smile again. She was beginning to believe this was actually real. Ted was here.

"It is lovely. I'm sure the ladies will enjoy riding in style." Angela squeezed his arm and he looked at her for a long moment. She wanted to be shy and look away but she was glad she didn't. His blue eyes were losing their shyness and she remembered all those feelings she felt last year.

The horses were harnessed and Ted let go of her arm and climbed aboard.

"Let me see how it handles before I let you on." Ted said. Angela nodded and watched him handle the reins. He pulled the surrey out of the livery yard and he pulled around to the street. He went a ways up the street and disappeared around the corner. In a minute Angela heard the jangling of the harnesses and then she saw him pull up next to her. The horses were well behaved.

Ted secured the reins and jumped down. He helped Angela up and joined her in the front bench.

"Lead on fair maiden." Ted said with a contented look. "The horses are easy to handle. We should be able to arrive in one piece."

"That is good to know." Angela said but her nerves were agitated. Her stomach in knots thinking about all she had to tell him.

She held on to his arm and gave him a few directions to get him started.

Chapter Seventeen

Varushkin Cabin

Pavel and Milo were outside next to the woodpile eating the buttered rolls they'd snuck out of the basket while Galina and their mother had been chatting with the blond lady who was still inside. They were boasting in between bites about how many squirrels they would shoot over the weekend. They both enjoyed school a little but they did agree that it interfered on their hunting time dramatically. They looked forward to the weekends the most, as long as they brought in game their mother didn't make them do inside chores too much. They would rather be outdoors. Even in the cold.

The boys had finished the stolen snack and looked around for anything to do, it was not yet dinnertime. Pavel noticed the man along the wagon ruts that was the road to their new home.

The man that walked along the road was taller than average, with shoulders that could carry a heavy load. He had a broad rimmed hat that was a dirty brown. The man had the tiniest hint of a limp in his long gate.

Milo walked closer to the road to get a better glimpse when he let out a whoop, then another yell and he took off running toward the tall man.

"Papa!" Pavel joined in the yelling and without pause turned and headed to the cabin to tell his mother.

Violet Griffin

Violet's heart was in her throat. A half hour before the Varushkin family had been surprised by the return of the head of the household from the gold fields of California.

She had felt so awkward standing there watching the family rejoice in the homecoming. Her heart was breaking in the reality of it. She should truly rejoice with them, husband and father home at last. She wanted desperately to leave, to pout or maybe even scream. It was her manners that kept her rooted to the floor. Unmoving with a smile plastered across her pale cheeks as she watched.

She finally got a chance to speak when the hubbub died down.

"I leave the decision up to you. If Galya would like the extra work I am certain that there will be plenty to keep her busy for at least a few days. Maria is due to give birth at any time. It would be a good experience for her to be there to help as well." Violet saw Mrs. Varushkin holding her husband's arm. Violet thought Magdalena was taking possession of it. Willing him to stay next to her. Violet knew she would have done the same if her Eddie had come home. If!

Slava, the husband, finally spoke to her. "Indeed, if the girl has work then she should be about it. I am back to stay, we can visit when the work is done. Until I can find another job here we will be needin' the help." His accent was thick but she understood him well enough.

His wife Magdalena nodded in agreement. Relief was written on her features.

"I have so much to tell you Slava. Ms. Violet has done so much for us, and the Spring Creek Church." Magdalena sighed and turned to Galina, who was stoically pulling her dark coat over her arms. "Go with Violet dear, you are such a good girl, helping your family."

"Yes, Ma'am." Galina spoke stiffly and nodded to her father before she stood next to Violet.

After a minute of 'thank yous' and 'goodbyes' the two young women left the cabin, both in stormy moods and trying to hide it.

It did not take long for Violet's tears to flow. She tried so very hard to tell her eyes to behave but it was no use. Her emotional upheaval was coming and she figured Galina was going to see it. The pain of the memory of Eddie burned through her insides. Seeing a man with the same motivation turn around and return to his family made the betrayal of Eddie's so much harder.

Violet took a few deep breaths to calm herself but every thought in her head was adding to the next and soon her heart was pounding.

"One moment!" Violet squeaked out, then sat on the cold ground and burst into tears. She wanted to pray but she didn't want to say the words that were threatening to spill. She was angry, actually angry. She hadn't allowed her thoughts to go to this dark place but her husband had been gone for so long.

"Are you okay, Violet?" Galina's voice was concerned and she placed a warm hand on her friend's head.

"No, I am..." Violet gulped to keep a sob down. "I am jealous." She uttered the sinful feeling and cried more.

"Your husband?" Galina had known Violet's husband had been gone longer than her own father, and now she was broken hearted. She understood the best she could. Being young and having never felt love. She could imagine it though.

Violet nodded and mopped her tears with the rough wool sleeve of her coat. She reached into a pocket for a handkerchief and tried to stand. She had to get a hold of herself.

"I am sorry friend." Galina said sincerely, sounding much older than her thirteen years.

"I apologize Galya, I should be rejoicing with you and your family." Violet sniffed and her breathing was still uneven from the heavy crying. She was calming down slowly.

"You needn't be sorry. I am so angry, I am glad to be leaving. I would have made a scene if I had stayed." Galina muttered and raised her eyebrows defiantly.

"Oh?" Violet was surprised to see the sweet helpful girl so riled.

"He deserves to sleep in the cold tent you found us in. He left us with nothing and if you and your church hadn't helped us we could have died." Galina let her own angry tears fall. "My mother and I had even spoken of giving up the baby so he wouldn't freeze to death." Her voice caught on a few words, she was on the edge of sobbing herself. "He has no idea of the pain he caused." Galina took a few deep breaths and swiped angrily at fat tears that raced down her face.

Violet realized that they were both in pain, feeling similar feelings. Her Eddie had left her behind with little too. She wanted to understand Eddie's need to leave but she still could not.

"I do not know why men do these things." Violet said with a heavy heart. There was nothing to say that was a comfort at this moment.

They linked their arms and wordlessly walked back to the Grant's cabin. They were lost in some difficult thoughts. Trying to calm their hearts so they could focus on the work that had to be done.

Ted & Angela

Angela pointed out a few things as they rode through town on the handsome surrey to the road south of town toward Spring Creek. She was working up her courage. Her mind had played over what to say so many times this past year. It had gone so many ways in her imagination but now was the time. She wanted no more secrets.

"I have some things to share." Angela said and he turned to look her in the eye. What he saw made him pull back on the reins. The surrey came to a stop.

"You can tell me anything, Angel."

The use of her angelic nickname made her feel worse but she decided to spill her heart. He would decide whether she was worth all the hassle in a few minutes anyhow.

"I moved into my own house yesterday." She stated. "I bought the land next to Grant's Grove."

Ted looked a bit confused. "You bought the land?"

"Yes. Before I came to San Francisco last year I received some news from Corinne Grant. She solicited a lawyer and he found my stepfather and convinced him to let go of the inheritance left for my brother Sean and I." She gulped, then carried on. "My family was not poor. I spent all those years in the work orphanage but there was money set aside." Angela had told him some harder things about her past. But she had never mentioned the inheritance, she felt awkward before even mentioning it.

"So you went to California to find your brother and tell him the news I suppose." Ted said and nodded. He didn't seem upset at all.

"Yes, but he wanted nothing of what I had to offer, relationally or financially. I suppose that his account will stay at the bank until he is ready to use it. It is no concern of mine anymore." Angela had worked hard on her feelings about her brother and his rejection.

Ted frowned a moment. "You mentioned in a letter that the reunion with your brother had gone poorly. Was he upset?"

"I think that he was struggling with some emotions. He said that I had already died, or some kind of nonsense. I keep replaying it when I cannot force the thoughts away. It was very confusing and hurtful. All that said, I used some of my inheritance to purchase land that had been forfeit next-door to my dear friend."

"I do know how close you are to Corinne Grant. Her and her husband…" He took a moment to recall his name. "Lucas?"

Angela nodded.

"They were very kind to me when I visited." Ted was making conversation but Angela could tell he was thinking.

"I am sorry Ted." Angela said meekly. She didn't know what he was thinking but her guilt about the land purchase was eating away at her. He had promised to come back and had come through on that promise.

"Why would you be sorry?" Ted asked, his eyebrows pinched in concern.

"I made a huge decision without you. I made plans, bought land, built a house. All without you." She confessed. Wondering when his anger would start.

"Without me…" Ted said slowly, his face without emotion for a minute. A slow redness crept up his cheeks. He paused a minute then asked the question that was hard. "You mean, you have…" He swallowed. "You have found someone else?"

Angela realized the implications. "Oh no!" She took his hand. "No one else, Ted!"

He let out a breath he was holding. "I don't understand. You seem to think I would be upset about you having money and spending it." He was beginning to grin at the corners of his mouth.

"Well, I thought you would feel betrayed. That I didn't wait until you arrived." She was feeling silly, a little, part of her still reserved doubts about his acceptance. Perhaps with time to think on it.

"Are you wanting to farm the land?" Ted asked.

"Well, yes. I have a business plan." She admitted.

Ted lifted his eyebrows and smiled. "I would like to hear about that."

"You truly aren't angry?" Angela asked.

"Not at all. I have questions though."

"Please, Ted, ask what you will." Angela gave him a sincere look.

"Alright." Ted grabbed the reins and clicked at the horses to move. There was a jolt when the horses took off and Angela grabbed Ted's arm tighter. He gave her a wink and let his mind form the questions.

"Some questions I have may be too soon. Having just arrived. I know I do not want to rush you in any way about our… about us. I guess I could start with the obvious. I would like to ask permission to court you, officially." Ted said without looking at her.

Angela wanted to laugh. After her big confession he was not angry, but instead wanting to confirm that they were courting.

"You have my permission, Ted." Her voice faltered, "I want to know you better, San Francisco was wonderful but I want to know your family and more about you. I will try and not be so shy and timid as I was back then." Angela had spent all these months away from him thinking about why he didn't know everything about her. She knew her own timidity had created the doubt in her heart. She wondered if he really knew her if he would still care for her.

"I agree Angel, we have time to know more. May I ask another question?" Ted asked quietly, he gave her a quick grin that said he was pleased with her answer.

She nodded before he looked away.

"Do you see me as a part of your plan?"

Angela felt her heart melt. Tears pricked at her eyes at the thought. So many times she plotted and planned with him in mind. "I see you everywhere Ted. I tried not to hope too much, in case I was disappointed again. But I hope you want to help me someday." She saw they were nearing the Spring Creek Church. She pointed it out. It was a good distraction and Ted promised to join her for Sunday services.

Once they neared the creek she pointed at her house sitting on the hill, unpainted but still a beautiful and grand vision with a few tall pines nearby.

"Oh my, you didn't build a cabin." Ted said, truly impressed.

"I had a dream of a big farmhouse." Angela said simply. She was proud of what she had done, even with so much work left to do.

They rode through the creek, the water reaching halfway up the wheels. They drove past the path toward Grant's Grove and the Harpole ranch further down. Angela reminded Ted about them.

"I do hope to get to see them all again soon. My opinion of Oregon was well established because of my visit with them. You have very good neighbors." Ted clicked at the horses to climb the small incline towards Angela's home.

"You see the porch around the west side?" Angela pointed to a corner of the house.

"Aye." Ted said and looked.

"I saved a seat for you, right there." Angela said wistfully.

The two rocking chairs sat calmly, waiting for a pleasant evening to watch the sunset over the western sky.

Angela was surprised by the warm kiss pressed upon her lips. She had just turned back to show Ted where to turn the horses. His kiss took her back to the sweet memories of San Francisco. She knew she wanted to make new memories with this man.

The kiss was over too quickly but without pause Ted found his way to the barn on the east side of the property. With a quick jump Ted was down and tying the horses to the rail.

"I smell fresh paint?" Ted laughed.

"Yes, Earl and the lads just painted the barn this week. It had just enough time before the rains came." Angela said. There was so much she wanted to tell him. She had such a good feeling that everything she wanted was going to happen. Her heart was light as a feather, ready to float away.

Ted took her hand as they toured the barn, they found Earl inside. Angela explained how Clive had found her the best manager.

She took him past Earl's cabin, Ted said he was glad there was a man on the property nearby, to keep an eye on her. She didn't mind his protectiveness. Clive, Lucas and John Harpole had all said the same.

The apple trees were young as they'd only had a few years to grow. But they appeared healthy as any tree in the pre-winter starkness could look.

"I see many apple pies in my future." Ted said and rubbed his belly in jest.

"Yes, I hope so. Part of my plan is to expand the orchard with almond trees." She talked about the Russian breed that Corinne had found. "We all are hoping they will be perfect for this climate."

"Knowing that you will have a buyer immediately for the almonds is a sound plan. Are you certain that you will get a fair price from your friend? Sometimes that can be tricky." Ted had been around for the bartering when his father had farmed, Angela was happy that he was willing to ask questions.

"Yes, she has a few people she is trying to buy from. Through correspondence she is finding the fair price. She agreed to pay me the same price or the average depending on what the fair market is. Earl has a lot of knowledge. I have some other plans for the land that I would love to talk with you about." Angela spoke fast, and the excitement was showing on her face.

"I am glad you have Earl to help. I hope someday I get to learn from him myself." Ted was feeling free to express his wants for the future, at least in small chunks.

"I am so glad you feel that way. I didn't want you to feel like well..." Angela stopped, her fears rising back to the surface. "Well... that you aren't part of this, I know you aren't yet." She was feeling foolish again. Jumping ahead of what was appropriate. She needed to hush.

"I am not feeling threatened. I am glad to see you have a successful plan, and that you have found a way to provide for yourself. Whether I am in your future or not." Ted said with all sincerity.

"Well, I have stipulations from the land committee. Clive co-signed but without a signature from a husband to take over the deed I will lose the land in four years." Angela felt her heart beat quickening. She said the word husband out loud. It was the last thing she had wanted to confess. A part of her wanted to be embarrassed, another primal part of her wanted to be angry about being forced to have a husband when her plan was sound with or without one.

Ted smiled with that charming boyish smile she remembered. "Four years." He nodded. "I certainly hope it would be settled long before that."

Angela's eyes were wide at his declaration. But she knew she shouldn't be surprised. Ted was not a man to play with her emotions. Some men were slower to commit. She thought of Ted as a man who knew what he wanted and driven enough to go after it. She would find out eventually, she thought to herself.

"I also want to know what your goals are. There is a lot of acreage. I have my plans for some of the land but long-term goals will take a long time to fulfill. I also have a portion of land set aside for Edith and Henry Sparks, they are moving here too. They took care of me. I would like to be close to them too." Angela walked around the barn and showed him the area that Earl and her had recently discussed. "A cabin there, and then with a few trees felled they could have a nice field for vegetables and…"

"You are very generous, my Angel."

"They have been the only parents I have known for the longest time. They may not be blood, but they saved my life." Angela looked up to Ted. Wanting him to be proud of her vision.

His arms were around her and she leaned into him. Their wool coats were bulky but the feeling of warmth was still there. Ted was really here, and he hadn't rejected her, even with all her schemes.

They walked up to the house a few minutes later. She wanted him to see her work in progress.

Dolly was standing at the front door and waving. Angela introduced Ted to her roommate and after a minute of chatting Angela and Ted started a slow walk through the house. All her plans and dreams were discussed as they walked arm in arm through the home.

"I know there is so much work to do but I am excited." Angela gushed. She was pleased to see his response to her ideas and he praised her constantly for everything she had done.

After the tour Ted made his way around the front porch of the house. The wind was cold but they took a moment to sit in the rocking chairs on the west-facing porch. They laughed at Angela's attempt to sit in the small rocker in the big dress with the hoop skirts.

"I can see this would go smoother with a less fashionable frock." Angela couldn't stop smiling. She ended up sitting on the very edge of the seat to keep her skirts from bending and warping.

Ted was quiet for a minute, a calm smile across his lips. He looked from her face to the land that lay before him. Down the hill lay the creek babbling happily. A willow tree drooped beautifully at the edge of the water. From the high point on the hill he could see the church past the creek and the dark rich earth of harvested fields.

"The land on that side of the creek is Corinne and Lucas's, on this side is…" she wanted to say 'ours' but instead she took a deep breath.

"Yours?" Ted finally spoke. Angela nodded.

Ted stood a minute later and took her arm again. They walked to the front of her house and she showed him where the Harpole ranch land started and ended. He now had the lay of the land.

It had been a peaceful end to their visit. Ted had kissed her hand as the sky darkened with dusk. He waved his goodbyes and was gone a minute later. The surrey he had purchased was squeaking and rattling as he crossed the creek.

Harpole Ranch

Corinne, Violet and Galina took the stone path from the Grant's doorway to the Harpoles'. They all wanted to check in on Marie. Violet had left a pot of stew behind for Lucas, and had an equal portion with her to serve to Cooper and John, as well as all the helpers. They walked into the front room. John was kneeling nervously in front of his son, Cooper, who had just turned eight years old. Angela and Dolly arrived a minute later. Everyone was chatting in the living room.

John whipped around and looked relieved to see the women at his door.

"I think Marie's time is at hand." John had a sweat sheen on his brow.

"You go get Doctor Williams, we know what to do." Corinne took a hold of her father's shoulder. She kissed him on the cheek and he visibly calmed.

Violet wordlessly made her way to the kitchen and stoked the fire in the cook stove. She found a heavy pot and Galina was there with a bucket of water a moment after. Dolly and Angela took instructions from Violet.

John was out the door and Corinne was holding her stepbrother's hand as they walked back through the spacious cabin to find Marie.

Marie was settled in her bed but she was wearing a grimace and panting softly.

"Father thinks it's time." Corinne said and sat on the cushioned chair near Marie's bedside.

Marie nodded and Corinne settled in with her stepmother and helped her get ready. It was going to be a long night.

Within the hour the doctor arrived and just after midnight a baby girl joined the community.

John proudly sat by his tired but healthy wife with Cooper as a proud big brother as they awed and oohed over the tiny girl.

Violet and Galya took charge of the linens and got a peek or two at the baby. The helpers stayed until long after dawn. Everyone felt the same nervous energy when a child was joining the world. Shortly before sunup everyone found a way to get rest, to catch a few hours of sleep before the day needed anything.

Chapter 18

December 1st, 1850
The Harpole Ranch

Violet woke feeling like she had sand in her eyes. The small sound that invaded her hearing was a shaking pathetic cry. It registered through her exhaustion. The baby… the new baby was crying, probably from hunger or a need to be cleaned or held. Babies had their reasons for things.

Violet pulled back the quilt and sat up from the davenport she laid upon at some point after dawn. Her neck was stiff. Violet sat up fully and stretched languidly, feeling the sleepiness roll through her like fluid. Every single part of her wanted more sleep.

"Need some coffee?" Galina used a harsh whisper to get Violet's attention from the kitchen.

Violet noticed that Galina looked as bleary-eyed as she herself felt.

"Desperately!" Violet said emphatically. She thought about standing up and going to retrieve the cup but her legs did not want to get up yet. Violet sat there dumbly and Galina brought the steaming coffee with sugar and milk already in it. "Awe…" Violet said with obvious gratitude.

"I pay attention. You like your coffee the same as I do." Galya shrugged. She took a spot next to Violet and they both sipped hot coffee to wake up. The baby's shaking voice had stopped her wailing and the house was quiet again.

Corinne walked out of a back room and sat opposite of Violet and Galina, her hair sloppily pulled back with a ribbon. Her wavy hair was in disarray, very uncharacteristic of her usually tidy ways.

"They finally decided on a name." Corinne yawned loudly.

Violet and Galya both shared a sleepy smile with Corinne.

"Oh?" Violet said after she took another sip.

"Yes. Abigail Marie Harpole. I have a baby sister." Corinne chuckled mildly.

Violet sat the cup down on the table next to the davenport and gave a healthy stretch again. She was beginning to feel life trickle back into her body.

"I cannot believe it is past 10:30 in the morning. I should go check to see if Lucas has burned down my kitchen." She enjoyed the pretend shocked look on Corinne's face. Even sleepy they all had a sense of humor.

"I thought I saw Clive through the window, heading in that direction. He may have come by here to check on Marie. He spoke with the ranch-hand and left down the path." Galina shared, she tipped her coffee mug all the way up and drained the last sip. "You girls can head home whenever you like. I can warm up a breakfast tray for them. You already have lunch made, too."

Corinne and Violet shared a surprised look, both impressed with Galina's abilities to take over the situation.

They nodded and within a few minutes they were headed out the door quietly. They wanted the family to get as much sleep as possible.

Corinne and Violet were inside the warm Grant's cabin a few minutes later. Clive was indeed there as Galya had predicted.

"Helloo, ladies." Clive said with a cheery tone.

Violet waved and Corinne said hello. They both plopped into a seat at the table with Lucas and Clive.

"Coffee?" Lucas offered, perched to get up from his chair.

Both girls shook their heads "no."

"Galya made some for us." Corinne offered and leaned against her husband's shoulder.

"I came to check up on the baby news and heard from Reynaldo, the ranch manager, that a girl was born." Clive said then paused. "I also wanted to chat with Violet and you folks about some news from town."

Corinne filled Clive and Lucas in about baby Abigail and the state of the family.

"So glad everyone is healthy." Clive smiled and patted Corinne's shoulder. "Yesterday was a busy day. Angela's feller came back, Marie had a baby. There is plenty to be thankful for."

Both Corinne and Violet clamored for more information about Ted but Clive held up his hands in surrender.

"I cannot believe that Angela didn't tell us last night." Corinne said with her forehead pinched in worry. "I hope it went well." She was obviously beginning to fret.

"I just brought the Greaves family from the boat into town. Angela got a chance to meet with the Greaves family herself. Ya'll can pester her." Clive laughed as both girls pouted simultaneously.

"I wanted to keep you all abreast of some happenings in town. I myself have no idea what is to be done." Clive took a more serious tone.

He frowned and ran a hand over his chin to pause, to reflect on what he wanted to say. "Violet and Angela went out for do-goodin' yesterday to pauper row outside of town and all the families were gone. Angela came to me yesterday to look into it. Well… I did and a part of me wished I hadn't."

He sat back in the chair and sighed, knowing that everyone was looking to him for an explanation.

"The families that were residing in the poor shanties have mostly been relocated to a warehouse that was empty down by the south side of the river. It was used to store access wool last year but has been empty for a while. The conditions are not very good. A few of the families had people to stay with, but some had no where else to go." Clive said with disappointment. His expression was grave.

"The families are each allowed two cots, no matter the amount of family members and the dirt floor is cold and damp. The warehouse is large and there is very little light from the few windows. I would never use it as a place of habitation. These folks were better off in the shanties. I spoke to one member of the council who filled me in on the decision. It is all going to be announced in the newspaper that is coming out in a few days."

The table was stunned into silence. Violet had tears in her eyes, knowing she could have been there with all those people. Corinne looked tired and angry.

"What is to be done?" Lucas finally broke the silence with an emotional edge to his voice. He had been on the losing end of the city council more than once. He wasn't a big fan of how the local government did things.

"I am not certain. I need to talk to others and perhaps meet with Mr. Jed Prince to find out the perticulars. I know they are being fed by the church in town, at least one meal a day. That is all I know. I wasn't allowed in beyond a foot or two. I would like a chance to talk to some of the folks staying in there." Clive said sadly. He had seen many things in his life but seeing human suffering at the hands of others was never to be tolerated for long.

"I was going to let Angela know the news as well. With her background I know this will be a hard blow. This place will probably bring back memories." Clive saw Corinne nod as they both knew the workhouse had been a living nightmare for Angela as a child.

134

They all chatted over ideas for a few minutes but they all knew they were speculating without facts. Actions needed to be taken and prayers needed praying. Lucas promised to tell the pastor and other families nearby to be praying. Since Sunday was the next day, the community would get plenty of chances to spread the story. It was the kind of story that needed to be shared. It was the only way that change would come about.

Angela Fahey

Angela lugged the heavy water bucket to the stove. Dolly was standing next to her in anticipation.

"You go get ready, Angie." Dolly was finally feeling comfortable to use the shortened version of her roommate's name.

"I wanted to get this going today. I don't want you to have to do everything yourself." Angela's voice was strained from the stress on her mind. Clive had just left after sharing the news from town. She had so few hours of sleep, after the excitement of the new baby and Ted's return her sleep had been hard won. Adding this new concern was a tipping point for her. She just wanted to sit down and bawl.

Dolly spoke up with a firm tone. "He is coming back in an hour. I can easily handle the washing up. You agreed to allow me to do the washing up when I have days off from work with Corinne. Do not force me to remind you every weekend." Dolly was trying to brighten her friend's mood but it wasn't working. "You need to go, I have got this part. You go take on the town council!" Dolly finally said, seeing the determined look come across Angela's face. It was what she wanted to see.

"I give up. You are right. I will be the grand lady again today and see what can be done." Angela wiped the moisture from her hands with a soft kitchen towel. "Perhaps nothing can be done…" She muttered more to herself than Dolly. She was feeling lost in her own thoughts and memories. Knowing that people collectively can do terrible things without considering others.

Dolly placed a hand on Angela's in a rare display of affection. "God is with you."

Angela sighed and nodded. "He is indeed."

135

She returned from her room in forty minutes, hair pinned back perfectly, a smart bonnet tied smartly around her chin, and a warm green velvet dress that seemed more suitable for a church service than a visit to town. The skirts flowed around her in a wide bell.

"You look elegant." Dolly stated emphatically as she was wiping away the water from a clean dish before she settled it softly on a drying towel.

"Fashion is a ridiculous waste of time and fabric. The fabric from these skirts and petticoats alone could dress at least three people." Angela huffed.

Dolly smiled at her friend in agreement.

"I know that people respect it somehow. I find it almost irresponsible and completely impractical. Oh, and the corsets." Angela rubbed a hand down to her waist and raised her eyebrows in emphasis.

"You will get attention in that dress for sure." Dolly said with her usual practicality.

"Yes, and attention is what is needed in this case. Perhaps I can woo my way into the warehouse downtown. I need to be an eye-witness for these people." She felt very strongly. She was stirred up. Her morning had been spent in a fog of happiness about Ted and babies, now her whole heart was turned away from the pleasantness of that to the struggle of those poor people affected by the city council. She knew there was nothing about the situation with Ted that she should be ashamed about. It was a natural reaction to affection and attraction. But how could she stay focused on herself when others were being treated poorly? She knew she couldn't.

Dolly finished up the dishes and sat with Angela at the dining table while they watched out the window for Clive to pull up in the buggy. He had said he would spend some time with Earl and come back with her in an hour. He was true to his word and Angela was helped into the seat next to Clive for the ride to town. The way there was spent in heavy reflection of what they both were hoping to accomplish.

Chapter 19

Oregon City

The stench of human waste was heavily mixed with the moist air that escaped the doorway to the warehouse. It had taken a good five minutes to convince the man at the door to let them in. Angela had summoned up a memory of Corinne's Aunt Rose, and spoke forcefully and elegantly to the man until he felt obligated to let the young woman pass.

Clive stayed silent and let Angela do her best, he was pleasantly surprised by the transformation from servant to lady that Angela had done. He knew this young woman was going to be a force to be reckoned with.

Angela tried to choke back a cough and fought the urge to hold a handkerchief to her nose. She had seen women do this when she had been a poor orphan at the workhouse in Boston so many years before. She remembered the shame she had felt. She never wanted to cause shame to anyone like that.

The room was very dark, two small windows allowed bright beams that did little but light the small area nearby. She could make out two wood burning stoves, one on each end. There was a young boy by each stove stacking the firewood nearby. She was making mental notes of everything; no detail was to be left behind. A woman sat on a cot a few feet away with a toddler in her lap.

"May I talk with you ma'am?" Angela asked politely.

The woman shook her free hand in a 'come over' gesture. Her face was dirty and the front of her dress stained.

"How long have you been here? My friend Violet had brought food earlier last week to the…" Angela saw the light spark in the woman's eye at the mention of Violet. Angela paused, not wanting to use the words shack or shanty. "The dwellings outside of town."

"Ah yes'm. Ms. Violet was such a kind soul, and Mr. Quackenbush." The woman paused. "I think it was three or four days later that they came. They held out a paper fer me to read but I cannot." She shrugged and shifted the child on her lap, the young child was just as dirty as the mother but happy to be held, she fell back to sleep against her mother's arm. "They gave me an hour to gather our things. My boy is over yonder." She pointed at the nearest wood stove. The boy that had been stacking firewood was probably close to six years old by his height Angela mused.

"What is the situation here? I heard there is food brought in?" Angela was slightly relieved when the woman nodded.

"Once a day the church in town brings by food, sometimes stew, sometimes bread or gruel. There is a man at each door who then rations out our portions. I didn't know what to expect at first, because I don't read but fer my name but a few young lads took it 'pon themselves to read the notice." She pointed to the paper folded on a crate nearby. The edges were dirty but Angela wasn't worried about dirt on her gloves.

She looked it over.

Notice: November 28, 1850 , Oregon City, Oregon Territory

All shanty homes squatting on city land will be torn down. They are considered hazardous to the health and wellbeing of the occupants and are to be evacuated on this day, November 28th 1850.

All occupants will be removed to a more suitable location.

Warehouse B on Farley St. All families will pay ¢2 fee per week, those unable to pay will have the weekly fee added up and paid back to the town upon request at a later date.

The Willamette Church of God agreed to provide meals to said families.

Doctor Williams will be brought out once a month to see to the medical needs of Warehouse B occupants.

Below the notice was the signature of the president of the town council, and the name of each member.

Angela was sickened by the notice and its implications. If all these families were being charged to live in this squalor... how would they ever afford to leave? She had been similarly charged for her care in her workhouse as a child. They had taken future wages for years after she had left. If Corinne had not gotten her own lawyer involved she may have

come to adulthood still as a servant and penniless as these people were
now.

Her brain was in a whirl as she turned to take in the sight of the
entire warehouse, her eyes finally adjusted to the darkness within.

"May I keep this ma'am?" Angela asked.

"Yes'm, I 'ave no need of it." She rocked the girl in her arms gently.

Angela murmured a thank you and gave the woman a nod. The smell
of the room reminded Angela of a thought.

"Where is the privy? Or outhouse?" Angela asked knowing that a real
'lady' would never ever mention such a thing in public but the woman was
not affected or ashamed to answer.

"There be none. There is a woods a ways to the south…" The
woman gestured. But the wind is mighty cold these days, 'specially at
night. Most are using a bucket. I seen a few young ins' use the floor. Tis a
pity." Her gaze was blank. Angela recognized the look. This woman was
giving up hope of anything better.

Angela tried to keep her face calm at the new knowledge she had
gained. Clive joined her a minute later. He had been talking with a young
man across the room.

"I will come back soon, is there anything you know that is needed
around here by more than one family?"

Angela pulled out her notebook as the woman listed off a few things
that came to her.

Angela looked over her list.

Fresh water
Blankets
Soap
Children's clothing
Children's coats…

The list continued and Angela wrote everything down. Clive made a
few suggestions when the woman paused to think.

"We have no ability to wash anythin' and even if we did everthin' has
the potential to be stole. The men in charge of the building have gone
through all our belongings and took anythin' they thought would be good
for ever'one." The woman shifted the toddler on her knee once more
after she spoke.

Angela nodded, knowing that was how her workhouse operated as well. Everything belonged to the community and no one was allowed to get ahead.

Clive and Angela left shortly after the list was made, armed with information. They got to Angela's buggy and she spoke the moment she hit the seat.

"I would like to go to the bank, please." Angela said dryly. She was trying to control her anger.

"You cannot start that way, Red." Clive said quietly.

"I would like to see anyone stop me." Angela gave a slow turn with her head and looked Clive in the eyes. "I will pay for the families rent as a start and get them some decent supplies."

"We have to do this the proper way." Clive placed a hand on her shoulder.

"How can I possibly go home to my warm house with food and water and A FLOOR..." Tears and anger were bubbling to the surface. She asked this knowing that he knew what she was feeling. She wanted to do something... anything that would help these people.

"They have no outhouse, they are living in filth... They were better off in their clapboard housing in pauper row. They were all cleaner when I saw them before. They could hunt and provide for each other."

"I know, Red." Clive's voice was quiet, his face contemplative. "Let us get further away from the ears here." He looked to the man sitting on the stool by the door.

He was wearing a dark wool cap and coat. She saw that the man was indeed listening intently. She nodded and acknowledged that Clive was right. Clive clicked at the horse and they were moving toward the general store. They needed to plan.

Chapter Twenty

Above the General Store

"Do you expect us to allow these people to live here?" Millie asked and gestured with her arms covered in lace and brown and red taffeta. "I am positive they are crawling with vermin and Lord knows what else?"

Clive and Angela shared a look of exasperation.

"Mrs. Quackenbush, that is to be expected but that is not the request. The conditions they are in currently are due to the town council's actions." Angela said firmly.

Millicent waved an arm. "Call me Millie, for heaven's sake child." Angela could see the pinched look on the woman's face and her heart calmed a bit. Millie was not as unfeeling as her words came across.

Angela sat back in the soft chair by the fire in J.Q. and Millie's home above the general store. It was a pleasant place with bright curtains on the windows and a lovely kitchen with the stove that matched her own that Clive had mentioned.

J.Q. rubbed his chin thoughtfully, "I heard rumbling about some business with those folks but only when Millie mentioned making food for them did the real news come out. Some of the church members were pretty horrified when they saw the place. Even just from the doorway." He sighed and shook his head from side to side.

"I would like to pay for their fees." Angela said. The conversation here was all conciliatory but not going forward with any kind of ideas.

"That is kind but doesn't help them out of the situation." J.Q. said practically. "We may have to make it a town folk issue."

Clive and Millie nodded but Angela didn't really understand.

"How do you mean?" Angela prodded.

"The right proper Mr. Jed Prince does not take kindly to interfering in his council decisions. He is now the head of the city council and enjoys the position." J.Q. said with a raise of his eyebrows. It was a gesture Clive used all the time.

"You think I should go talk with Mr. Prince, I have heard that he is not very movable on his positions." Angela wondered aloud.

"Yes, but no matter what he says you and Clive could be a witness. No one meets with Jed Prince without the whole town knowing about it.

It could get the talk started and action could follow." J.Q. finished and took his wife's hand. "I know how the word could easily get about town about the tragic condition of those poor souls." J.Q. spoke in a higher tone mimicking a woman.

Millie smiled and nodded. "I think if I share your experience, Miss Fahey, then people will take it seriously. People know of your background. No one wants the repeat of that kind of insensitive bureaucracy here. There is enough politics already. I will start with the prayer group meeting tonight. The governor's wife will be there." Millie winked victoriously at her husband, showing Angela a conspiratorial side. Angela let out some of the tension within her.

"Please, Millie," Angela smiled in a gesture of friendship. "Call me Angie."

"I will set up a meeting with Mr. Prince for early in the week with me and Angie." Clive stood and nodded to his son and daughter-in-law. "Blessed is he that considereth the poor: the Lord will deliver him in time of trouble. Psalm 41:1"

"Amen!" Millie and Angela said together and smiled at their timing.

"I still want to pay their fees." Angela said as she was being helped into her wool coat. She tied the bonnet strings under her chin and gave Clive a serious look.

"I believe you will do as you wish Red. But I recommend a waiting stance. We will move in the direction of helping these souls. Let us see what the town can do to right this wrong."

Angela nodded and said a thankful prayer for her good friend Clive. He was a source of wisdom when she needed it.

The bell over the door jangled as Angela went through it. The cold wind reminded her of the people struggling to stay warm in the warehouse. She needed to remember that they were in God's hands.

Angela looked down the street and saw the new home of the Greaves just a few doors down. She got an idea to invite them to Sunday service tomorrow.

"I will head home in a few minutes, Clive. I want to make sure the Greaves feel welcome to join the Sunday worship." Angela grinned nervously as her stomach flipped at the thought of a moment to say hello to Ted and his family.

"I will join you in the invite. I 'been wanting to peek in on 'em anyhow." Clive placed a warm wool cap lined with fur over his salt and pepper hair. He wiggled his eyebrows like he was being mischievous. "Have you two shy lovebirds had a proper reunion?"

Angela felt the heat rise in her cheeks but she answered him calmly, trying to avoid any more embarrassment.

"Yes, we have been able to talk some. I showed him my new home and property." Angela sighed after she spoke, part of it out of memory and another part of exasperation. She did not know what to feel.

The last two days had been a whirlwind of activity. She had moved, reunited with Ted, heard of Marie's childbirth and then the issue with the poor people in that dreadful warehouse. Her brain was a jumble of thoughts, feelings and the need for a good cry.

If I had a spare minute I may just cry my heart out. Angela said to herself.

Clive knocked on the Greaves door a minute later. Angela was glad she had worn a nice dress since she was seeing Ted's family again. She wanted to make a good impression.

The housekeeper Beatrice was at the door with Sophia lingering right behind, she peeked over the ample woman's shoulder and grinned.

"It's Clive and Miss Fahey!" Sophia's blond waves jumped around as she skipped forward to take Angela's hand. "So glad you came!"

Angela could see the warmth and genuine cheer in the girl's smile and pushed her own timidity aside.

"I am so delighted to see you again. Clive and I only stopped by for just a moment. We do not want to intrude on your rest at all." Angela said to Sophia but with a glance she could see the whole family was in the sitting area of the front room.

Ted had a blue cotton shirt on casually unbuttoned, his shirt sleeves rolled up. He stood once he saw her. The expression on his face was endearing. Angela took a moment to capture the look to keep as a memory. He was very pleased to see her.

"I wanted to see if you all had any needs. I think Angie here wanted to make sure you were welcomed to Sunday services. Since I attend the same church I would offer you all a ride. If ya be needin' one." Clive took off his hat and gave the slightest hint of a bow.

Olivia Greaves stood and nodded. "I do believe my sister wants to go to the church in town, but since Ted and Sophia want to attend where Miss Fahey goes I would be glad for the ride. I have heard it is just a few miles out of town. I would love a chance to see the lay of the land." Olivia smiled at her niece Sophia as the young woman stifled a giggle.

"My conveyance would fit all of ya." Clive said politely.

Amelia Greaves stood a moment later and cleared her throat, capturing the attention of everyone in the room.

"Miss Fahey, I was hoping tomorrow you would have dinner with our family after the worship services. It's time we get to know the young woman that Ted has spoken so much of." Her voice was without much emotion but Angela took the invitation as a good sign. "You are welcome to come along Clive." She added, probably to avoid rudeness.

"I beg your pardon ma'am. I already have plans with my granddaughter's family. Chelsea and Russell Grant." Clive said and smiled at Angela. "I hope you can meet them soon."

"I would love to share dinner tomorrow." Angela said softly, she looked Amelia Greaves in the eye, trying to be sincere and set aside her nervousness.

Amelia nodded and harrumphed. Ted took his mother's hand as a thankful gesture. After a moment he looked Angela in the eye. Everyone in the room was staring at the lovebirds. They were too caught up in each other to notice anyone else.

"I do hope you will be able to come to dinner some night this week Mr. Quackenbush. Perhaps Wednesday? I know we would love to talk about business and learn more about this budding community." Olivia spoke up and cleared away the nervous energy floating around the young couple.

"I have no plans, and please, call me Clive, Quackenbush is such a mouthful. I would have shortened it long ago but never had the nerve." Clive smiled and enjoyed the chuckles from the room.

Amelia had turned and taken a seat back on the davenport and folded her arms in front of her chest. Olivia took the moment to smile at Angela then Clive.

"Miss Fahey, I will see you tomorrow morning at church and again for dinner." She turned her face to Clive and gave him a pointed look. "I will expect you to be here at six thirty on Wednesday. Please be on time." Olivia smiled the briefest of smirks.

Clive and Angela both bade a brief farewell and left. As they walked back to the general store and Angela's buggy, Angela's eyes were wide. She had just witnessed the most amazing thing.

"I remember a ways back you shared a proclivity with me Clive." Angela said when she couldn't hold in her thoughts any more.

"Oh, what was that? I do have so many." He chuckled to himself, suddenly in very good spirits.

"That you have a liking for strawberry blondes." Angela said with amusement.

Clive frowned at his young friend. "Oh hush, ya meddling female." He grinned in spite of himself and took her arm tighter.

Chapter Twenty One

Angela Fahey

A soft word turneth away wrath.

The Bible verse flowed through her like a balm, for a minute and then the hurt returned. She was at a loss of what to do. The dinner conversation had gone so very wrong. The church service with his Aunt and sister had been a delight, introducing everyone there to them. Getting to show off her 'beau' to her small church. The morning had been perfect.

When she arrived at the Greaves' townhouse she had been given a tour by Ted and Sophia, who was always nearby. Being the younger sibling, Angela understood why Sophia wanted to be part of the fun. She had a suspicion that Sophia was hoping to be friends. She still did not know many people in town yet.

Sophia wanted to show off a lace project she had been working on and also show Angela a surprise.

Angela was delighted to have an escape and the two young women went alone to the front parlor where Sophia showed her the lace she had been making that day.

"I have a gift for you. I worked on in while in California, waiting for the steamship. I hope you like it." Sophia bent over a basket and peaked inside and pulled out a large lace collar.

Angela gasped over the fine work. The design of full roses was clearly seen in the pattern.

"I am working on a series of roses in different states of blooming. This collar has the two cabbage roses in full bloom. I went with the off white because of your coloring. Ted has talked about your hair and your alabaster complexion for months." Sophia sighed and laughed the way a sister would.

The camaraderie the brother and sister had made Angela think of her brother with the slightest wish that the relationship had not been broken.

"This is so lovely. I cannot imagine how one would do this. I cannot draw roses on paper, and here you have created this masterpiece that clearly represents the flower so well. I am stunned." Angela praised the artist for a full minute before they joined the others in the dining room.

"She loved the collar!" Sophia announced and both Ted and Olivia cheered.

"It is extraordinary work. I will be so proud to wear it. I hope it makes all the ladies in town envious so they have to have one too." Angela said with a mischievous grin.

"I may use the cabbage roses again but not on a collar. That is yours alone." Sophia crossed her heart in a pledge.

Angela couldn't help herself and gave the young lady a hug in appreciation. Dinner was served a minute later and the conversation quickly spiraled downward.

"I heard from Ted about your new home and land purchase." Amelia stated when she received her soup bowl. After she spoke she raised an eyebrow then with a steady move she grabbed her soup then took a dainty and silent sip of broth.

"Yes, I was telling Ted about how I used my inheritance to get land next to my friend's property as it became available." Angela wasn't sure how much information that his mother would like to know.

"A few people in town are talking about how foolhardy and impulsive you are. Only just Eighteen and thinking you can farm the land." She continued.

Ted tried to speak but Angela silenced him with a look. The noise that escaped his lips sounded like "ugh" before it was cut off.

"I know not everyone will understand my intentions but I believe I have a solid plan and with God's help I will see a fruitful harvest, Lord willing." Angela had had naysayers before, she could handle it now. She hoped.

"You intend to snatch away my son from me and will have him working your land soon." Amelia Greaves spoke with a vicious tone that stunned Angela speechless.

"You are unfair Amelia." Olivia chimed in and her sister stared at her coldly. Olivia harrumphed audibly.

"Mother, I do not appreciate the tone you are using to attack Miss Fahey. She has made no pressure on me in any way. When I left the west she would not allow me to make any promise or engagements because of her feelings for my family back home. Saying otherwise in this case is untruthful and not appreciated." Ted placed a hand on Angela's shoulder as a show of support.

Olivia leaned and whispered in her sister's ear, only to be batted away.

147

Angela heard most of it. 'Your foul mood is not welcome here…'

"I just want to make sure my son has his eyes open about the type of child he is attaching his feelings to. Olivia, you *are* his Aunt but you have no say in this." Amelia squinted and focused on eating her soup as if nothing happened. Sophia sat silently with tears brimming at her eyes. She dabbed at her cheeks then her eyes with the cloth napkin. Angela wasn't sure if the girl was embarrassed or sad for her.

Angela held in the frustrated sigh that wanted to escape. She was warmed by the protection in Ted's and Olivia's speeches. It covered some of the sting of the words, "foolhardy and impulsive." She supposed that gossips in town were always going to have to say something.

She wanted to defend herself but with Ted's mother she was feeling unsafe. This woman had been through a tremendous loss and perhaps the move had been hard on her. Angela was going to try and give the woman a chance to warm up.

Ted tapped her on the shoulder and mouthed. 'I'm so very sorry.'

Angela nodded that she knew. This was not what she wanted. She wished that everything had been smooth and flawless. She would go home and pray after dinner. God would help her through this. It was the only hope she could cling to.

The dinner ended soon after the outburst. Angela felt uncomfortable and any attempts at conversation were awkward and stunted.

If there were any plans for after the dinner Angela cared not. The moment everyone was headed to the front parlor Angela spoke up.

"Thank you all for the visit. I do intend to visit my dear friend Marie. I was hoping to get a peek at the new baby and check in on the mother's recovery." Angela tried to pull forth any false cheeriness to her voice. Somehow it had not worked fully. The pinched foreheads of all her potential allies in the room gave away their concern.

"May I accompany you?" Ted asked with real desperation in his voice.

Angela wanted to tell him no. She wanted to be alone, perhaps cry… Instead she nodded weakly, knowing how it all would go.

A few minutes later they both were bundled in their wool coats. Angela had her smartest bonnet on over her hair and ears, feeling remarkably foolish about how late she had lain awake the night before thinking about how to do her hair for today.

Silly female… She said to herself.

"I don't have a clue what to say Angela." Ted took her gloved hand and tucked it into the crook of his arm.

"I don't want you to spend this whole conversation apologizing." Angela said a little more harshly than she meant to.

"I can concede to that." Ted said as they stepped off the porch. Angela looked toward the livery where her buggy was kept.

He was aching to do everything the way she wanted, she realized. Wondering if that was going to make her feel worse about how she felt.

She wanted to be angry... Shouldn't she be allowed a moment or two of self-pity and anger over accusations and slander, especially from a person that she had never said a contrary thing about? Angie felt a tidal wave of different emotions overwhelm her at the implications of Ted's mother's words.

"She does not approve of me." Angela said without looking at Ted. It was her worst fear, she realized. She was reliving the feeling of her brother's rejection and the pain in her stomach was burning hot. If she could have sat and sobbed just then it may have helped with the pain, but Angela would not allow the eyes of the townspeople to have that luxury.

"I do not care what she thinks." Ted answered and tried to pull her shoulders to look at him.

Angela pulled away, trying to hold on to any shred of self-control she had.

"You would defy her?" Angela asked quietly, her legs kept moving toward her goal.

"I have honored my mother in every way I could. I helped her get a fresh start. I will provide for her in every way I can. Her unhappiness is beyond my understanding." Ted sounded as frustrated as she felt.

Angela was overwhelmed and she wanted to be left alone suddenly. She just wanted to step away from this situation and not have to always defend her every action.

"Ted, I am not sure I can handle this." Angela turned and finally faced him. They stood before the livery. "I do not want to make a scene and have even more gossip stirring around about me." She didn't want to see the pain in his eyes.

"I am s..." Ted cut off the apology to abide her wishes. "Please don't be sad. She is a very unhappy woman. I know in time..." Ted ended his speech lamely, knowing that he knew nothing about what the future would bring.

"I need to go Ted. Please let me." Angie was so tired and her tears pushed past the wall she had tried to put up.

"I love you Angie, I will give you the time you need." Ted leaned toward her to kiss her but Angie pushed away.

"No Ted. I cannot defy her wishes. I will not be happy knowing…" Angela stepped away and nearly fell. Ted's arm was there to steady her but she pulled away. A sob escaped and Angela covered her mouth to try and muffle its sound. "Please go!" Angela said with whatever nerve she had left before more sobs escaped.

Angela had managed to get her emotions under control after a mile of reckless buggy riding. She was glad the horse hadn't veered off the road while she was blinded by tears. She felt foolish and terrible for what she had said to Ted. The heartbreak on his face when she had sent him away had been her undoing. How she had asked for the stable manager's help with the buggy she wasn't sure. She was positive that everyone in town would know her business by tomorrow.

Angela gulped down a few breaths and wiped the cold tears from her cheeks. The dry cold air would be dipping close to freezing any day.

She crossed the creek and saw Corinne and Violet walking along the road. They waved and Angela regretfully pulled her buggy to a stop. She was thankful that her horse obeyed her suggestions.

"We were coming to chat. We weren't sure if you were home yet from your visit. We knew we could visit with Dolly until you got back… Are you alright, Angie dear?" Corinne said with sudden concern.

"To be perfectly honest, I am not. I am at my wits end." Angela said without any humor in her voice. Her face told the true story, red and blotchy, her eyes swollen.

"You go on ahead. Violet and I will be one minute behind you. We will get some tea on and figure this out." Corinne reached a gloved hand and patted Angela's.

Five minutes later Corinne gave a deep bear hug to her friend and let her sob onto her shoulder. Corinne didn't need to know the reason behind the tears; she knew enough to be quiet and was ready to listen.

Violet joined the hug and all three rocked a little in the way of women. It was comforting and a part of how they instinctively knew what was needed.

Angela broke free from the embrace when her tears had run their course. She grabbed a kitchen towel and mopped the moisture from her face. Violet took the teakettle and filled it from the fresh bucket of water on the counter.

Dolly said 'hello' from upstairs and joined the women.

"Let's go in the parlor. I have barely used it yet. I bought cushioned chairs and a davenport for visitors." Angela said weakly. Her voice wavered but everyone pretended not to notice.

"I will bring in the tea." Violet offered.

"You are my guest." Angela did not want Violet to feel like a servant in her home.

"Today I am a friend." Violet said with a genuine look of concern and care. Angela could not argue with that.

Angela and Dolly puttered around with the fireplace and got a small fire started, it made the room warm and the yellow flame brightened up the space. The clouds were getting darker outside as the rain threatened to steal the sunshine for the winter doldrums.

Violet brought tea and a tray of cups for everyone. She was so excellent at her job. Angela thanked her over and over.

"I don't know what to say." Angela offered finally when she was settled into the chair looking at her friends expectantly. "Today was terribly overwhelming."

She began with talking about Ted. "I don't want anyone to think badly of him, or his family." She paused a second, wondering what was allowed, to be polite and not gossiping. "Ted's mother does not approve of me." She stated simply. She took a deep breath then a sip of tea to keep the lumping in her throat from turning back into tears.

"How is that even possible?" Dolly shocked them all by saying.

Corinne and Violet nodded in agreement with Dolly.

"I want to say that Ted was completely supportive, as well as his Aunt and Sister. Everyone seemed mortified and apologetic for what Ted's mother said." Angela wanted to protect Ted and his family members that were kind to her.

Corinne prodded her for a minute to spill what was exactly said. They all gasped over the 'foolhardy' and 'impulsive' comments, as well and the implications of stealing Ted with womanly wiles.

Corinne sat her teacup down and clenched a fist in frustration. "She does not know you in any way. How could she have that kind of opinion based on nothing?"

151

"Ted thinks she is angry and sad about losing her husband." Angela offered. "He said it doesn't matter to him about her approval."

"That is a good man." Violet added. "If she cannot be happy with you as a daughter-in-law, no one could please her."

"I am not sure I can be happy knowing that she disapproves so greatly." Angela said, her voice breaking with emotion. This was a truth within her that hurt so badly.

"Love can overcome a lot of things." Corinne said wisely. "I am so sorry that this has happened sweet friend." Corinne stood and took a step over to Angela's chair and sat on the arm, resting her own arm over Angela's shoulders. "God can find a way through this battle too. He has been there for me through the impossible."

"And I." Violet said.

Dolly smiled and nodded too. "I am only just learning to trust in God. But His word says 'The Lord is my strength and my shield; my heart trusted in Him, and I am helped.'"

Angela wiped away a tear and closed her eyes. She let the verse sink in. "The Lord is my strength and my shield." She took a deep breath. "And I am helped!" She stated and opened her eyes again. She felt shaky start towards peace.

She looked to the friends around her. She knew God had blessed her in her friendships.

"I do not know what to say to Ted, yet." Angela said a few minutes later when she was calm enough to talk about it again.

"I think he knows that you may need some time and space to let this heal, if not you can let him know. I am sure he has his own struggles to get through, too. That would have been very hard on me if my father had treated Lucas disrespectfully." Corinne furrowed her brow in thought.

Violet stayed quiet for a minute, she seemed lost in thought for a bit. She finally muttered a sigh and spoke. "Sometimes the betrayal of one's family has a way to cut the deepest wounds. The memory of words spoken in haste can last a lifetime." Violet wiped her own tear from her cheek, displaying a rare sight of her own emotion. "I know this will be equally upsetting to Ted. I can imagine he would want to be anywhere else right now."

The women all agreed.

"We all should pray for his mother. If she is truly so unhappy as to wish unhappiness to everyone around her than she needs the Lord's help." Dolly offered.

They all vowed to do that very thing.

The warmth of Angela's parlor shown through the windows as the cold storm slowly crept over the mountain and the daylight passed into dusk. Violet and Corinne eventually made their way back to Grant's Grove before the heavy rain came. But it was not before the women's heartfelt prayers were spoken together. Angela and Dolly stayed cozy in the parlor until it was long past time to sleep. Dolly read the bible aloud for a while and Angela talked and crocheted. Her heart felt lighter than it should have. But the Peace that passes all understanding was her comfort for the night.

Chapter Twenty-Two

Galina Varushkin

Galina's boots were coated with thick mud. The cold from the wind and rain was seeping into her bones. Her wool coat was handed down a few too many times. The holes along the seams allowed so much wind and moisture in. She turned her shoulder to the eastern wind and marched up the road to Angela's home. She had a heavy laundry bag slung over her back that her father had handed her.

"You can work on the family laundry too, I'm told." He had said so briskly. Galina had already known she was to take it but his reminder got under her skin. He did not yet have employment, and it made him irritable. She was the only one earning any good money. It did not seem so fair for him to be so bossy with her when he only just got back a few days ago.

He was eating food and resting under a roof that he did not earn. She thought ungratefully. Knowing she herself had not earned it either.

Oh Lord, forgive my wicked thoughts. She prayed in her head.

The heavy bag was slipping and fell off the precarious position resting its weight on her hip and swung out in front of her awkwardly, she nearly dropped it. Galina gasped and used force to swing it back into a semi-comfortable position.

She looked up ahead and decided to try and guess how many more steps to Angela's back door. She decided on the number two hundred. She began to count aloud. "One - two - three…" She closed her mouth after she said three because the cold wind actually hurt her teeth. She told herself that snow was coming soon, and she resumed her counting of steps quietly. She grabbed the scarf with her teeth and tried to pull it awkwardly over her face and slightly succeeded. It covered half of her mouth and most of her neck now. It would have to do, her hands were full and she did not want to stop or move the bag again.

The step count was actually two hundred forty seven when Galina reached the back porch. The sky was grey and dark but the young girl knew that it was almost eight a.m. certainly. She was glad for the work and excited to get to know Angela better. The walk may have been uncomfortable but Galina was glad to be away from her home. Since her father's return the cabin was full of tension.

Angela was at the door a minute after Galina knocked.

"I have been looking forward to you coming since I moved in. I am so glad you can come and help me." Angela pulled the young girl in and snatched the laundry bag with her own strong arms. "Oh my, that wind has a bite to it today."

"Yes Ma'am." Galina said politely, suddenly feeling awkward.

"Oh no, that will not do." Angela smiled. "I am Angela, or Angie. Formality is not allowed here."

"I forgot. So sorry." Galina nodded.

"No need for that. Come have some coffee or tea?" Angela settled the bag in the back room and grabbed for Galina's coat.

"Coffee please." Galina smiled. Her mother let her have coffee on cold days, but her father wouldn't allow it. "With milk?" She asked while shaking off her wet mittens.

"I have cream or milk. I love having my own cow." Angela gave a wink to Galina. "I can say that easily because I did not do the milking. Though I want to learn. Just not today." Angela gave a shiver and Galina laughed.

Once they got to the kitchen Angela pulled a stool from under the counter and patted it as an invitation.

"You just missed Dolly by about thirty minutes." Angela poured two mugs full of coffee then settled the small pitcher for cream and the bowl of sugar on the counter next to Dolly. Angela fished two spoons from the silver drawer.

"Mmm." Galya said. " I saw Dolly head into the laboratory as I crossed the footbridge." She savored another warm sip of her coffee. "She and Corinne are always so smart about everything."

"Indeed." Angela said. "They are so very inspiring. I had the hardest time getting up this morning. But once I remembered you were coming it cheered me dramatically." Angela confessed.

"You jest."

"I do not! I would never make that up. Had a bit of a rough day yesterday. Knowing that I get to stay home today and visit with you actually cheered me up. I promise." Angela patted Galina on the shoulder.

"I need something sweet to make amends for my bad day. I shall I bake scones before we start."

Angela pulled out a recipe that Edith Sparks had shared with her almost three years before. Seeing her handwriting on the paper made Angela feel loved and the memories of Edith's sweet mothering flooded her. She wished to have her to talk to, knowing that they would be coming west cheered her heart.

Angela showed Galina to the pantry and the two gathered ingredients, the scones would come first, laundry later.

Angela's apron was messy and her hands were slightly sticky from rolling out dough. The pan of scones had been placed in her oven when there was a knock at the front door.

"It's always something when you are looking your best." Angie said sarcastically and was rewarded with a giggle from her young new friend. "Pardon me while I get the door."

Galina sat back down on the stool and sipped at the second cup of coffee.

Angela wiped most of the sticky dough from her hands with a dishtowel. She wiped at her apron but knew she would only make a mess if she continued. She went to the door just as she was.

She was amazed when she saw Ted's face peeking through the lace curtains. She waved and opened the door a moment later. She had no words.

"Hello." Ted said simply.

Angela muttered something resembling a reply.

"I am not staying here long, I just wanted to let you know I was on the property. I came to see you last night but I saw you had company. Instead I ran into Earl, he invited me over today."

"Oh yes, I..." Angela struggled with what information to process first. He had come to see her. Her heart melted a bit. "My friends were here." She said, finally proud she could speak at all. "We prayed."

"Prayer is good." Ted smiled and his eyes lit up in a way that nearly took her breath away. "I did some of that myself."

"I feel like I need to apologize for being so blunt yesterday." Angela started.

"You faced some heavy insults. You are allowed to be upset." Ted said with sincerity.

"I just didn't mean…" Angela faltered, still confused about what she really felt. "I am not angry with you at all. I don't want to be angry with anyone. I am definitely hurt, but I am working through it." Angela looked back to see Galina contentedly sipping coffee at her counter.

"I will let you spend time with your friend. We can be introduced some other time. I need to go to see Earl. If you need time to think, pray or whatever, you have it." Ted settled an off-white cowboy hat over his blond curls and tipped it politely in a goodbye gesture. "You mind if I keep the horse in the barn?" He buttoned the top button of his tan leather coat, the bright white wool lining made Ted's smile stand out all the better.

"Not at all." Angie nearly lost her voice over the effect of Ted's new hat and coat. "You come by after your visit with Earl. I have fresh scones in the oven. Be sure to tell Earl and Warren too."

"Will do." Ted walked away with a calm gate. He was steady as a rock.

Angela and Galina spent some good time in the kitchen, getting to know each other a little better. Angela wanted the girl to feel comfortable in her home. Her thoughts were mixed on hiring help but she knew this girl's family would be blessed by the money her work provided. Angela pushed back her mixed feelings and instead focused on the girl.

Once the scones were pulled from the oven the ladies got busy doing the 'hot' work. The stove in the washroom was piping hot when Angela had stoked it earlier. The large stockpot was beginning a rolling boil.

Galina took the lid off the big water barrel just outside the back door and filled the large washtub with six inches of cool water. She knew if they only put hot water in the tub, the water would steam away and they would have little water to work with. Angela took charge of watching the water pots.

"You get your family's clothes first. We will do mine as the second batch." Angela offered and was pleased to see the girl smile.

"Only if you are certain." Galina wanted to be sure.

Angela nodded emphatically.

Galya sorted through her family's things. Angela scooped hot water from the boiling stockpot into the washtub. It was going to take a bit of time to get it up to the right temperature. A second stockpot was started next to the other pot and that was starting to produce steam. The room was going to be very warm, very soon.

Chapter Twenty-Three

Angela Fahey

Washday had gone remarkable well. The big pile of clothes, sheets and dishtowels had been handled properly. The water drained with the special system that had been built into the washtub. 1It allowed the water to go out after the plug was pulled, through a clever trough. That trough led to a small door that flipped up against the wall. The water then traveled out the side of the house and over the hill into a harmless group of trees. Clive had seen the system in a bathhouse once and had incorporated it into every home he had built. He passed the design along to his friends. It was becoming a popular way around town to handle the washing.

Galina had surprised Angela by having a sharp sense of humor and she was an excellent storyteller. Angela felt she knew the girl very well after they had spent so much of the day together. Angela felt bad when she offered to share her small library of books with her.

"I can barely read, Angela." Galina stated simply. To Angela it seemed she had given up on the hope of changing it.

"You are such a smart girl, Galya. We shall have to see about that. I'm certain you can catch up in no time." Angela let the matter drop when she saw the dejected drop of Galina's shoulders. She would not press the issue for now but she would certainly be praying about how to help her. She knew that being uneducated would hold this girl back needlessly.

Earl and Ted stopped by while the gals were hanging the clothes on the line strung through the washroom. Angela kept the stove warm, not as blazing hot as before so the clothes would dry overnight. The wet bed sheets were still sitting in a heavy wicker basket, ready to carry upstairs to an empty bedroom. They would need to string a clothesline across the room and allow the sheets to dry up there.

The girls were glad the visit from the men had given them a moment to pause. Laundry was hard work and arms and backs were beginning to ache from the heavy labor. The scrubbing, squeezing and twisting of fabric to help it release the water was hard on the body.

"You ladies have been busy." Earl stated as he stood at the open back door of Angela's house. She was glad he felt comfortable to come into the mudroom without knocking. She wanted Earl to feel like he was family.

"I would be lost without Galina's help. She is an amazing helper." Angela said and leaned against the wall next to her.

"Well, you take a breather ladies. We shall visit and eat scones, then maybe we can help you finish up with the hanging." Earl said giving a glance behind him to Ted, getting a hearty nod from the younger man.

"Sounds good to me." Angela sighed and saw Galina's wide eyes stare at the men first and then at her.

"My father has never helped with the wash, ever, even when he is home with no work." Galina shared. She grimaced when she realized that she was perhaps over sharing. "Pardon…" She finished softly.

No one said anything but Angela gave Galina's shoulders a squeeze to let her know she was in a safe place.

Earl and Ted led the procession through the mudroom passed the pantry then into the open kitchen and dining room. Angela passed the small mirror in the hallway and saw how the humidity from all the steam had turned her pinned back hair into a halo of frizzy red tendrils all around her face. She frantically tried to save her hair by patting it with her hands, but the damage had been done.

Phooey! She said to herself. She had laid out a large white neckerchief on her dresser this morning to tie over her hair. Could she escape quickly and cover up the mess on her head?

"Oh dear, I am such a mess." Galina declared. "May I take a moment to wash up, Miss Angie?" Galina winked at her friend.

"Yes, you ladies take a moment. I know my way around. Ted… be my extra hand here and grab some plates from yonder." Earl said. He gestured with his good arm to the cabinet full of china.

"Be right back." Angela stated as an afterthought. She was so thankful for the chance to escape.

Angela led Galina to her own room where she had fresh water in the washbasin and pointed to the hand towel for her as well.

"Thank you for speaking up. I was just noticing the state of my hair." Angela said with a laugh after she closed the door behind her.

"I saw my own hair first and was feeling self-conscious. I saw that yours had reacted similarly."

Angela grabbed the comb from a bedside stand and repaired the damp tendrils and then wrapped the large neckerchief around her head. She handed the comb to Galina.

160

"I have another one of these in my wardrobe. Thank you sweetie." Angela didn't need to explain why she was thanking her new friend. She had been flustered from the male company.

Galina fixed her hair and smiled at Angela in friendship without speaking. She felt useful and good inside. It was a simple pleasure, being appreciated.

Angela tied the dark green cloth around Galina's dark hair and they took a moment to make sure their appearance was acceptable.

Ted Greaves

Ted had watched the girls disappear into Angela's private room. He took a deep breath and let out the tension. It didn't seem that Angela was angry with him. They had both seemed to go backwards since that first night he had been home. He really felt closeness with her once they had worked past the nerves. She had walked with him around her property and held his arm possessively. Now she seemed nervous around him again. He was more than frustrated about how to handle his mother. He had spoken to her sharply when he had gone back home after that horrible scene in front of the livery. He never wanted to see Angela hurt like that again.

Earl had been a good soul to talk to today. Ted would have liked to pester Clive today but the man was gone early according to son J.Q.

'Town business' he had said.

Ted said a few prayers on his ride over to Angela's. Trying to forgive his mother was the biggest challenge.

After seeing the flustered look on Angela's face at her door he knew his decision to give her time was a good one. But there was a part of him that wanted quick answers.

I want to be with her now! His thoughts said in frustration over and over. He had to constantly push away his impatience. He was usually so levelheaded and practical and he was upset with himself for his inner struggle.

His meeting with Earl today had been good. Discussing the land and the plans for the future of it was actually quite enjoyable. Earl felt a bit protective of Angela and Ted was amused when Earl had questions about his intentions. The conversation turned when Ted got brave enough to share the events of the previous day.

"Well, you do have yourself a predicament son." Earl scratched at the scruffy beard on his chin.

"Yessir," Ted nodded. He was sitting cross-legged at the rough table in Earl's cabin and he shifted to get more comfortable.

"The challenge you have before you is a common one. You get to choose to follow your own happiness or obey the wishes of a parent. Each path will have its heartache." Earl shared, his eyes showed he knew this from his own experience.

"I know what I want, but with yesterday's escapades I fear that Angela will be unwilling to accept now. She was clear that she didn't want to displease my mother." Ted grabbed his knees in frustration.

"You seem like an easy going bloke." Earl looked him over.

Ted nodded, "I used to be." He laughed a little, somehow finding the situation humorous in a tragic way.

"Find your inner patience and give Angela some time. You don't have to avoid her unless she asks you to. But you can lower the pressure on her having to make a decision right this moment. Sometimes us fellas can come on pretty strong. We need to remember that God has a plan and it isn't always full speed." Earl stood up from the table and grabbed the coffee from the warm stove. He poured them both a refill.

Ted took a deep breath and didn't feel the need to speak. He knew that Earl was right. He needed to calm down and wait.

The conversation over the morning led to other things, the plans for the land and a walk through the cold misty morning over to the orchard to talk over the best way to grow an orchard. The frost crunched under Ted's feet and he enjoyed the frosty white covering on the trees to the east on the bluff. The dark barren trees looked haunted with the white frost clinging to them. The white mist enhanced the image. He looked along the bluff and saw tall pines and further east the mountain snow caps were declaring boldly that winter was on its way. This land that Angela bought was perfect. The rolling hills were picturesque and the land was fertile and dark. He couldn't have disagreed more with his mother's criticism. Angela had chosen wisely. He was proud of her. He would pray about how he could tell her.

Now that he was back in Angela's house he felt that rise of frustration coming close to the surface again. He wanted to have everything be perfect once more. Before his mother's interfering. He reminded himself of Earl's advice and allowed a quick prayer asking for peace to keep his thoughts busy.

He saw Angela and her young friend leaving her room, their hair wrapped protectively. He hid a smile that wanted to escape. He had seen Angela's curls earlier, he was sure she was self-conscious. She shouldn't have been, the curls framing her face were beautiful. Her cheeks turned red from the warmth of the room. He hadn't been able to look away.

Angela introduced her friend.

"Hello Galina," he said cheerfully. He shook the young lady's hand. "You must be a great help with all you got done today."

The young lady blushed under his praise.

"You can call me Galya, everyone does." She surprised everyone with her bold answer. She was not shy as the blush indicated.

"Then you must call me Ted."

The introductions were complete and everyone sat down to the table. Angela forced Earl to sit and let her pour the tea. The scones were already on the table with small bowls of jam and butter presented in the middle.

"You set a good table gentlemen." Angela laughed a little in surprise.

"My wife always said I was raised by wolves, must be Ted that has the manners." Earl chuckled at his own joke. Everyone else did to.

The buttery scones were good and the jam provided by Mrs. Quackenbush was the perfect compliment. Everyone exclaimed over them.

"I am determined to learn more about canning this year. I know some ladies at church who will teach me." Angela shared. "There is so much to learn."

"My mama makes some amazing canned vegetables, her stewed tomatoes with garlic and onions are very good." Galina said with an emphatic nod.

That began a whole conversation from the men about their favorite foods. After they exclaimed about canned peaches, sauerkraut, smoked salmon and candied yams, Angela pretended to whisper to Galina.

"You know, my dear caretaker, Edith Sparks, declared that the easiest way into a man's heart was a pretty dress, but the way to keep him was through his stomach." She said loud enough for everyone to hear.

"She is a wise woman." Earl laughed heartily.

"I do hope she comes next year to Oregon." Angela said wistfully. " I will tell you all about her sometime." She told Galina, not wanting to leave her out of the conversation.

The conversation continued as they cleared the table and prepared to finish the rest of the laundry.

163

"I beg your pardon for all the work that still needs done. You volunteered to help not knowing what was involved." Angela declared when she grabbed a broom from the back of the pantry.

"Pssshh." Earl said as if that was all that needed saying.

Angela shrugged prettily and she gave instruction.

"I need an armload of firewood. The wood stove has not been started in that room. It needs a good sweeping too." She held up the broom and grinned sheepishly. "I hung the hooks for the string a few days ago, but have been in town so much I never got the string up. It should only take me a few minutes to get the room ready."

"Lead the way." Ted said, he wanted to say much more but he decided to keep the conversation neutral. Even if the others hadn't been in the room he knew he needed to keep his tongue under control. Any pressure may ruin the fragile state of their relationship.

Ted was the tallest in the room and easily took over when the plan for the laundry line was explained. He only needed a step stool to reach the ceiling.

Angela and Earl worked on getting the fire started while Galina glided her way around the room with a broom. She started telling them all a story about a laundry incident that had happened the year before.

"My brother Milo had been hunting outside the small camp of families. We were there because the men were doing lumber work; either as lumberjacks or at the mill further down the river. He had himself a bag full of squirrels and a few doves, he is a fine hunter with his sling." Galina bent down and picked up a nail from the floor and handed it to Angela. She picked up the broom and continued her story. "My mama had just gotten the whole line full of clean laundry, it was a pretty spring day and the breeze was going to do quick work of drying the extra laundry my mama took on sometimes. We were right next to the dirt path the men used to travel in and out of the camp. We all had nice little wooden huts to live in, my mama was proud that we didn't have a dirt floor anymore." Galina scooped up the dirt into the trash bin in the hallway and came back in.

"Please continue, Galya." Angela prodded.

Galina seemed pleased that everyone was listening.

Everyone grabbed a few pins from the linen pouch that Angela had carried up and the all grabbed a wet item from the heavy basket. Angela was grateful that all personal items were already hung up downstairs. All that was left were the large bulky items, like sheets and towels and a few odds and ends.

"Well, my two brothers are excellent hunters but they had made a mistake in determining the…" She paused for the right word. "Deadness?" She shrugged and continued. "The bag of game had been settled at the foot of the empty laundry basket and we were just admiring the lovely spring breeze when a high pitched squealing was coming from the tightly tied up bag."

Ted and Earl already were starting to chuckle softly.

"My brother Milo grabbed the bag and saw that something had come back to life and was making a fuss. The critter inside was jumping like his feet were on fire." Galina had mirth in her voice and she bent down to get another towel from the basket. Everyone in the room was looking at her expectantly.

"The bag was tied so tightly that my brother couldn't untie it, especially when the creature inside was flopping around so. My mama tried and just shrieked the entire minute, which made my brothers giggle endlessly. I ended up grabbing the bag and loosening the knot. I still don't know how I managed it with all the racket and wiggling going on. But the knot was loosened but I didn't know what to do. I handed the bag over to my brother. I was going to tell him to take it back to the woods to release the critter but before I could speak my brother released the crazed squirrel and his wild journey began. First the furry thing leapt on my mother,"

Earl's barrel-chested laugh rang through the room which prompted everyone else to laugh the way they wanted to. Galina picked up her volume so everyone could still hear. "Second, he bounced to me. I screamed and flung the creature anywhere to get it out of my hair. The creature landed in the muddy path. I saw on my hands that the creature had been injured for the drops of blood. I told my brother to catch it to put it out of misery. Which began the chase. My brothers joined the creature romping through the mud, then a leap across the yard to the first curtain that hung on the line. It left a trail of blood and mud along the clean sheets, the underthings, and my family's Sunday best. My brothers tripped over themselves, pulled down the laundry line to fully finish the hope of any article on the line remaining clean. The critter was frantic and bounced around for several minutes, even the neighbor children heard the ruckus and join the chase. After a long battle the poor thing must have been crazed and disoriented because he jumped over every obstacle and stood on the line post near the washtub and while cornered he fell in. He got tangled in clothing in the water and perished by drowning." Galina ended with a curtsy. The laughs and cheers were profound.

"No," Earl finally said after his laughing had subsided. "The wee thing died after all that."

"On my honor!" Galina giggled and made a cross over her heart.

The laughter continued and the job was finished. They all went downstairs.

Angela split the remaining scones and offered it to her guests. "I can make fresh ones anytime." she said.

Earl gladly took a few. Ted passed claiming his housekeeper was always making treats.

"I will be fat by the time that winter is through," Ted declared with a smirk. "I will head out. But I will be back in a few days Earl. I can help with those tasks in the barn. Warren and I can follow instructions, certainly." Ted said to Earl. He gave a nod to Galya and Angela. He tried to keep his face clear of all emotions. "It was a pleasure ladies."

"Goodbye Ted." Galya said. She looked up to see her friend and tried to discern how she was doing.

Angela did not seem as casual as Ted was but she revealed nothing with words. Ted could see she was torn. "Pardon me. " She said softly and took Ted's arm.

They walked out to the front porch. Angela could see Earl and Galina cleaning off the table from the corner of her eye. *God bless my helpers*. She thought.

"I wanted to say thank you for the help and the visit." Angela said finally, her voice was a little thick with emotions that she didn't understand.

"I am glad to help you in any way." Ted wanted to declare his love, apologize again and just hold her, but he refrained.

"I don't want you to feel you have to do work here." Angela said. Her voice was a soft whisper.

"I had already made arrangements to talk to Earl. I am learning from him how to run a farm. I am grateful for the tutelage." He said sincerely. "My father would be teaching me this, but..." Ted faltered, realizing the mistake in mentioning such a personal subject.

"I know, Ted. Perhaps I care too much about what other's think. I will work on that. You are always welcome here." Angela said and with the look on her face Ted could tell she was sincere. "I want to speak to your mother again. I do not think I feel as strongly about what I said. I

166

don't think I can end a relationship with you just because of a few heated words from your mother. But I do want to speak to her. A part of me needs to know that we can live peaceable."

Ted felt his heart expand over her words. Hope bloomed within him. She would not give up on him. "Beautiful and wise, my Angel." Ted said simply.

"For now I will give her some time and space. I will see you in a few days perhaps. I heard there is going to be a barn dance next month. Perhaps by then she will be in better spirits." Angela said.

Angela gave him a slow grin that had his heart pounding in his chest. He felt like a young boy around this woman.

"I can respect that."

They said goodbyes simply, without any embrace. But Ted rode home on his new horse with a promise of better days in the future.

Chapter Twenty- Four

Sophia Greaves

Olivia bounced around the room, fussing with the open boxes and doing her best to find a few things to make the house start to feel like a home. Her strawberry blonde hair pulled back into a loose bun, the curls ready to burst out of their pins if given a chance.

Sophia enjoyed watching her Aunt flutter around. Sophia wanted to be like her, bouncy and full of life. She had seen her Aunt struggle through her own loss but when the time came to set aside the grief over the divorce and public scorn she did. Olivia was a complex creature.

Sophia saw her mother stroll down the staircase. Sophia noted there was a significant squeak from one of the boards. She would ask Ted to take a look at it. Sophia wrote the thought down then looked up to see her mother looking at her with a raised eyebrow.

Those eyebrows can say paragraphs. She thought. Her mother's eyes had a way of piercing straight through her as if she knew her every thought. Sophia lowered her gaze to keep her thoughts to herself. If she appeared meek it always worked out better for her.

"I will be going to see Angela's new house in a day or two. I hope you didn't scare the sweet young thing away permanently." Olivia spoke to her sister. "I had hopes to call her my niece soon. You squinting and grumbling at her will not do well in convincing her of our good regard."

"She has not earned my good regard. Olivia, Ted is *my* son. I will judge the character of any girl he courts. It is not your concern."

"Amelia Sophia Greaves, is that really how you want to start your new life here?"

"You mind your own, Olive. I will think on it." Amelia said with a huff.

Sophia looked from her mother to her Aunt, noting how much they looked alike in so many ways. Both had the curly golden hair with the hints of the red peaking through. Both had handsome cheekbones that she had luckily inherited from them. Her own hair was a yellow blond, though.

The two years between the sisters showed up differently on their faces. Just this last year since the death of Sophia's father, her mother has lost the bloom in her cheeks. She had always been opinionated and in charge of everyone around her, but now it had taken on an edge. Sophia prayed often for her mother to be happier and to let joy come back in.

Sophia had her Aunt to talk to sometimes, when it was a moment alone. Her Aunt gave her hopeful thoughts to dwell on, like given time, her mother may be happy again.

Sophia's eyes were wide and she left the room to escape the tension.

Ted was back from his visit with someone. Sophia hoped it had been Angela. Somehow she felt such pain at the thought of Ted losing Angela over words spoken from her own mother. It was a painful thought to ponder. No one wanted to say anything to Mother lately, she seemed above any comments or reproach for her actions.

Sophia felt so torn, she had been raised by the woman who taught her that there were consequences to attitudes and actions. *Had sadness really changed her so much?* Sophia wondered.

Sophia felt lonely all of the sudden, the house was full of tension and she had family surrounding her but she felt a bit lost.

Chapter Twenty-Five

Angela Fahey

Angela had spent the next few days gaining a routine. Her life had been in chaos since she had moved and everyday she had been busy. She started her morning by talking to Warren, the hired hand, when he dropped of the pail of milk at the back door. She said goodbye to Dolly as she headed over to Grant's Grove, then she skimmed the cream from the milk and poured it through cheesecloth to catch any debris. She had yet to make butter. But she wanted to try soon, she thought. Violet had been spoiling her by bringing some every few days.

Galina came by after she worked at Marie's the day after she had helped at Angela's to pick up the clean laundry. Angela enjoyed seeing the young lady again and had a sincere hope of a long-term friendship. Angela had handled her laundry and folded the Varushkin's family laundry into a nice stack. Angela wondered aloud when Galina arrived if they needed to get the girl a small wheel barrel to carry items back and forth.

"The idea is a good one. I am not sure we can afford that kind of thing yet." Galina said cautiously.

"Well, Michaelmas is coming…" Angela said with a wink.

Galina shook her head. But Angela would not be dissuaded so Galina dropped the subject. She then asked if Ted had been by.

"Not today. I am, in a way, grateful. He flusters me completely." Angela confessed.

This brought out the giggles in Galina and she showed her young age for a moment. It brought joy to Angela seeing Galina look like a girl. Her own childhood had been cut short and she hated seeing anyone lose their youth over hardship.

After Galina left with her loaded bag, Angela was back to work. She had many boxes to unload, a pantry to organize, a root cellar to go through and many more little jobs that required her attention. She poked the fire in the stove and began making a stew. Earl had been to town the day before and brought back a freshly slaughtered lamb from the new butcher. Oregon City was a small town, but just this week rumors of a butcher and a grocer were circulating. Every new business made their small town more and more certain of becoming civilized.

Angela set herself to work and the day flew by.

———◆•◉•◆———◆•◉•◆———

Wednesday morning the same duties called to Angela. The pail of milk waited for her at half past seven. Dolly was gone just minutes later. Angela enjoyed her coffee with fresh cream and sugar, thinking absently about whether Ted would come by.

She wasn't disappointed when there was a knock at the back door. She was pleased to see Ted and Clive waiting for her.

"Hello Red!" Clive said cheerily. "I was on my way to see ya when this lad in a fancy new hat passed me by on a pretty white horse."

"You both are welcome." She welcomed them in and served them coffee at the table.

"I am only staying for a cup and I am off to meet with Earl and Warren." Ted said.

"I am here for a brief chat if ya have the time, sweet lady." Clive plopped his hat down.

"I always have time for a chat."

They discussed pleasantries over coffee, the weather and the new newspaper that would be releasing an issue in a few days. Everyone was excited to be able to have news, even with the fairly reliable word-of-mouth that was around having outside news was precious to everyone.

Ted made his goodbyes after his coffee cup was empty and was out the back door a minute later.

Clive jumped on subject immediately.

"We have a meeting with Jed Prince, the head of the town council, on Friday. It took some convincing. He is not very happy with our interfering, according to a few people, and he wants to ignore us. But with a brief mention to his second in charge at the lumber mill about the new newspaper and public opinion, I convinced him that a meeting was a good idea." Clive said and wiped a hand in a nervous motion through his hair. "Not sure what good we can do but we have to try for something. I looked into a few things, to have a backup plan in place but I am at a loss."

"What sort of backup plan?" Angela asked.

"I sincerely want to find a way for these people to be clean and safe so I was thinking aloud with my son for a bit and we came up with a thought. The boarding house in town, usually a busy place, has twenty rooms available. I spoke to the lady who manages it and was hopeful that she might have an idea or two on how we could help these folks." Clive shared.

"That might have merit, if she has enough rooms open we could get these people into a safer environment then we can work on helping them be self-sufficient," Angela said. She had thought about those people in that horrible warehouse constantly.

"It would have been a grand scheme but the boarding house is not solvent as a business currently. With the gold boom in California most of her tenants were male and they left town. A few of the families that had been boarding with her are now in that warehouse. The proprietor, Mrs. Gemma Caplan, is nearly bankrupt and contemplating selling the building. She says she loves the care taking of people in her stay but the money problems are just too trying. She is a widow and was using the boarding house as a way to make ends meet. She despises the situation. Struggling to feed yourself is hard enough, she feels partly to blame for the downcast state of some of her former tenants." Clive said thoughtfully.

"That is too bad, I know that the boarding house was a busy place over the last few years, families would arrive from the wagon trains and have a place to stay. I have heard of many families starting out there while their cabins were being built. She serves breakfast, lunch and dinner to guests. So sad to know that Mrs. Caplan is struggling to keep people in the building." Angela thought silently for a moment. "We cannot give up yet. God has faced down tougher battles than this." Angela was trying to focus on the positive, but her heart was very heavy.

Clive left shortly and paid a visit to the barn to see the progress the men were making on the building of a hayloft. So far the barn was a bit large for the buggy, one horse and one fat jersey milk cow. Ted and Warren were heaving boards up to the second level using a pulley system. Clive and Earl chatted below for a while before Clive felt the itch to move along.

Angela was nervous and agitated about the meeting. Friday morning her stomach had been in knots. Clive promised to come by and he brought his two-bench conveyance wagon. It had button down flaps on the side to keep the wind out. Angela still brought two blankets and her warmest fur hat to keep the cold away. While they were driving along the road to town Angela commented on the first snowflakes of the year.

"I could smell the snow in the air for days now." Clive said with a grumble. He was not ready for the weather to turn cold. "I myself could use another month of Indian summer this year."

Angela laughed and agreed. Her mind was only halfway in the present conversation though. She was thinking of what to say to Mr. Prince.

Jed Prince's main building was whitewashed brick building with fancy windows he had bragged about being from Boston. His office overlooked the river and Angela was impressed by the grandness of the office, in a small town it was rare to see such a nice building.

"I hear you all are taking offense to the town council's decision about the vagrants." Jed Prince had welcomed both Angela and Clive to sit but he didn't join them. He was pacing the room with his hands clasped behind his back. Angela could not help but feel slightly intimidated.

"Calling them vagrants when they weren't breaking any laws seems harsh." Clive said casually, his tone not in the least controversial or on edge. His tone seemed to relax Mr. Prince and he leaned on his desk in a more relaxed pose.

"I can see that. It will soon be a law that that part of town is public land." Mr. Prince suggested.

"When that part of town becomes public land, the town council will be replaced by a mayor and we will be a state. We do not know when that will take place. Displacing these people was perhaps a bit premature." Clive added.

Angela felt the back and forth between them was a little tenser than she realized. The tone was calm, but she felt the power and influence.

"I am certain you can see how the committee had to take action, when we heard that one family was living in a tent and in danger from the winter cold..." Mr. Prince stood again.

"That family was well handled." Clive interrupted. "That family was given the help it needed, a cabin was repaired that was going to waste away and the church had plans to help other families in any trouble."

"Perhaps your little church is interfering in public duty." Mr. Prince interjected.

"Perhaps the town council knows very little of the personal struggles of the poor and abandoned." Angela words burst out, her tone not calm

173

at all. "Maybe while stripping them of all cleanliness, dignity and hope, you might take a moment and put yourself in their shoes."

Mr. Prince's eyebrows were raised and he even gave a bewildered look to Clive for a moment before his expression changed.

"Young lady, I doubt you have the wisdom or experience to lecture me on public affairs." His voice was on the edge of laughter.

"I do not think you know the extent of her experience." Clive said in a low voice, there was no anger and Angela was very impressed with his demeanor and tried hard to adopt it. She took a deep breath.

"I was born of a wealthy family, Mr. Prince. But due to an unscrupulous man, my brother and I were sent to a work orphanage in Boston when I was very young. My stepfather sold us for a profit to this institution. He succeeded in failing his responsibility to call a lawyer and handle our money in a trust he unlawfully kept for himself." Angela said with a quieter tone.

"That is a shame Ma'am but I do not see how that pertains to the situation at hand."

"I saw first hand the type of system you are creating here. You are taking advantage of these people in a tragic situation. By charging them for the uninhabitable surroundings and leaving them unclean. It makes them trapped and unable to find decent work. Have you been to the warehouse where you have forced these people to live?" Angela asked.

"I had visited that warehouse before we ever made the decision with the city council." His tone had an edge. She felt he wanted to say more but he was holding his tongue.

"You should go back, the place is disgusting, there is no water for cleanliness, no privacy for the families. There is not even a privy." Angela said, knowing that he would be shocked that she mentioned something so wholly unladylike.

"I can look into the matter Ms. Fahey but I would appreciate you remember my position here."

Angela could see by the way he folded his arms obstinately that they were losing their audience. Angela looked to Clive and saw that he was certain of the same thing.

"Mr. Prince, all we are asking is that the people have a improved circumstance and an offer to pay their fees. They will have a better chance to get out of the impoverished state they are in." Clive stood, his body language showed that he was nearly ready to leave.

"I allowed you both into my office as a politeness. I do not want to be lectured on how to provide for the people under my care. As head of the town council it will be my decision how to handle them."

"Your insensitivity to their plight is my concern as Christian, sir!" Angela stood to her feet as well. She wanted to remind him about all the verses the bible mentioned about taking care of the poor.

"If I were you, Ms. Fahey I would concern myself with finding a husband to secure your own property. We agreed to allow you to be a landowner at the town council's discretion. If you want to interfere in my business then perhaps I will be persuaded to interfere in yours."

Angela felt the threat down to her toes and Clive gave her a look that silenced any retaliation.

"I do hope you understand our concern is not a criticism of what you were trying to accomplish Mr. Prince, just the way it was handled. As Christians we all want to do our part." Clive was ever the peacemaker.

"Agreed." Mr. Prince's tone stayed cold but he nodded to Clive. "You can be assured we will do what's necessary, I would greatly appreciate you allowing us to handle this in the future." He said and gestured it was time for them to go.

Angela and Clive walked quietly back to the livery. They where a mile up the road before Angela felt the need to speak.

"We really accomplished nothing but alienating the town council." Angela felt defeated.

"It may seem that way, but we spoke up. There will be a ripple in the community about this." Clive said and gave Angela a grin that eased her fears. Somehow she knew that Clive had handled harder issues than this, remembering his role he played in Indian affairs. He knew how to ease his way through political situations without ever getting dirty.

Varushkin Cabin

Galina watched her father and mother embrace just moments after he had ducked through the front door of their cabin. Her father had picked up her mother and swung her around with a smile that Galina hadn't seen in a long while.

"I have found work Magda." He said to her but loud enough for everyone to hear.

175

The boys were sitting by the fire warming up after spending hours chopping wood to trade with the neighbor. They both cheered and joined in the celebration.

Slava began to hum an old Russian melody and shook his hips in a dance that had even Galina smiling. She had longed for the tension over their father's presence to be gone and wanted to see her family living a happy existence again.

"Where will you work, papa?" Galina asked politely. She had barely spoken a civil word with him in days and everyone turned to see her with a bit of a surprised look.

"I will be working for Lucas Grant, of Grant's Grove. You have not been wrong in your opinion of these people, Galina. They have offered me a good position." He walked over to his oldest and placed the palm of his hand on her head in a loving gesture.

Galina closed her eyes and accepted the affection offered. It was a healing moment for her.

"I will be working the land, the way I love. Clearing acreage for the Grants. It is a blessing, indeed. I will be clearing trees and will get a percent of every tree felled and sold." Slava said and his smile was large.

It made Galina think about the many times her mother had tried to explain how a man is not himself when he doesn't have work.

"I start on Monday. We have so much to be thankful for." He moved across the room and sat on the floor next to the boys warming up. He scooped up his youngest and held Radimir to his chest. The baby was enthralled by his father's growing whiskers and got handfuls of hair when he could.

Galina watched and prayed for her family in that moment. So much had happened in the last year. She knew they were in a better place now, but she wondered why the suffering time needed to happen. She had learned in the last months to have a portion of faith in God. She wanted more but she knew she would understand little if she could never read the bible. It was her greatest desire. She did not know why she wanted to so badly but it burned within her that she had been denied the opportunity from her teacher, and now her circumstances. She would pray about how to approach her father about attending school again. Once he was working again perhaps she could go back to the primary school. She would put up with any comments about being too old for children's school. She could still do extra work at night and on the weekends. She would do whatever she had to.

Chapter Twenty-Six

Oregon City

The newspaper, The Oregon Gazette, came out with its first edition on Saturday and the town was buzzing over every detail. The grocer advertised canned goods from local farms, preserves from well-respected women and root vegetables. The new butcher offered pork, beef and lamb at affordable pricing according to the large advertisement on the bottom of the front page.

Across the dinner tables and the store counters, everyone was also talking about the town council's decision to clean out the Pauper village outside of town. The opinions differed in heated debate in many cases but most people also knew about Clive Quackenbush and that Fahey girl having met with Jed Prince. The rumors of the conditions of the folks in the warehouse had spread far and wide. Some exaggeration always occurred in a rumor mill, but the general consensus was that they were concerned about the welfare of these people, more than the town council had been.

By Sunday morning worship the townsfolk of Oregon City, the rural community of Portland and Salem were all settled on their own opinions of what needed to be done. At the church in downtown Oregon City when Jed and Ellie Prince arrived to worship at the Willamette Church of God, the whispers and stares were prevalent. Ellie was a popular member of the ladies' prayer group and felt the sting of the wagging tongues. Her words to her husband at Sunday dinner were harsh and disapproving.

The Spring Creek Fellowship Church had a different experience. Tongues were still talking about the business in town but everyone was very proud of the actions taken by two members of their own congregation.

When Angela sat in the third row pew, she was patted on the shoulder by everyone who could reach her. She gave a look around and saw many approving nods. Clive gave her a bold wink, the rascal, and she couldn't help but smile.

The row was open next to Angela and after a few minutes she saw Ted slide in next to her, followed by his sister, his Aunt, and his own mother! Angela's eye grew wide and she gave Ted a look.

Her eyes asked a question.

Ted's grin told her she would have to wait to find out.

Lucas played a sweet melody on his violin to open the service and Violet sang along after her played for a minute, she sung the words of Psalm 62.

My soul, wait thou only upon God; for my expectation is from him.

He only is my rock and my salvation: he is my defense; I shall not be moved.

In God is my salvation and my glory: the rock of my strength, and my refuge, is in God.

Trust in him at all times; ye people, pour out your heart before him: God is a refuge for us.

The words were sweet to everyone there and the sermon began from the same Psalm. Pastor Whittlan preached about leaning on the Lord when troubled times come. Counting on Him who gives strength to stand up and fight for what you believe. Pastor mentioned the people that were suffering in town. He read aloud Deuteronomy 15, verse seven and eight.

"If there be among you a poor man of one of thy brethren within any of thy gates in thy land which the Lord thy God giveth thee, thou shalt not harden thine heart, nor shut thine hand from thy poor brother: But thou shalt open thine hand wide unto him, and shalt surely lend him sufficient for his need, in that which he wanteth." Pastor said and let the words sink in.

Angela felt the call in her heart strengthened to help those in town. Her mind had been pondering what ways that she could help. She knew it was impractical for everyone to come and live in her house. It would burst at the seams. She would certainly not have enough food to keep them fed this winter. She let her heart settle in trust that God would guide her.

After the service she visited politely with the Greaves family. Glad to see his mother making an attempt to be sociable. Amelia Greaves still wore a frown for most of the church service but she hadn't uttered one thing that was impolite or critical. Angela took that as a positive sign moving forward.

She was given a handshake from every member of the church, including Governor Pritchlan and his wife. Angela was introduced to his wife, Henrietta. Angela took a moment and introduced the Greaves to the smiling couple. Angela noticed that Ted's mother could smile at the Governor and his wife.

The governor shook her hand warmly. "I have been brought abreast to the happenings in town. I have been spending a lot of time in Portland, Salem and other towns that are growing in Oregon. Hearing that you stood up to the likes of Jed Prince and the town council is quite impressive. I will certainly be addressing some concerns I have with actions taken by any town that affects people so vastly."

"I am relieved, Governor Pritchlan." Angela felt tongue-tied and humbled. She had only done as she felt was right. Everyone was acting as if she had truly made a difference. Those people were still in exactly the same position as they were. "I felt the need to act, I still do."

"I believe that a solution will present itself when we all do our Christian duty. I believe prayer is the best way to find these answers. God can move like a mighty wind and perform miracles still, do you think?" Governor Pritchlan said and a crowd was gathering around to hear. A few people muttered 'Yes!' aloud.

"Yessir." Angela said, a flood of emotion came over her. Perhaps just relief in knowing that others felt the same way she did.

"I am glad to be in town at the right time to know about this. My wife and I will be staying in Oregon City through the winter. I do hope to see this situation solved in a matter of days. We made a visit to this warehouse just yesterday, my wife and I were also horrified at the conditions."

Clive joined the group and placed a hand on John Pritchlan's shoulder.

"I paid him a visit, just to let him know how the meetin' went on Friday." Clive said and got a hearty nod from the governor.

"I heard through the grapevine that your house is now lived in." John said.

"It is. Only just over a week." Angela shared. She gave a self-conscious glance around to see everyone's surprise at her still conversing so easily with the governor.

"I have yet to hear about a house warming young lady." The Governor said. She gasped in remembrance from a month earlier.

"I did promise you an invite. I have been so distracted. Moving is a lot harder work than I ever thought..." Angela said.

"Well, if you need help planning a housewarming then I would be glad to help. Everyone is talking about you young lady. I would love a chance to get to know you better." Henrietta said. Her eyes were kind and Angela felt the offer was very sincere. Angela nodded her agreement.

"I would enjoy that." Angela admitted.

"Also I think a meeting of minds may be in order about this business in town." John said, first looking at Angela, then at Clive.

"How about we all meet at my office at the Hudson Bay store?" Clive offered. "Tomorrow at five would work well for me. What say ye'?"

Both Angela and the Governor both agreed. Angela was relieved a minute later when the gathering dispersed when everyone starting making their way to the door.

Angela invited the Greaves over to Sunday dinner but Ted's mother declined. She was still weary from so much travel and unpacking. Angela sent her off with well wishes. Clive offered her a ride home so the rest of Ted's family could enjoy dinner with Angela.

"I am still unpacking myself. But I have a lamb stew warming on the stove and fresh bread rising." Angela hoped they wouldn't be disappointed with her simple meal.

"That would be wonderful." Olivia Greaves stated. "After all that chatter with the governor I am fascinated to hear about everything that has happened." Olivia snatched her arm away from Ted and led her out the door, chattering away. Sophia and Ted just followed with a smile. Angela found Dolly and let her know there would be guests. Dolly passed on Sunday dinner herself too. She had been invited to spend the day with Chelsea and Russell Grant. Angela embraced her friend and even said a brief greeting and introduction for everyone with Chelsea and Russell. Angela wanted the community to know them and welcome them whole-heartedly.

Galina Varushkin

The Varushkin family walked home from church. The school building that the young boys attended during the week was nearby. Galina stared at it as the family walked. Her desire to read was at the forefront of her thoughts. Since her father was starting work in with Lucas Grant the next day she knew that their financial woes would be lessened dramatically. The weight of worry had been with her for so many months and she knew at thirteen years old that she should not have that on her shoulders. She had to fight off the anger of what her father had done every day, many times a day.

He was back now. She told herself. He would take over the responsibility of the family and she could be there for her mother and do odd jobs but she didn't have to miss school anymore.

It was a few minutes later, when they were nearing the creek that she got brave enough to ask the question that had been bubbling up inside her.

"Father, since you now have work again, I was hoping I could attend school during the week. So I could learn to read the bible." Galina said sweetly. She had been working so hard on using a softer tone with her father.

"You have work." Slava said gruffly.

"I am certain I could make arrangements to work around it with my friends." Galina said.

Slava began to laugh and it had an edge that Galina did not appreciate. It seemed like he was laughing at her.

"You think they are your friends. Durak!" He muttered and laughed again.

Calling her a fool in Russian had done what he had likely intended. Galina's shame was evident by the dark red staining of her cheeks.

Magda had a hold of her husband's arm and she leaned in to whisper something that Galina didn't hear.

Galina's anger was stewing inside her. All the words she had wanted to say were sitting bitterly in her throat, ready to spring out.

"All I have done is honor my family. Why is asking to be educated as well as your sons too much to ask?" Galina said and was proud that she hadn't lashed out, but instead spoken softly. She wanted to cry but she held those emotions back. Her father did not respect emotional females.

"Honor?" Slava yelled. He broke his contact with his wife and with two huge steps he forcefully grabbed Galina's shoulders and lifted her off her feet. His fingers squeezing into the flesh of her arms, burning into her the knowledge of how strong he truly was. "You have treated me with dishonor every moment since I have returned. You will do as I say and be thankful for the roof over your head."

"The roof that was provided because you abandoned us?" Galina said foolishly.

A minute later she was on the ground, her father's boot on her back. Her face was in the cold wet grass, the high weeds around her. They were in the wild fields between the church and their home. No one would see what happened.

Galina could hear her Father's angry voice but mostly she listened as his belt buckle jingled as he removed it.

The fear was hot as it raced through her body. She knew what to expect. It had happened before. Her coat had been pulled off and her brother Milo was holding it next to her. Her father was talking to Milo about discipline. He wanted Milo to watch to learn what disobedience would earn.

The belt was felt across her shoulders, the whistle of the leather through the air could be heard before the slap and incredible white-hot pain ripped through her shoulder blades. She reacted immediately by screaming and squirming. She reached up and instinctively covered her head.

"Do not move again." Slava yelled hoarsely. He then cursed in Russian.

Galina obeyed… and the belt continued to fall.

The slow walk home was painful. It had been difficult to pull her body up from the cold and wet ground, even more so when her coat was handed to her. She moved in slow increments to get each arm through the sleeves. Her parents began walking towards home without her.

Her brother Milo looked at her with big eyes that held pity, he muttered. "You are bleeding."

His words had been spoken softly but still she put a finger to her lips in a shushing motion, her arms and shoulders burned mercilessly. This had been her worst punishment.

Milo walked with her, every few moments looking up at her with compassion in his eyes. Galina was thankful for the show of support but silently wished that Milo had gone with her family ahead. He did not need to be seen showing any type of support for her if her father was beginning to go into an angry phase again. Galina would gladly take the discipline if her father would leave everyone in the house alone. She prayed silently that God could calm her father's heart.

The cabin was warm by the time Galina and her brother made it inside. Her mother was getting supper prepared and her father was seated on the floor with Radi in his arms, he tossed Radimir a few inches up and caught the boy, which produced a few belly laughs from the baby. Slava chuckled himself and repeated the toss a few times more.

Galina stood still for a minute, feeling the pain course through her bruised and battered self, watching the household go on about it's normal routine. She remembered now the way of things. The beating would now be forgotten, the acting as if nothing happened would continue.

In one way it was a blessing, all the anger had been channeled and her father was calm and happy now. The tension eased. Galina would not be lectured or reminded at all about this punishment. Instead, as long as she went along with the charade, everything would return to normal.

But Galina had seen this before, and she wasn't always the one with the bruises.

"Go get cleaned up for supper, Galya." Her mother's voice was almost musical. Galina felt pulled from her trance to look at her mother's face.

Her mother was wearing a forced smile, the sing-songy voice a pretense. A brief look crossed her face. It said volumes.

'Please do not draw his attention.'

Galina took a deep and pain-filled breath. She let the air out slowly in effort to clear the anger from her heart. She took a few steps toward the water-basin. She would begin acting, she would hide the pain and keep the peace.

Angela Fahey

Flurries of snow fell all afternoon as Angela visited with the Greaves family, minus one member. She was flooded with stories of Ted growing up, and silly jokes from Sophia, who loved to make people laugh. Olivia was such a pleasant woman, helpful and engaging. Angela felt hard pressed to think of Ted's mother as the sister of such an enchanting woman. Olivia was vivacious and endearing.

The day flew by and when dusk came early because of the season they all were sorry to end the visit. Dolly came home just as the Greaves were bundling into their warm coats.

"I am sorry to have missed the visit." Dolly shared when everyone began saying their goodbyes.

"We would love for you to come to our place in town next week, after service if you like." Olivia offered. "You and Angela." She said. Her smile was sincere but it fell slightly when she saw Angela's face turn a few shades whiter.

"I.." Angela stammered and stopped. Not sure what to say.

"I know you haven't had the best treatment there. I have been working on my sister. She knows that you are respected in this town. She will come around." Olivia said.

Ted placed his arm around Angela's shoulder, the first really affectionate touch she had had from him in many days. It was warm and protective.

"I will always defend you, Angel." He said softly next to her ear.

"And I." Sophia said boldly, grinning over her brother's flirtation.

"And I." Olivia said and leaned in to kiss Angela on the cheek, taking her completely by surprise.

Dolly and Angela agreed to dinner in a week's time. She watched them load into Ted's conveyance and roll away. Angela bundled up herself, grabbed the extra bread rolls and leftover stew and told Dolly that she would be back shortly.

She walked through the cold across the creek and knocked on the Varushkin's door.

"I come bearing gifts and news." Angela said when the door opened.

The stew was well received and the home was in pleasant spirits over the news Slava had of work.

"Corinne has been a dearest friend for years and when she offered me a job a few years ago as her ladies' maid it changed my life." Angela shared a little of her story.

Magda and Slava seemed to enjoy hearing her and the boys sat by the fire.

Galina kept her hands busy and her eyes down. She seemed a little upset and her cheeks were red like she was overly warm.

After a short visit she explained that the usual Monday laundry would have to be postponed, but she paid Galina for her time anyway. Galina and Magda protested but Angela was determined.

"I am changing the time, it is not for you to go without the income. If Galya has extra time on a different day we can catch up." Angela could see they were happy with that settled.

Angela tried to make eye contact with Galina but was not successful. The young girl seemed to be in a sullen state.

Angela said goodbye to the family and in a last second of boldness asked the girl to speak with her outside.

Galina pulled her threadbare coat on wordlessly. Her eyes were glassy and sad.

They shut the cabin door when they got outside. The snow was falling softly around them.

"Are you well?" Angela asked, noticing Galina's head was down again.

"I am fine, Angela." Gainyla said stiffly.

Angela placed and arm on Galya's shoulder and the girl could not help but wince.

Two fat tears escaped Galina's dark eyes and ran fast down her red cheeks.

"You are hurt!" Angela exclaimed in a harsh whisper.

"Please do not ask. I was foolish and it was my punishment." Galya said very softly. Her countenance was bent over, trying to crawl within herself. Angela watched her take a few deep breaths.

"I will let this go, but if you need a friend you know you can come to me day or night." Angela said and the girl nodded but her eyes never looked up.

Galina went back inside the cabin. Angela took one step and something made her wait.

Angela took shallow breaths and just listened.

"What did you tell Miss Fahey girl?" The father's voice boomed.

"Nothing father." Galya's voice was meek.

"You must learn to respect my authority in this house again young lady. You better not be telling tales."

There was a minute of quiet and Angela felt the urge to walk away. She had heard all she needed to hear. Galina had implied a few times that her father was firm. Angela somehow knew that that firmness had caused him to lay a hand on his daughter.

Angela talked to God the entire way home.

Chapter Twenty-Seven

Monday, December 1850
Angela Fahey

After straining the milk and cream and seeing Dolly off to her own work, Angela peeked out the front window to take a look at the sky. She had asked the stable hand, Warren, to ready her buggy and she bundled herself up. She saw patches of snow under her boots but wasn't sure if the cold would stay. The sky was clear and the breeze wasn't as cold as it had been.

Angela made her way to the barn and said a greeting to Warren and gave the jersey cow a pat on the rump. It was the extent of their relationship but Angela promised herself to learn more about farm work. She knew there was a lot to learn.

The buggy ride to town was quicker than she expected, her thoughts were busy on details as she made her way past the general store, the Greaves residence and she turned down a secondary road.

She pulled the buggy to a stop and said a sincere prayer for guidance.

"Lord, I am ready to be impulsive and foolhardy. Please stop me if I am doing the wrong thing." She prayed aloud in the crisp morning air. Since her heart felt led to move forward she tied her horse to the hitching rail and went forward with her plans. She just hoped that she was doing the right thing.

Hudson Bay Store

The Hudson Bay store was taking on a new appearance. Clive had mentioned that he was keeping the Quackenbush sign but changing some things around the store. When the hint of a grocer and a butcher were floating around town in early October Clive and J.Q. had put a business plan together. They wanted to slowly transition the store into a fancy goods store like the one he had in Portland.

Clive showed Angela around as they waited for Governor Pritchlan to show up.

"Small towns grow and sometimes a business has to adapt and grow with it. We have a milliner to make hats for the ladies, and a tailor and now a lace shop thanks to the Greaves ladies." He gave Angela a teasing wink. He noticed that she was a bit distracted and didn't smile at the teasing. She was listening, though, so he kept talking. "The grocer will gladly handle the flour, fatback, coffee sacks and sugar. All these things are wasted in my store shelves in a redundant fashion."

Angela nodded, seeing how that could be true.

"I just think the town is ready for more from its general store than the basics." Clive said.

"You are a wise man, Clive. You have such a good sense of the right time to move forward. I pray that it rubs off on me." Angela said and sighed deeply. Her brow had the slightest furrow.

John Pritchlan arrived precisely at five o'clock sharp. His mood was light and he seemed ready to talk.

Clive's office was warm and Clive had pencils and paper set up at the table.

"I want to jot down any ideas we have tonight. It can all be confidential. I just don't anything good to pass us by if it gets mentioned." Clive offered. Both Angela and John nodded.

"First, I would like to ask a question. I am not trying to be impertinent but why am I here?" Angela asked. "I am not important or a decision maker in a any way. If you asked public opinion about town I am barely out of the child category in some people's eyes." Angela felt foolish for bringing the topic up but she had been wondering all day why she had even been invited.

"You sell yourself short chile'." Clive said softly. He said nothing else and Angela wondered why he didn't explain further. Clive stood up and walked to the corner where a water pitcher stood. Clive gestured a question to both his guests and with two nods he poured water into two glass mugs. Angela felt the time was moving slowly and she was still wondering what she could possibly contribute.

"Your life experience and compassion make you a good person to be here." John Pritchlan said and smiled.

Angela breathed in deeply and accepted his simple answer as good enough. She planned to do a lot of listening.

"The main goal is to get these people into a safe place which is clean and healthy for all involved." John said, his voice was firm and Angela could begin to see how he had been voted as governor over the territory. "Public opinion is on the side of doing the right thing. That will make working around the town council a little easier."

"I am concerned about the repercussions of any actions Red or I take so soon after being told in no light terms, to back down." Clive admitted. "I own my property outright. Having been here longer than most, I helped found this town when it was no more than a few trappers and a lumber camp. But Angela has a lot more to lose, especially still being under the thumb of the land council which ties right in with Mr. Prince and his lot."

"I am hoping that public opinion will curtail that eventuality. Jed Prince can try and swing the power hammer around here but it won't look good on him." John stated. He had a pencil and a piece of paper in front of him and he was doodling in the corner of the paper. He put the paper down when he realized what he was doing.

"I have been running ideas through my head and even brainstorming with my brother and his wife." Clive said and folded his hand in front of him. He seemed a little frustrated. "One idea is to do what Spring Creek Church did under the Violet Griffen scheme." He paused. "To find a suitable cabin for each. Pay for land and let them all have some time to find a solution. I looked around town and found a few potentials but there are only two properties with that kind of option. Both cabins are in horrible disrepair and would require more work, if not a complete rebuild. I went through my mental inventory of the families in the warehouse and wondered which ones had the capacity to farm the land. Two families included mothers of small children. Another had a lad of ten who was actually bringing in a little bit of money from chores around town." Clive sighed. He was not seeing any good solutions in front of him.

"There are a few larger homes in the community, perhaps with good Christian folks doing their part, we could see about parceling people around town. Some people could take charge of a child or take in an adult." John pitched the idea but his eyes said he didn't like it. "Splitting up families is just not what I was hoping for as a blessing." He was shooting down his own idea.

The room stayed quiet and Clive gave Angela a look. He was giving her the floor. Should she tell them her idea, she wondered? Her insecurities and fear bubbled up inside her. Her days of being unheard as a servant had taught her to say nothing and just respect her betters. It had been a few years since those days. She took some deep breaths and fought off the panic rising in her stomach over her actions of the day. Had she done the wrong thing? What would they thing of her irrational choices.

"I bought the boarding house today!" She said aloud.

Chapter Twenty-Eight

Oregon City

If there had ever been gossip in the small town of Oregon City it had been put to shame by Tuesday afternoon. Any person with any connection to anyone had heard the news of Angela Fahey taking on the town council.

"I heard that Angela bought the boarding house and Mr. Prince threatened to burn it down." Said the butcher to several of his customers buying the fresh pork that had been slaughtered that very morning.

Doctor Williams talked about how proud he was that Miss Fahey had done what no one else thought of. 'She was going to help those people even if she loses her own beautiful house.'

Angela had met with Millie and her closest friends in town and told her own story on Tuesday morning. She tried to quell the rumors and set some positive actions in motion.

"There is so much to be done ladies, and we need every Christian in town to do the good work of the Lord." The ladies clapped at Angela's speech and everyone agreed to do their part and spread the word.

Even with do-gooding and the well-intended Ladies prayer group going door to door the rumor spread misinformation about town. But every word made Angela look like a hero, and the town council looked vindictive.

Something was going to happen, and everyone in town wanted to be there for it.

Angela Fahey

Angela had her list in front of her. It was expansive. She felt a headache coming over her brow. After her meeting with the Ladies church fellowship committee she felt vindicated for all her actions from the day before.

The visit with Gemma Caplan, the former owner of the boarding house, had gone so well, she felt God was with her. But her doubts sprung back up when the bank manager had given her a seriously doubtful expression when the money was exchanged.

Mrs. Caplan had been thrilled with the idea of running the place after their long discussion. She loved being a caretaker for people. She felt it was her gift. But the administration and the money problems had been her downfall. Angela hired her on as manager and head housekeeper. Mrs. Caplan was pleased with the arrangement and was glad to still be a part of the business in a positive way.

Angela had looked over every room of the place and made a few notes about her own thoughts of where people could stay. What needed redoing and how to go about making the boarding house a successful business as well as a potential home for a few families who needed a little charity.

She had sent Clive to let the church family know what was needed and what needed accomplishing. Angela prayed fervently over everything that had been put on the list and knew if this project was going to be successful it would take many hands.

Angela wanted a place to think and someone to bounce ideas off of. She knew Clive and John Pritchlan were unavailable. JQ was an option but she wasn't sure if that was the right person for the moment. She could talk more with Mrs. Caplan but she wanted a fresh perspective.

Angela stood in front of the livery in the early morning pondering who in town would be the best to talk to. Within a moment her eyes fell to the front porch of the Greaves' house. She could tell the fresh snow had been swept off the front porch, meaning someone in the household had gotten up early enough to do that chore. There was ample smoke coming from two chimneys. Angela took a deep breath and found her inner courage. She knew that she may face a little opposition from Mrs. Greaves but Ted would be good to talk to just now.

With a decision made in her heart, she sought out the front door and gave it a firm knock. Olivia Greaves was one who greeted her.

"Oh dear Angela, you need not knock, we are a storefront now. You are welcome here anytime." Her grin was infectious and Angela's heart felt lighter. Olivia just had an encouraging way about her.

"I had forgotten that. I am here to speak to Ted if he is available." Angela smiled as she saw the other two Greaves ladies busily at work. There was strings, pin and lace bobbins in front of Amelia and Sophia Greaves. They both looked up from their work for a moment to acknowledge Angela. Amelia went back to work after a nod and smile.

Sophia said a brief hello and then in a swift move cleared her lap of every pin. She placed the pins neatly into a bowl at a side table.

"It is a pleasure to see you. Everyone that has been here shopping for lace in the last day is talking about you." Sophia gushed.

Angela smiled a little but didn't know how to reply. She had heard a few of the rumors, some of them wild and inaccurate.

"I could not be prouder that my brother is courting the local heroine. You make us proud." Sophia reached out and took Angela's hand.

Amelia Greaves stood and cleaned away her pins. "I couldn't agree more, child." Her voice was still clipped, even if her words were positive.

"Thank you." Angela muttered, wondering what turnabout had happened.

"I may have been harsh about you in the past but I will admit to jumping to conclusions." Mrs. Greaves said, as she got nearer.

"I, um, thank you." Angela said lamely.

"Your actions lead me to think you have a generous Christian heart." Amelia said, and Olivia put her arm around her sister's waist in a sign of affection. Amelia smiled first at Angela and then her sister. Each was pretty in her own way and Angela could see the resemblance between the two even better.

"I will admit the words you said to me stung. Foolhardy and impulsive have stuck with me, and I will agree to having those traits every once and a while. This week perhaps being the strongest example." Angela smiled and continued. "Buying that boarding house is probably not the wisest move I have ever made with my money, but I feel God will bless my intentions." Angela finished and let out a sigh that held so much tension and released it all.

"Please forgive me for my words. Your patience with my attitude has humbled me. The Lord is gently dealing with me on my anger. It has burrowed deep in my heart over the loss of my husband. I fear I have not been very kind as of late." Amelia's cheek grew red and her eyes misted over with her confession.

"You have been forgiven." Angela said, feeling tears come to her own eyes. She knew how hard it had been for Amelia to say such things. Angela had worked on forgiveness every day and she was glad to have given those feelings over to God, where they belong.

"Bless you girl for that. We have heard that you need help with getting the families to your boarding house."

"Yes, Ma'am." Angela said respectfully. "I do."

"Come sit, let us know what is needed before we send you out back to fetch Ted." Amelia said, gesturing to the davenport.

Once seated Angela brought out her list and reviewed a few things with the ladies.

"I am asking all parents to see if they have any clothing for youngsters that have been outgrown but are still in good condition. I am also asking women of a medium to small stature for a spare blouse or skirt. Simple things are fine. We just need clean, dry clothing for these families to wear. The condition of everything they own is now dirty and potentially contaminated from that horrible place they live in." Angela saw all of the ladies nod. The word had spread through town about the warehouse and now many people had stopped by to witness the situation for themselves.

"I have many things that need to happen simultaneously to make this work properly. I don't want any of these people to feel shamed for the condition they have found themselves in. My wish for them is to have them bathed and in fresh clothes before they come to their new home. If any items they have need to be laundered then I am hoping a family can take on that duty. Since the boarding house has furnished rooms and they are served all meals in the main dining room there is no immediate need for some things. Getting them clean and fed will be the focus of the first few days. Getting them equipped for daily life, the children ready to attend school again, and jobs and such for those that are able will be forthcoming." Angela finished her speech, wondering if they were as overwhelmed as she.

"I am amazed that you have put all this together, Angela." Sophia spoke, her eyes bright.

"How are you planning to get them bathed? Is the bath house available?" Olivia asked.

Angela tried not to make a face. The local bathhouse was owned by a member of the council. Though it would be the quickest and most ideal way to get everyone clean it was just not wise.

"It is not available at this time." Angela said curtly.

"I heard that the town council has threatened to take away your land if you interfere." Amelia said and surprised Angela down to her toes.

"It was not the entire town council..." Angela spoke slowly then paused, not wanting to disparage Jed Prince, even if he deserved it.

"I see you are trying to handle this rocky situation with as much decorum as you can muster." Olivia said with a chuckle. "I remember dealing with a church that had turned against me for the divorce I sued upon my husband."

"I am trying, it is not always easy." Angela was glad for the sense of camaraderie she was feeling suddenly. This conversation was restoring her faith in people.

"So you need some homes to be available to set up bathing and laundry?" Amelia asked, getting straight to the point.

"Yes Ma'am. I am hoping to have enough clothing donations that everyone has a clean set of clothing for that first day. I want the process to be as seamless as possible. Clean faces, clean clothes, and renewed hope."

"Please mark us down for that duty." Amelia said firmly.

Angela felt no shame for the tears that fell from her cheeks. She turned to a blank page in her notepad. She wrote down Mrs. Amelia Greaves, bathing and laundry services. She showed it to Amelia and saw her nod.

"I cannot thank you enough." Angela said through a tight throat.

"I thought while you were sharing, about that box of clothes I kept for so long with Ted's old things. It was a shame we left it behind in New York. It was a cumbersome item to bring along. But when I heard about the bathing and laundry I knew we could bring that about. This family has had to start over ourselves. We even stayed in a boarding house in New York. Unless Ted had brought back the monies he did, we would still be struggling to make ends meet. Our lace sales were keeping us alive, but there was a lot more competition for our skill set there." Amelia shared.

"The West is a good place to begin again." Angela said sincerely, she felt everyone's agreement through the nods and smiles on their faces.

"I will be contacting you soon then with more details. The ladies prayer group from the church in town is busily trying to find clothing donations. I am sending someone soon to speak to the families in the warehouse. I need to know what is needed for each family. I am hoping Ted would be up for the challenge." Angela said, seeing his mother set her chin proudly at the mention of her son, Angela continued. "Once we assign a family to you, I will send the clean clothing to you for every member of that family. If any mistakes are made or anything is missing please send word to the boarding house. I am organizing everything from there for now. The family will be sent through the back door and we hope that you can be ready with a bath and perhaps a simple meal for them.

Since it will take some time to get everyone clean from head-to-toe."
Angela shared, hoping that she was not being too bossy.

"Is the pantry of the boarding house stocked?" Olivia asked.

"It has a decent selection of dry goods, but it will be hurting for fresh
items like eggs, meat and dairy. There is a large root cellar below it and
has enough items to last past Michaelmas, but I may be purchasing more
from the new grocer. There is so much to do." Angela put a hand to her
cheek in exasperation.

"Do not fret Angela dear. This town has been humbled by your
generous actions. I cannot imagine that this day will go by without seeing
a miraculous outpouring of generosity come out of it." Olivia put her
hand on Angela's shoulder.

"I thank you so much for the encouragement. I really needed to talk
through my plans and this was the perfect remedy." Angela closed her
notepad and stood.

Amelia, Olivia and Sophia all stood up with her.

"Would I be presumptuous to ask if I can pray for you now?" Olivia
asked.

"Oh please do."

The women took each other's hand and stood in a small circle in the
parlor. They each bowed their heads.

"Dear Lord," Olivia prayed. "Your daughter is moving forward doing
your work to bless the poor. I pray your divine hand on this town as we
fight to right the wrong that has been done in our midst. I pray you give
Angela strength and courage to complete everything that needs doing here
Lord. Please give us all the strength and the provisions needed to
accomplish your work in this community. In Jesus' name we ask, Amen."

Everyone in the room said 'amen'.

Angela was flattered that they all had made her feel that she had done
the right thing. She knew that making the boarding house a profitable
venture was unlikely at this point, but using her money to help the poor
was going to be worthwhile.

She said goodbye to everyone and was shown her way to the back of
the property, where Ted was splitting wood. He was wearing a thick
insulated flannel shirt and a warm wool cap. He looked up from his task
to see Angela and his face split into a handsome smile.

Angela was very glad to see him.

Chapter Twenty-Nine

Galina Varushkin

The bruises on Galina's body were a distressing reminder of the previous day. She tried to put the violence from her thoughts but found it very difficult to do. Galina had cried herself to sleep on Sunday night. But after a fitful night of sleeping and praying she had a fresh perspective. There was nothing that she could do to fix what had happened, her mouth had caused the situation and she would be the daughter that she needed to be so that it would never happen again. She had learned a few years back to pretend. Pretend that she was loved, pretend that she mattered to her family, pretend that she had any kind of importance to the world. She was the uneducated daughter of a Russian lumberjack. Her brothers were the future of the family name. She knew she held very little influence in her father's eyes, if any at all.

Her mind, though, was her own and her prayers to God were also hers. She quietly went about her day with silent prayer. She placed a blank look across her face and once she had dressed in her simple skirt and blouse, she grabbed a slice of bread and said goodbye.

She was thankful that Brandon had been sent over late last night from Grant's Grove. Violet was hoping for extra help from Galina. Without asking or even looking at Galina, her father had sent the messenger back to Grant's Grove with an affirmative.

Galina ate the bread as she walked, now thankful for the snow falling prettily around her. The stillness and beauty was not lost on her. She thanked God for her work and promised to be good. She would not hold on to bitterness anymore.

Galina and Violet finished the washtub full of clothing and hung it as speedily as they could. Vowing they would finish the untouched laundry another day.

The entire conversation while they scrubbed had been about the warehouse in town and the folks of Pauper Row. Galina's family had heard the news over the weekend and had discussed it at length before and after the Sunday services. Galina had tried hard to use that as something to think about instead of thinking about herself.

She felt she had earned the punishment she had gotten. These people in the warehouse had done nothing to deserve the suffering they were now enduring.

Violet asked Galina to walk with her to the nearby laboratory, Violet was distracted and wanted to talk to Corinne and Maria to see what could be done.

Galina was happy to tag along, wanting to see what her family's heroes would do. They had been there to help her own family. She knew they would not disappoint in taking action when others were hurting.

"I am glad you are here. Dolly and I were going to get you and go talk to Marie, there is nothing more important I can do here today. We were simple organizing the back room. That can be done once this is settled in town." Corinne said once Violet and Galya had reached the laboratory.

The group of four made their way quickly to Marie's house. She had hired a cook and housekeeper at her husband's urging and was in the baby's room.

Marie made a lovely picture with her baby girl in her arms, the baby was nearly asleep and the ladies were quiet as Marie stood up and placed the sleepy girl into the crib.

The group made a quiet exit from the baby's room and settled themselves in the sitting room by the fire.

"How fairs the new mother?" Corinne asked, beaming to see her stepmother looking so happy.

"Tired but so very satisfied. The last few nights have been easier. I was frightened that she slept so much last night, the five hour stretch was the longest she had gone without feeding." Maria settled into the rocking chair and sighed.

"You look rosy and healthy." Dolly added.

"Thank you Dolly dear, I am doing better this round than with Cooper. I have bounced back a little quicker." Marie shared.

"Have you heard from Clive?" Corinne asked.

"Yes, he met with John and Reynaldo, the ranch manager, first then he peeked in on me and shared the news too. He has moved along to share with the rest of the farmers and ranchers in the area." Marie said.

"I was hoping we could brainstorm together for ideas. I wrote down the things Clive said were needed to make this event a reality. We need to act posthaste to be ready for Angela's plan." Corinne said then pursed her lips in thought.

"I have a few items of Cooper's that he has outgrown that can be easily sent to town. I may not be up for the trip myself yet, but if someone is willing to take them for me." Marie said.

Corinne eased her concern. "That is a forgone conclusion Marie, you need not concern yourself. Your job is here now, resting and mothering."

"I also have been told we have an abundance of root vegetables in the root cellar. I may part with some for the Boarding House for food stocks."

Corrine nodded and joined with Violet in a discussion about what could be shared from their pantry.

Galina sat back wordlessly as each person had ideas. She remembered vividly the days of her family's move. She recalled how much her own family had been given from not only the church family, but the surrounding farm community as the word spread. The Varushkin household would survive the winter because of the generosity of these amazing people.

Marie had a moment of inspiration and energy and led the ladies to her closet first and then a spare room that had been taken over with shelves full of fabric and sewing projects. Galina could definitely tell that sewing was Marie's passion.

"Oh if I had a month then I could have everyone dressed. Well, I could at least try." Marie sighed and ran a hand over several bolts of fabric lovingly.

"You need your rest." Corinne admonished.

"Oh, your father has made me promise not to sew for another month. I have a horrible habit of staying up all night to finish a sewing project if I get obsessed." Marie confessed and bit her lip in a way that made her look like a young lady that needed scolding.

Everyone laughed a little at her admission.

"I have a few things that I can dig out that are in a completed state that would work." Marie stated.

"Let us do the digging. You just sit and instruct." Violet pointed to the stool next to the sewing machine cabinet.

Marie put up her hands in surrender and 'instructed' as she was told to do.

Within a few minutes the outgrown boys' clothes were found as well as a few crocheted shawls, scarves, a few blouses and a new woman's wool coat.

Galina reached for the wool coat and folded it and held on to it for a moment. The wool was really good quality and the outer buttons were very attractive. She felt a pang of longing as she realized it was a size that would fit her and was vastly superior to her own threadbare coat. She had to remind herself of how much her own neighbors had endured in that warehouse in town. She resigned herself to set aside her envy of the beautiful coat, knowing that was not what God would want from her. She was so thankful for everything that God had provided. A warm home, a dry bed for everyone in her family. She had much to be thankful for.

As Galina placed the coat down and resumed her folding of the items from Marie's closet. She had missed the glances that everyone had shared around the room over her reaction to the coat.

Later, after the clothes had been crated up and readied for transport to town Galina was getting ready to go. Marie called her over.

"Come back to the sewing room Galina dear." Marie had a lilt to her voice. She was such a sweet woman and her cheery tone made Galya feel welcome in this expansive home.

Galina followed Marie after giving a look to Violet, letting her know she would be a minute more.

"I'll return her right away." Marie saw with a muffled voice a room away.

Marie stood with a measuring tape in her hand.

"Once I am allowed by my husband to sew again I had the thought to make you a blouse or two. With all the work you do it would be nice for you to have several to use every week. Am I right?" Marie asked.

"Oh. No." Galina stated. Not wanting Marie to take her precious time and waste it on her.

"One thing you will learn about me dear, is that I never offer sewing unless I intend to do it with or without your cooperation." Marie grinned and looked Galina up and down. "I can either wrestle you to the ground and get your measurements, or I can guess." Marie looked pleased when Galina giggled.

Galya surrendered and let Marie have her way. Marie was finished penciling down numbers a minute later. Galina held in all winces or gasps of pain when Marie pulled the measuring tape across the bruises on her back. If she didn't breath it wasn't too bad.

A few minutes later Galya was headed back home to her family after they loaded the wagon in the barn with provisions for Angela to distribute.

Galina had been praying more and more these days, she had lots of time alone on the walks she had to her many different jobs. She enjoyed the quiet time to pray or think. Today she wanted to pray. Her heart was so very troubled over her neighbors from Pauper Row. It had been in her thoughts non-stop and she wasn't sure if there was anything for her to do.

She sincerely pleaded to God to give her a way to help someone, in any way. She desperately wanted to atone for her bad attitude. She had dishonored her father with her thoughts and with her mouth. She had said disrespectful things about him to more than one person. She had hated him and she knew that was a sin. She knew from church that God's forgiveness was real and felt at peace when she asked for forgiveness. But she was confused at how someone could go about earning the forgiveness. She had a weight of guilt on her heart. Her father was always lecturing on sacrifice. What could she sacrifice to earn forgiveness?

Within a moment she knew that she had something to give. The dress she had been given by Angela, the blue dress with the cream lace would be a perfect fit for one of the mothers that had lived on Pauper Row. She'd had a petite frame and would be able to fit into the dress easily.

Galina was sincere in her desire to bless them but her young heart did mourn the giving of such a precious item. She had not worn it as an every day dress but instead used it for her Sunday best, but only a few times. She had worn it to church and felt such pride in looking her best. Tears streaked down her cheeks as her heart dealt with the joy and pain of giving. She had heard the story of the woman in the bible who had given her last cent as a gift to the church. Galina wanted to be that kind of person. Even if it hurt for a moment, she would be generous. Her new friends, Angela, Violet, Corinne and Dolly were all that way. Galina was just getting to know Marie and was amazed at how strong she was. Galina had always thought that people that had money were selfish and cruel. She had been proven wrong at the Harpole home. Their cabin was enormous and their ranch and stables were impeccably kept, but they were well known in the area for being kind and generous to a fault.

Galina wiped her eyes before she walked into her family's cozy cabin. She didn't want to answer questions about her emotions just now.

She filled in her mother about the news she had heard while with Violet. Her mother allowed her to changed out of her work clothes. Her blouse and skirt had gotten damp while helping Violet scrub the laundry.

The skin on her hands was a little chapped from all the contact she had with the drying soap and warm water so often.

Corinne Grant had given her a balm that was creamy and contained some frankincense in it. It made Galina think of the story of Jesus when the wise men brought the child gold, frankincense and myrrh. Galya would wait until after her chore to put on the balm today.

She quickly found the dress and was so glad she had not worn it since she had cleaned it last week. There was another dress in her closet from Angela and Galina ran a hand over the velvet material. It was a lot fancier, with petticoats and a small hoop to go with it. Galya's mother had declared it to be a little too old for her as of yet. But perhaps when she was fifteen. It was not very appropriate for any occasion that Galya had ever attended. She would feel a bit foolish wearing it now.

Galina had tears streaming down her cheeks as she took the scissors to the hemmed section of her favorite dress. It had been the gift she had been given by Angela back when her family was moving into the new cabin. The dress was the nicest thing she owned, and in her heart she was ready to give it away. She carefully cut the thread that hemmed the dress to the shorter length her mother had asked her to do.

'You are far too young to have that length of dress.' Her mother had said lightheartedly. Her mother knew that the years would fly by and Galina would be a young woman.

Galina knew the people in that warehouse and had been brokenhearted to know that they were in such a place now. If her family had not been saved from their own tent in Pauper Row her own family would be in the squalor along side all the others. She shed tears with Violet as they heard about the plan to save these people. They even prayed together, sitting there with wet hands, hovering over the washtub full of clothes. They prayed for these people and for the community to step up and take on the work of God's kingdom.

Galina sat on the cot in her small room in the loft of the cabin and quickly removed the hem. Her tears began again as she working her way through every stitch she had made.

"I am doing this as unto the Lord." She said softly to remind herself to set aside her emotions.

She swiped at the tears and finished her job with a promise to herself that her crying was over.

She shook the dress out and saw that the hemming had made a crease in the bottom. She would need to iron it before she sent it off with the other provisions.

"Why ever would you give away your nicest dress?" Galina's mother looked confused when Galina asked for the use of the hot irons.

"I prayed and just knew that I had to give it. It is the right thing. You know perfectly who could fit into this dress. Does she not deserve to be clean and well dressed?" Galina asked.

Galina's mother nodded, thinking of the same woman that Galina had.

"You are right and good, child. Go on." Her mother gestured to the trunk in the corner where the irons were.

Galina busied herself with warming the irons in the fireplace and getting the crease out of the dress. Once she was done she folded the dress neatly to minimize any wrinkles. She had Pavel write the name of the woman the dress was intended for and pinned the paper to the collar of the dress.

Galina went back to her trunk in the loft and found her best pair of tall socks and included them too. She had a few pairs and with all the laundry she did she could easily wash one pair while she wore the other. She wished she had more to offer but was satisfied with what she gave. It was all she could do but it felt powerful rising within her. It was a good thing to give. The joy of the experience was beginning to bloom inside her.

Chapter Thirty

Angela Fahey

Wednesday dawned bright and cheery for Angela, she walked down to the barn and saw Warren milking the jersey cow.

"I wanted to let you know I was hoping to leave soon. If you like you may take the portion of milk and cream to your family today. I have not the time to deal with it properly." Angela said.

Warren looked up from his task with a broad smile. "My ma will be glad for that. She could always use some extra. She may make cheese from the whey. It is so good on biscuits in the morning." Warren was a big lad for being only fifteen but the smile across his face showed him to still have the heart of a lad. Angela found his smile infectious.

Warren stood and moved the stool back with a scrape along the rough planked floor.

"Come on Lady…" He patted the cow's hindquarter and backed her out of the stall. He led her to the larger pen in the back with a door leading to a fenced outdoor area. Angela knew that Earl had plans of expanding the fenced area and adding another milk cow if necessary.

"You call her Lady?" Angela asked.

"Yes, well…" Warren blushed being put on the spot. "She is the cleanest cow I have ever worked with. She avoids getting dirty. It's the strangest thing." He chuckled nervously and Angela decided to let him be about his work.

"You be sure so say hello to your ma and sisters." Angela said as she was leaving.

"I will do." Warren waved after he closed Lady into her pen. "I will have your buggy ready for you in a jiffy."

Angela fetched her notebook inside and ate a left over biscuit from her dinner the night before. It was not as soft as it had been but Angela was distracted with many thoughts and plans and barely noticed. Today was going to be a big day.

The air was a little warmer than the day before. The snow was gone and the mud had cleared from the roads.

The ride to town went swiftly. Mrs. Caplan was waiting in the front parlor for Angela at the boarding house.

They made quick work of the plans for the day and then Angela was pleasantly surprised by a knock at the front door.

Clive was waiting for her on the porch.

"Whatcha want with all the loot, Red?" Clive asked mischievously.

"You can bring it into the main dining room here. We can sort through everything there. Any idea when the others will be along?" Angela was hoping to have many hands for help with the sorting.

"They are just a minute behind me, in John Harpole's fancy rig." Clive wiggled his eyebrows and was pleased when Angela couldn't help but chuckle.

Angela sighed and pushed the door open wide. Clive began unloading.

Within five minutes a flood of people were welcomed into the boarding house. Ted had joined Clive in the unloading process. Crates and bags were flowing into the dining room faster than anyone knew what to do with.

A few minutes of chaos reigned as Angela parceled out assignments left and right. She furiously scribbled on her notepad, 'name- job' – with a box next to it for completion. Angela had thanked Clive over and over with all the organizational advice he had given her. He could have taken charge, but the respect he gave her and encouragement said that he knew that she could handle it. His trust in her gave her the courage to face the challenges of the day.

Corinne, Violet and Dolly were set to organizing the donations. Clothing set on the dining room table, to be sorted through and eventually settled into family stacks. Each family would have enough for at least one set of clothing. Angela was hoping to have shoes for the children too. She had seen many without on her visit to the warehouse. She wanted all of these children to have the opportunity to go to school.

Reggie Gardner was put in charge of food items. Anything donated for the pantry or root cellar was to be moved to its proper home. Angela gave Reggie a quick tour of the places where she wanted things to go. He had a good head for common sense and was quick to take charge and get things moved around efficiently.

The ladies prayer group came by at nine a.m. and dropped off more clothes and pantry items. As well as a few bibles, slates for school age students and a heap of knitted scarves and mittens. Angela thanked everyone profusely and was charmed by everyone's goodwill.

Doctor Williams stopped by and was able to have a brief talk with Angela about maintaining the health and well being of everyone involved.

"I have been twice to the warehouse to check on everyone's health. I do not see any disease that anyone should be concerned of. But the poor conditions may make for some poor health for a few weeks after the transition. If people have raspy coughs or high fevers then please fetch me." Doc said.

Angela nodded that she would.

"Are you feeling fair, Miss Fahey?" He asked to be thorough.

"Yes Doc. Just dealing with the cold this year. My old leg injury does not enjoy the cold and wet weather." Angela shared. The doctor had known about her accident on the Oregon Trail and was always good with advice on how to take care of herself.

"Be sure to eat your vegetables everyday and you may see if Clive has any of those rubber hot water bags. They are advertised in the papers out east a lot. If not keep a warm compress on your achy leg at night. May help you sleep better." He pinched his lip with his forefingers in thought. He patted her on the shoulder. "You are doing a good job young lady." He said proudly and left.

Angela joined Corinne, Violet and Dolly in the sorting room and reached for a crate herself. She saw some pantry items on the top and placed them near the kitchen door where Reggie could see them easily and retrieve them. He came through every few minutes and left with a crateful of goods. Angela noticed that Dolly was aware of Reggie's shy smiles on every trip.

The very cautious flirtation reminded her that she needed to thank Ted later for all he had done.

Angela got to the bottom of the first crate she sorted, so very pleased with the town's generosity. She picked up a linen bag and opened it in on the table. She pulled out a neatly folded dressed and gasped. The dress she had given to Galina was neatly folded with a note pinned on the collar and a pair of stockings was under it.

Angela had heard more than a hundred thank you's from Galina over that dress. The phrase, "that dress is my favorite thing I have ever had…" had been uttered by the young woman more than once.

Angela was tempted to put it away, to give it back to Galina and thank her for the generous gift but it was unnecessary. But Angela suddenly felt the weight of the sacrifice that Galina had made. Angela had lived with very little and she knew what it was to share when you had next to nothing of your own. Angela settled the dress and stockings into the pile for the proper family. She made a note in her notebook to do something special for the girl at some point, she swallowed at the lump in her throat.

Angela was pleased with the progress an hour later when the clothing stack for one family was complete. She sent Ted to his home with the crate of clothes, a special jar of perfumed shampoo made by Dolly in the lab, and instructions.

The families that offered to help with bath duties were to have the baths ready by noon, 1, or 2 pm. The families in the warehouse had been told by Ted to be packed and ready to go. Ted had been casual as not to cause alarm with the men posted at the doors of the warehouse. He brought firewood and took his time unloading it. Every family he spoke to agreed to be ready. Ted took notes on every family. He wrote down the general size of each person in the family, any special skills of any person in the family.

Clive took crates to seven more families who had volunteered for bath duty.

The last family on Angela's list was the hardest to complete. The woman with a young baby, and toddler twins were the last stop toward Angela's completed goal. The baby had several changes of clothes, and lots of clean nappies. The toddlers clothing was not here. Angela knew that youngsters were generally hard on clothes and sometimes hand-me-downs were difficult to find.

After finishing the last of the donated crates she knew that the pantry would supply a few months worth of meals. A side of beef hung in the root cellar to be butchered later. The meat donated by the butcher himself with a promise of more as needed over this winter.

Angela glanced at the watch pin on her dress. It was past 10:30 and she wanted to have everyone to have a bath by mid-afternoon.

Angela talked with Clive and the ladies organizing and decided on a course of action. There was a dress shop just two blocks down the road. The owner made suits, dresses and children's clothing. They also did custom dressmaking and tailoring. His wife was an excellent milliner, whose hats and bonnets graced nearly every woman in towns' head. Angela knew the owner by reputation only, he was an excellent craftsman, a dear friend of the Prince family, and a long sitting member of the town council.

Angela had no choice but to seek out the clothing needed in the lion's den. Her heart pounded in her chest but she refused to back down. She would accomplish her goal.

◆•◦•◆•◆•◆•◦•◆

Angela was back at the boarding house in less than an hour. She had a bundle in her arms and a flush to her cheeks.

Clive and Corinne were chatting in the parlor. Dolly and Reggie were visiting at the dining table amidst the stacks of things that still needed to be organized. Everyone was waiting on instructions from Angela.

"I finally have everything we need for the last family. I even got a few extra things that surprised me." Angela settled the heavy packages.

"They were civil?" Clive asked.

"More than. Even apologetic. Which surprised me the most. Mr. and Mrs. Goodall were amiable and generous. I was even given notice of a job offer to any of the women who had decent mending skills. He has recently been bombarded with work. He complained that even with the Gold Rush there are still many male only households. The farmers claim to be always too busy to do their own mending. The lumber and mill workers too. He has plenty of work to share." Angela said and began unpacking the parcels.

She peeked inside one and saw what it was and handed it to Corrine. "This is the toddler's clothes, and this..." She paused and grabbed a package from the bottom of the stack. "Here are two coats that should last them the winter."

Corinne settled the parcels in the crate especially packed for the last family on the list.

"That should do it. We can send these off and then work to get this place ready for visitors." Corinne settled everything into its place and heaved the crate off the table and walked outside to the front porch of the boarding house. Clive followed her and they both left soon after the delivery.

Ted came into the front door a minute later.

"There is enough firewood for the winter in the back of the building. Is there a box inside, or crates for me to settle a portion inside?" He gave Angela a wink that everyone else saw too.

"I know there is a wood box in the kitchen, I think there is also one upstairs."

Ted and Angela went together to the kitchen to search for the wood box. Angela tried to let him know with a silent smile how much she appreciated his support on this day full of challenges. He seemed to smile back and Angela was satisfied.

Violet was in the kitchen helping Mrs. Caplan sort through a few things that had been donated. Some fresh herbs in pots were sitting along the back window.

The wood box was located conveniently next to the back door. There were a few tablecloths and odds and ends piled on top of it so Ted and Angie tackled the piles to make room.

The volunteers were fed at lunchtime with the help of Violet and Mrs. Caplan. The jobs were parceled out again for those who stayed. Angela had been informed that all the families were out of the warehouse and in private family homes being seen to. Everyone at the boarding house cheered in relief to hear that their labors had not been in vain.

The rooms that Angela had prepared needed only minor work to make them livable. Mrs. Caplan had done a good job of maintaining the place. Clive and Ted made a few rounds about the building, noticing little areas that needed fixing. A brick was loose on the north-facing chimney. The siding would need a whitewashing or a coat of real paint in the next year or so. A windowpane had a crack on the second floor. All things were manageable and Angela wrote everything down. She had moments where she wondered what she had gotten herself into. She was only eighteen. Mrs. Caplan was a grown woman with so much more experience and this had been beyond her skills to keep going. Angela felt the words 'foolhardy and impulsive' sweep over her again and again. *What had she been thinking?*

The first family showed up and Angela was happy to see that every volunteer made them feel welcome but didn't smother the new tenants. Angela wanted them to feel comfortable.

She saw that the mother was in a clean and simple dress with a warm shawl wrapped around her shoulders and a bonnet. The children were neatly attired with shoes on their feet and clean faces.

"I would love a chance to show you around. If you like my friends here, Corinne and Violet." Angela nodded to her friends in the parlor.

"They would be happy to entertain your children while we discuss business."

The woman looked thankful and wiped a tear from her cheek. "Yes, please." She said softly.

Angela took the woman the dining room table and brought out a notebook.

"You are Frieda Warhan?"

"Yes," the woman replied.

"I want to make this transition as smooth for you as possible. My friend Ted Greaves came by a few days ago and talked with you about this move, correct?"

Again she simply said 'yes'.

"I do not want you to feel beholden to anyone. I was brought up in a work orphanage and know the feelings that come from being stuck in a hard situation." Angela saw the many emotions on Frieda's face and just let her be. She would explain everything and let the woman process everything on her own time. Angela knew she had to get through this with eight families. "You only just got to the warehouse a little more than a week ago."

"Yes, I had heard from the others there that they had all been evacuated from shacks outside of town. I lived near Salem Oregon in a lumberjack camp when my husband worked there. Our home was given to another family after my husband died a month ago. We had nowhere to go. Someone told me to come here. I was so confused and lost, I just started walking and hitched a ride on a delivery wagon with my two young boys." Her tears dried up but the grief was written in her eyes. "When I got to town I was told that they had a shelter for the misfortunate. That we would be fed and cared for." Frieda stopped and looked to her hands.

"I know that place was not what you expected."

Frieda nodded and said nothing.

"I want to discuss how you would feel most comfortable. I purchased this boarding house as a means to helping out everyone that had been forced into that dreadful situation. I want to be able to help you out, just as I was helped once." Angela took a deep breath and continued when she could tell that Frieda could hear her. "I am more than willing to allow you to stay here as long as you need. Some women that are coming today have husbands gone of to the gold fields of the California territory. You are in a different situation. I want to try and help you, in a manner that is timely and appropriate, to find work so you may provide for your family."

Frieda nodded with more vigor. "I would like that very much. I have been so afraid."

"We can talk more at a later date about that, such as what you would be interested in doing and your skills. For now I would love to show you the rooms I have picked out for you, to see if they would be suitable." Angela stood and took Frieda's arm.

She led the way to a first floor apartment. It had a large bedroom with two drawer chests and stand with a washbasin and curtains at the window. It also had two large cots.

"Will your boys be willing to share a cot?" Angela asked.

"They always have. This is far nicer than they are used to." Frieda said.

The sitting room had a simple davenport and a rocking chair that sat near the small wood stove.

"All meals can be taken downstairs or if you want to eat in privacy, you are allowed to get a tray and bring it up here. Right now we do not have a large staff to help but I am hoping that everyone will understand that at first." Angela felt foolish for jabbering. She just wanted everyone to be happy and feel comfortable.

"This is wonderful." Frieda started crying again. "This is more than suitable."

"I will need to be notified of any repairs that need to be done or issues you have with anything. Do not be afraid to go to the proprietor, Mrs. Caplan. I will be here as often as I can to check in on everyone." Angela led Frieda back downstairs.

Frieda was introduced to Mrs. Caplan and given a tour of the building and then she was told about the code of conduct rules.

This was the part that Angela dreaded the most, but Mrs. Caplan insisted that it was necessary the first day so that everyone knew the rules.

1. No stealing of any property belonging to the Orchard house or its occupants.
2. Everyone should be treated with respect.
3. No running or roughhousing by the children in the house.
4. No storing or hoarding of food in the rooms, to prevent infestation.

5. All valuables may be kept in the Orchard House safe, cleared tagged and labeled with the proprietor and the owner as the only key holders.
6. Breakfast is between 6 to 8 a.m. Lunch between 11 to 1 pm and dinner between 5-7 p.m.
7. All laundry will be done Tuesdays and Thursdays - the washtub and soap provided.
8. Absolutely no foul language or cursing on the premises.
9. Please be respectful of other guests. Yelling or disrespectful behavior is not allowed.

Mrs. Caplan is the manager of the Orchard House and the former owner. She will be in charge of the running of said establishment. She welcomes everyone to feel at home here.
Saturdays anyone is welcome to join in on a tradition at this boarding house, music, storytelling, and other fun activities will be planned for. She is open to suggestions and creativity. She wants this place to be full of happy adults and children

There was a spot for every adult to sign or make their mark if they agreed.

Frieda was the first to print her name on the line. After that she gathered up her children and her few belongings and showed her young boys their new home. She was promised a delivery of her laundered clothing by the family that had opened their home earlier. She was given a fresh start.

———◆—●—◆——◆—●—◆———

Angela was exhausted and emotionally drained by the end of the day. The boarding house had eight full apartments and the place was much tidier than Angela expected. She drove her buggy home wondering half-heartedly if she had thanked everyone enough for all the help.
One of the women immediately offered to work with Mrs. Caplan in the kitchen. Her children were old enough to be at school during the

daytime hours and were responsible enough to behave. Since that meeting had been with two families that had arrived at the same time, the other mother offered to care for the new cook's children while she worked. Both were pleased to be earning their keep, as they put it, and Angela was relieved that all the work wouldn't fall on Mrs. Caplan.

Time would tell if the situation would work out smoothly. Some of the residents were emotional and dazed and would need time to adjust. Angela been promised by Pastor Whittlan that he would be making visits to all the residents over the next few days. Just to minister to them and see if they had any needs.

Angela forced herself to stop thinking as she drove the horse toward home. She was completely spent.

Chapter Thirty-One

Angela Fahey

Angela pounded out bread dough and watched the flour spread around her countertop. Her apron and brown calico day dress was covered in flour, gravy and even a little tea she had spilled earlier when she over poured a teacup. She enjoyed the quiet in her kitchen. The windows facing the road showed the snow falling softly outside, but Angela was very warm from all the cooking she was doing. This last week had been busy but she was determined to obtain a peaceful stance in her new life.

The Orchard House was working toward running smoothly. According to Clive, no business is ever smooth, and expecting it to is setting oneself up for failure and disappointment. Angela took Clive's advice as gospel and trusted his wisdom.

Today was a new day. She was having Ted and Sophia over for dinner with her and Dolly. Angela was determined to enjoy every minute of domestic bliss.

She got the bread in the bowl and covered with a towel to set and proof. She stoked the fire on the wood stove in the washroom and got several bucketfuls of water into the washtub.

She put a few drops of lavender in the water and thought pleasantly of Corinne's lavender crops in the summertime, the rows of purple splendor that looked and smelled of heavenly inspiration.

It was nearly an hour of waiting but the tub did get full. Angela picked out her outfit for the evening and locked the backdoor for privacy and made good on the promise she had to herself for a long and leisurely bath.

Soon her fingers were very pruny. She was relaxed and at peace.

She dried off with a soft towel and got into the dress she was planning to wear for the night. She would wear a fresh apron over it to try and keep her dress clean while finishing the preparation of the meal.

Angela sat near the fireplace on a stool combing through her wet hair when she heard a knock at the front door.

Angela figured it was Earl or Warren, she had forgotten to unlock the back door after all.

Jed Prince was standing tall in the doorway when Angela opened the door, a woman stood next to him.

Angela's eyes grew wide but she remembered her manners. The two adults walked in.

"The house is certainly the nicest in Oregon City." The woman said. The woman gave a glare to the man and nudged him with an elbow.

"Your coats?" Angela offered, feeling a little self-conscious about her wet hair. "I do apologize. I…"

"Don't fret yourself none about that, I haven't been introduced. I am Ellie Prince. My husband must be struck dumb just now." She stated sarcastically after she pulled her coat off and handed it over to Angela. Mr. Prince handed her his hat and coat wordlessly.

She hung everything neatly on the stand near the door.

"I do love the design of your home. It has so much potential. And I am green with envy over that cook stove. I heard a rumor that Millie Quackenbush just had to have one when she saw yours arrive." Ellie said.

Angela smiled and nodded. She gestured to the parlor and again wished she had a moment to pin her hair back.

"I do not want to take up much of your time, Miss Fahey." Jed Prince finally spoke. He took a seat in the chair by the fire and Ellie sat on the green velvet davenport.

Angela stood, feeling ready to take flight if Jed Prince came all the way to her house with bad news.

A moment of silence filled the room awkwardly. Angela looked to Ellie for any clues on whether the visit was from friend or foe.

"My husband and I wanted to visit to clear the air about some unfortunate happenings in town this week." Ellie hinted and gave a serious glare to her husband.

Did Jed Prince actually almost flinch at his wife's glare? It was the minutest movement across his eyes but Angela had thought she had seen it.

"Yes, indeed, my wife is correct. I have been made aware by some members of the town council and some of the citizens of our young town that we brought out a dispassionate course of action in dealing with the residents of what people are calling Pauper Row."

Angela wanted to nod vigorously in agreement but fought the temptation. She figured a small grin was polite and showing she was listening, without exulting in the news that people in town found him in the wrong.

217

"We were all stuck on a solution when he heard the news yesterday that the warehouse is now empty of occupants." Jed Prince spoke with the hint of a sarcastic edge to his voice. Angela wasn't sure if it was mocking or not.

"Yessir, I have acquired a new business. I have already hired on workers and found jobs and was able to barter for room and board with several families." Angela said innocently.

Jed Prince's left eyebrow quivered then shot up. He wasn't buying her story.

Ellie Prince spoke up to diffuse the mood. "I am certain Mrs. Caplan... who ran the place is eager to have help. She has a giving heart but she has asked for many prayers at the Ladies Prayer meetings about her trying to run that place alone."

Angela let out a slow breath. "Indeed she was very relieved."

"Whatever the reason the town council feels responsible for the purchase you made of the boarding house. It was a great scheme for getting the poor into reasonable housing." Jed Prince said, his tone approaching a general sense of normal sincerity.

"Thank you." She said simply. Her stomach was feeling nervous from the pent up anxiety. She grabbed at her wet hair and let it go lamely. There was nothing to do about it now.

"The town council is offering to take this burden off of your hands. We are willing to pay you the full buying price you paid for the business plus a bonus for all the work you did to get the provisions taken care of." Jed Prince had a friendly grin that surprised Angela. It only took her a moment to realize that he was a businessman. He knew how to fake a smile to make a good deal.

"I do appreciate the offer sir. But I do have plans for the business. With the news of the gold rush going so poorly for some folk in California I thought to take an opportunity to advertise. I have a lot of things to work out but by Spring I hope to encourage people back into the area. There is plenty of work in these parts for a strong back." Angela said trying to hide the smirk that was threatening behind her lips.

Ellie placed a hand on her husband's arm. Angela assumed it was to keep him in line.

"If you are certain on your course and that is your decision." Jed Prince said simply.

"I am appreciative of the offer, Mr. Prince. I just want to see it through." Angela lightened her tone to take a more generous approach.

Mr. Prince nodded. He stood and took his wife's arm to help her stand as well.

"If I may, I would like a little peace of mind about my land." Angela felt the fool for saying it but she wanted the worry off of her mind.

Ellie was the one to speak. "I am certain that from this moment on you needn't give it another thought."

Angela watched them walked out of the parlor wide-eyed. She was amazed that Mr. Prince had married such a dynamo. She would laugh about the dynamic between those two all day.

"Thank you for coming. I will be having a house-warming party soon. I will be certain to send an invite." Angela said to be friendly. Ellie Prince was certainly an interesting character. "I know the governor and his wife will be here too."

Both Mr. and Mrs. Prince looked at her in surprise. Perhaps they suddenly realized that she was a force to be reckoned with.

Chapter Thirty-Two

Angela Fahey

December passed with snow and wind over the mountaintops. Angela went to visit in town whenever the weather was fair enough for her to make it. Earl and Warren both kept mentioning that the livery had sleigh rails available once the snow got heavy. Angela held off for a heavier snowfall.

Corrine had taken her to town a few times when she went to check for mail or supplies.

Every week she was able to get in a visit with Ted, and the bond between them grew. Sophia was begging to stay with Angela and was promised that it would happen soon. Angela was beginning to plot a time when Sophia and Galina could meet. They may have seen each other at church, Angela mused, but they were the only two females in that age group in the area. Even with differences in their social status Angela thought it was worthwhile.

The annual winter barn dance was announced in the Oregon Gazette newspaper. Everyone was planning out what they would wear and what special recipes the womenfolk would bring. It was a time to show off cooking skills and Angela wondered if she could compete at all with some of the seasoned cooks in the area. She knew the basics and a few things she had learned from Violet while living at Grant's Grove.

The large sign for Orchard House had been finished at the woodworkers and replaced the original sign. All the minor repairs had been done by Clive and Ted, who stubbornly refused payment, at least in the traditional form.

Ted did offer to take the payment in kisses, and Angela pretended to be coy before settling on one kiss on the cheek. Ted had no complaints.

Ted's mother had warmed up to Angela over the weeks since the Orchard House opening. At least in Angela's opinion she had come to terms with Ted courting someone. Angela knew from the look that would come across Ted's face that he was a little impatient with her still for her attitude sometimes. But her anger had subsided a little and she seemed to have crossed into a new sadder phase.

When Angela had talked it over with Clive, while seeking advice, he had a few words on the subject.

"Grief over a death is tricky. Everyone has their own way of grieving, some grow angry and bitter for a long while. When I lost my first wife, I poured myself into work, probably to an extreme. My poor kids had to fend for themselves a little too often when I would go off on a trapping run for days on end. My guess is that Amelia Greaves is entering a new stage to get through. To grieve over what is lost is normal. We can all pray that her heart will heal."

Clive had been to visit Angela at least once a week, and usually made the rounds to see Corinne, Violet and Dolly, then after he stopped in to chat with John Harpole and his wife. He would also stop and chat with the manager of the Harpole Ranch, Reynaldo Legales. Word was that he was a man with a lot of wit and charm. Usually after a visit with Angela, Clive would go a few miles down the road to Russell and Chelsea Grant to see his grandkids.

Angela enjoyed the slower pace the weather allowed her. She took time to write letters, and decorate her new home. She had so many plans that she was dreaming of for the following year, with the Sparks family arriving with their newly extended family of adopted children. She also had hopes of visiting Portland and staying a day or so with Gabe and Amber Quackenbush, who she had stayed with in San Francisco the year before. They now ran the first fancy goods store in the territory. Clive had bragged about shipping off his second shipment of lace purchased from the Greaves family lace makers. The first shipment had been a huge success.

Angela was enjoying the simple life and felt peaceful finally in her new place in the world. Her days of forced servitude were over. Now she wanted to contemplate what it was to serve people out of the goodness in her heart. 'As unto the Lord,' the bible stated.

Every Monday Galina would come by and they would have a wonderful time visiting over the laundry duties.

Galina shared her frustrations, how her father was not allowing her to spend any time on any kind of schooling. She had never mentioned how she had been punished, but instead focused on asking for prayer. Angela had promised to pray about that with her. Angela made a note to herself to get a slate for Galina to practice her letters with when she came to visit.

Angela had taken the time to visit with each family at Orchard House to see how they all were fairing. Each family had its own struggles but Angela could see each of them showing more spunk as the weeks went by. All the school age children were taking classes in town and Angela was relieved to know that she had been part of something so big.

Mrs. Caplan had gushed over the help she was getting from all the families. Every child old enough to do chores wanted to help out, and the women were also helping each other out in their own way. The job at the tailors with extra mending had every woman pleased. Angela was told by three families that they would be paying for their keep soon. There was a part of Angela that was hesitant to take their money. But as she prayed she began to understand that there was a pride in earning your own way. She promised to listen to God speak within her when she wanted to be stubborn about things. She never wanted to insult these people who had been through so much.

The barn dance was on a Saturday and everyone in town was talking about it. This year the governor had volunteered his barn, and it was certainly going to be full. With more than three hundred souls in Clackamas County, the dance would certainly be a crowded event.

Angela had decided to wear her burgundy gown with the wide hoops, it had been declared as Ted's favorite earlier in the week. He said it made her eyes shine. That was certainly enough flattery to convince her.

Corinne and Marie had new dresses that Marie had made. Violet fought off the idea for more than a week to wear a dress with a corset and hoops, declaring herself a simple girl who would look silly in a fancy gown. Corinne finally persuaded Violet into wearing Corinne's less ostentatious gown that was a pale green. The hoops weren't as wide as the current fashion but in the West the fashion didn't have such a severe timeline. The dress was light and bounced, it could easily be considered a summer dress. Everyone made every excuse they could think of to convince Violet to agree. "It is always too warm at these types of events." Everyone had agreed that she would be the most comfortable. Violet, laughing at their lame excuses, agreed finally.

Dolly was a holdout and she promised meekly that she would wear the dress that Chelsea had sewn for her. It had several petticoats and was full at the bottom without the use of the cumbersome hoops.

The Friday before the barn dance a secret plan was unleashed with Angela and her friends on a poor unsuspecting Galina.

It was the day that Galya came to help Violet with extra laundry she had taken on for the Harpoles, since Marie had given birth. It gave them extra money in their pockets. Violet was saving for when her husband returned and Galina gave every penny to her family.

Galina was surprised to see Marie, Angela, Violet and Dolly all staring at her with smiles when she had arrived to work.

"Are we all doing laundry today?" She asked with a bemused expression. She took off her threadbare wool coat and hung it on the hooks in the wall.

She kicked the little bit of snow clinging to her boots and smiled suspiciously at the females all grinning at her.

Corinne took charge. "We wanted to thank you for all the hard work you do and for the sacrifices you make every week to be such a great helper." She gestured for Galina and everyone to go to sit near the fire.

With everyone seated Galina felt free to speak. "I appreciate my work and you are always more than generous with me and my family. My father is very pleased to be working again, with your husband Mrs... Corinne." She corrected.

"We wanted to thank you and surprise you. It is too early for Michaelmas but we wanted this to be a well timed present." Angela said and walked around to the other side of the chairs. First she pulled out a sky blue dress, with puffed long sleeves and white and gray pinstripes. It was a warm material that was soft and a fine quality. Galina gasped when Angela handed it to her.

"Go put it on." Violet clamored. Galina shot back into the back bedroom.

She was glowing with her young radiant smile when she came out. She asked for help with tying the bow in the back.

The color made her cheeks bright and her dark eyes stood out even more.

It was declared the perfect dress for the barn dance. It was a few inches above her ankle, just the right length for a young lady. Marie was certain that Galina's mother would approve.

"We have one more thing for you." Marie said. She held her sleeping child but she seemed very excited. "I have prayed that it blesses you."

Angela went back to the same spot behind the davenport to retrieve the charcoal gray coat. It had a black mink lined collar.

"Between us and Clive's trapping skills we were able to make this for you." Marie stated when she saw Galina's jaw drop.

223

Tears ran down her cheeks. She wordlessly put on the coat. It fit her perfectly and was long. It would keep her body warm through the long walks in the winter months. She was stunned to own such a nice coat.

"I am not sure how to say thank you for such a gift. It is not enough to say." She said, her eyes were pink-rimmed and full of emotion.

A few ladies got up from their seats and a group hug commenced. Galina cried unashamedly. She was simply overwhelmed by her friends.

Chapter Thirty-Three

Pritchlan Home

The Governor's farm was handsome under the dusting of snow and the two story cabin had a large front porch with every window lit with lanterns. The evening sky was clear and the road was an easy path for everyone to travel.

John Pritchlan and his wife welcomed everyone in.

Corinne rode with Angela and Ted, her husband Lucas had left early to be a part of the large band playing music. With so many musicians they all hoped to take turns and have a bit of time to participate in the dancing.

The women were greatly outnumbered by the men but it just gave every woman a chance to be admired all the more. More than one hundred people were all stuffed inside John Pritchlan's fancy barn. It was perfectly cleaned and the lanterns and decorations made everyone feel like they were part of a special event.

Clive jokingly announced that the 'Governor's Ball was ready to begin.' The music began and the dancing commenced.

There were tables full of food and apple cider to drink. Some of the men hung back from dancing, preferring to watch and eat the food prepared.

Ted and Angela were one of the first couples out on the dance floor that had been built. Clive snatched up Violet, who had been trying to hide in a back corner. She seemed nervous and edgy but Clive had her warmed up and smiling after a few minutes.

Dolly danced with Reggie the first dance and Reynaldo Legales on the second.

The dark and handsome Reynaldo was making his rounds as a great dancing partner. He danced with Corinne while her husband played the violin on stage. Then he danced with Violet after seeing she was without a partner. He was not flirtatious, but he was friendly and knew how to be a good dance partner. His handsome Latino looks, with dark eyes and slicked back hair did not make accepting his offer to dance a difficult one for any lady. He even danced with Sophia and Galina, setting their cheeks to blushing and fits of giggles.

He was making a good reputation around town as being a good man. John Harpole bragged about him constantly and by the end of the night he was introduced to everyone. He had only been working on the Harpole Ranch for a short while. But his reputation and skills would earn him his own place in short order.

After an hour of dancing Angela decided to take a break and got a plate to eat. She found an empty seat on a bench and it was only a minute before Ted joined her in the tight space.

"Have I told you that you look radiantly beautiful yet?" Ted asked. He placed a hand on her arm.

Angela grinned and nodded. She took a bite and chewed quietly while grinning. Ted was staring.

"You did tell me when we danced." Angela said finally.

Ted blushed a little and kept his hand on her arm. He seemed content to be near her. The music began again with a playful jig and Ted tapped his feet next to her.

"You do not have to wait for me Ted, I waited too long to eat today. I am famished. You can go dance if you like."

"I prefer to stay with you. I want the next dance. Whenever that may be." Ted declared, leaning close to her ear so he could be heard over the music.

"Suit yourself." She said with grin. Knowing he had been staring at her while she danced with the handsome Reynaldo. Ted had no reason to be jealous but a small part of her was pleased over the attention. It made her think hard about what she wanted from Ted. She wasn't sure if she even knew.

After she finished her small plate of food, Ted immediately offered to take the plate away. He ran with the plate and returned in short order. He was most attentive.

He offered her his arm as a new song started.

It was a waltz and Ted was a good partner, leading her around with a gliding step.

"I need to tell you something, Angel." Ted said with a serious look.

Angela wasn't sure if she could tell if it was good or bad news, her stomach flipped nervously. Perhaps his mother had made him reconsider the courtship. It had been going very slowly, Angela had some guilt about that but she was unable to figure out a way to make it any better.

"You needn't worry darling. I can see it written on your adorable face." Ted said as they continued to glide through every turn. "I just needed to tell that I still love you, my Angel."

Angela held her breath a moment. Ted's stare was intense and serious. He broke the serious look with a playful smile.

"I…" She spit out and stopped herself from saying anything more. She knew a part of her loved him, but another part was holding her love back. She couldn't say it aloud.

She knew that Ted was hoping and waiting for her to say it. Angela felt a pain in her chest over her inability to say what he needed to hear.

The dance ended and Angela stood there dumbly just staring at Ted and feeling the pain over the slightly hurt look that crossed his face. It was subtle, but definitely there.

There were no words but so much was said in that long moment. She wasn't ready, and now Ted knew it.

Would he give up on me? Angela wondered. She wanted to tell him that she didn't deserve his love. That she was a coward. But she was mute.

A jig started and John Pritchlan walked up and asked to borrow Angela in a dance. Angela gave Ted an apologetic look and then plastered a fake smile on while she danced with the governor. She had no idea what to do. She would pray.

<hr />

The barn dance had been a huge success, and everyone had left with full bellies and with fun memories.

Corinne rode home with her husband, Dolly went to stay with Chelsea and Russell Grant and Ted and Angela were alone for the buggy ride back. The night air was crisp but there was no wind or snow.

Angela felt so very sad about the declaration of love. She somehow wished he had waited just a little longer.

She wondered what Ted was thinking but was not brave enough to ask.

The horse's hooves clopped on the cold hard ground and was the only sound invading the silent night. Ted finally turned and gave her a long look.

"Have I overstepped?" Ted asked simply. So many emotions crossed his face, he probably wanted to ask more but that was all he could say.

"I don't know. I think that there is something wrong with me." Angela confessed.

"Am I being presumptuous to think that we are in a courting relationship?" Ted asked and sighed deeply. There was fear in the question.

"I consider you my beau, we are courting." Angela said, trying to make this better on him.

Ted looked to the road. He took another long minute before speaking again.

"I am glad." He stated simply. He tried to give her a smile but it was forced.

Angela knew from his expression that she had hurt him. He had traveled so far for her, had defended her against his own mother, had been helpful and courteous in every way without having every placed any kind of expectations on her. She was a fool. She should tell him right now that she loved him and that she was lucky to have his affection. Instead she sat silently until he dropped her off at her home.

She cried as she sat in her room and lit the fire in the wood stove, her room felt as cold as her heart.

Chapter Thirty-Four

Oregon City

The newspaper every week was full of local news and big stories from the rest of the country. There were political rants from the Oregon territory about the state of each town and how parts of the west were ungoverned and in a state of vigilante law.

Oregon City residents discussed this at length over breakfast tables, when visiting neighbors and even in letters. They were proud of their town. Having together dealt with the warehouse situation, knowing that they had come together for the good of others had proven that they were civilized. The town council had not been savage law but susceptible to the will of the people.

The territory Governor John Pritchlan spoke all over the territory about the responsibility of its citizens. To write to the United States congress and demand that it be made a state. He was a good man and a great motivator. His many articles in territory newspaper held his call to action; to make the West, especially Oregon, a frontier to be proud of.

Grant's Grove

At Grant's Grove a new project was underway. Corinne and Dolly had finally agreed that is was time to stop talking about the book project and begin to make it happen.

Corinne's stack of journals and notes about herbs and plants was the main inspiration. All Corinne and Dolly had learned was useful and beneficial but was scattered and not cohesive enough to share with anyone else. Both Corinne and Dolly had a decent drawing hand, so they decided to begin working on publishing a book for every home on how to use herbs and plants for everyday use.

They were both very excited about the process and asked for prayer on Sunday at church.

With pen and paper they both vowed to work hard, pouring over every thing they knew and had learned over the years. They joined forces with the town apothecary and knew that the end result would be worth the work.

Since the winter months held less work at the laboratory, Dolly worked in the greenhouse in the mornings and on some days came home early, she would lose herself in her work, drawing plants, reading through journals and writing.

Angela Fahey

A week after the barn dance Angela received a letter from Ted. She had been wallowing in her own guilt over her inability to say what he needed to hear. She had been to town once but had not stopped in to see his family. She wanted to give him space if he needed it.

She opened the letter, partly dreading his words. Perhaps this time he would finally give up on her as she had expected to happen all along.

My dearest Angel,

As days and hours pass I think of you and of hoping that your affections turn to me. My admiration of your independent spirit and honesty in every situation has me mesmerized. I feel like a buffoon when I talk to you, so shy with my words and glances. Certainly you must find me to be a dullard.
Your hesitancy towards my affection is felt most keenly, but I will give you the space and time you need. If I must admire you from afar I will. But know my thoughts are never far from you.

I dream of walking this world together with you, as equals in all things. I would throw myself from the highest peak before I would harm a hair on your head. To earn your heart is my greatest prayer.

Sincerely Yours,

Thaddeus Greaves

Angela knew she had a lot of praying to do herself. She had hurt Ted and was continuing to do so with every day that she withheld her feelings from him.

As she went about her daily life she made her requests to God to heal her heart. She knew somehow that she was broken.

———✦•❈•✦————✦•❈•✦———

Galina clasped a paper in her warm pocket. Her time with Violet that day had been good, not only for her reading skills, which were improving in small steps, but in her heart as well.

She had read through the words slowly.

*For by **grace** are ye saved through faith; and that not of yourselves: it is the gift of God: Not of works, lest any man should boast.*
Ephesians 2:8-9

She struggled on several words but had read it again and again. Violet was patient and helped her through without ever making her feel awkward.

"May I ask a question about this?" Galina asked after she had been through it a few times.

"Of course!" Violet offered and her smile was sincere. Galina had been told by her father that these people weren't her friends. But Galina was beginning to doubt his words.

"It says that we are saved by grace. Yes?" Galya said. She wanted to know. "What is grace? I have never heard anyone explain."

Violet paused, her face in serious reflection. "I once asked Helen Whittlan, the pastor's wife."

Galina nodded, she knew Helen from church services.

"She said that Grace is the undeserved blessing of God." Violet let the words sink in before she continued. "We cannot earn this favor from God by any work of our hands or giving or being well-behaved. We only get it by believing in it."

Galina swallowed as she understood.

"But how can that be, in this world everyone is judged by what they do?" Galina had misty tears in her eyes. She couldn't understand why she wanted to cry over these words.

"I think Jesus came to show us forgiveness as God offers it. Not the way the world does." Violet said. "Do you remember bible stories about the temple, how for every sin people had to take animals to the altar to be sacrificed. Blood had to be spilled for every single sin."

Galina nodded, knowing the Old Testament was full of stories of sacrifices.

"We as people can fall into the trap that we can do enough to be good. That if we are forgiven then we have earned it. God's Grace is the reminder that His love, blessings and favor are ours because He gives it freely for believing. It says that God does not respect persons… that we are all equal in His eyes." Violet said. Her light blue eyes showed the emotion Galina was beginning to feel over the words. Like saying these words had reconfirmed her beliefs in her own heart.

Galina let the tears fall as Violet's words sunk in. If the bible was true, then she had the Grace of God on her, because she did believe in these words. The very reason she wanted to read was so that God's words of the bible could be in her daily life. To God she was worthy of Grace. She felt herself lean into her friend and then wept into Violet's shoulder as she dealt with her emotions.

She had already been forgiven… but now she felt free from all the guilt and shame.

As she walked home she held on to the verse that Violet had written down for her. She would use the slate that Angela had bought for her to practice writing each of the words of this verse.

Her world was one full of hard work and sometimes a lot of struggle, but today she felt as light as air. God was with her.

Chapter Thirty-Five

April 1851

The winter months crept by, the snows were mild in the valley, only a few inches at a time. Every week the clouds would darken and folks would prepare for a storm, but it never came. The wind would howl but everyone was pleased that it was a mild year.

Every week Ted would visit a few days. He would ride from town, sometimes bringing his sister along. If he did, Sophia would stay with Angela and help her throughout the day. Angela enjoyed getting to know the young lady. One visit included Galina on a laundry day and Angela was pleased to see the girls were fast friends, even through their social differences.

Sophia was sympathetic about Galina's father and agreed to loan her any books to help her in her quest to learn to read. Galina had spent a few afternoons every week working on her letters with Violet and Angela.

It became a weekly event from the first afternoon with both girls that Sophia wanted to be there whenever Galina was.

"My mother is not always understanding about my need for a friend my own age." Sophia shared. Galina nodded in agreement.

Sophia brought over some of her lace work, when her mother protested over her leaving the shop. She was allowed to come as long as her work was accomplished. Sophia enjoyed the challenge of her work but the daily grind was sometimes tedious to the young lady. She wanted the chance to be a child for a little longer.

Galina and Angela were fascinated to watch Sophia's fingers fly with the strings, bobbins and pins. She made a long, thin row of lace a lot quicker than anyone expected.

After finishing the laundry work, Angela let Sophia and Galina have the parlor to themselves to talk and visit, for reading lessons or anything they needed. Angela remembered the days when she and Corinne would lock themselves in Corinne's bedroom for as long as they could get away with. That had been years ago when Corinne lived in her Aunt Rose's mansion in Boston. The days had flown.

Seeing the camaraderie between the young girls made Angela wish for visits with her friend. She found herself bundling up and walking over to visit with Corinne more often.

When Ted was finished with his weekly visits with Earl, the land manager, he would come back over to see her. She was beginning to look forward to his visits more and more.

She wondered what had gone so very wrong when he had left San Francisco? He had stayed true to his promise to return to her. But she had lost something in her heart when he left, and she felt a certain sense of guilt about it. A pit in her stomach whenever he would give her a look that said how he felt about her.

He had been very patient and not pushed her, but she knew how he felt. His letters from New York had been full of his adoration and preference for her. She enjoyed reading them again and again but perhaps she wondered now, she had never really believed he would come back for her? Her heart had grown so used to disappointment.

Since the dance at Michaelmas where he blurted out how much he loved her she had been doing so much soul-searching.

The explosion with his mother had sent her affection away, she knew that now. She still had cared for him deeply, but the hurt had chased her into a hiding place like a scared rabbit. She felt ashamed of herself for that, but she wasn't sure how she could repair it. She prayed a lot over that hurt and confusion, knowing there was no subject that God would find silly or insignificant.

With every visit her heart was growing fonder of Ted again. His handsome smile was always charming but it was his calm demeanor that won her over. He was somehow a protective presence, without ever treating her like she was incapable.

"I trust your judgment." Ted would say whenever she had any ideas. That trust he gave her was the sweetest balm to her fearful and hiding heart.

As the spring thaw came over Willamette Valley, Angela felt her own heart melt.

It was a Wednesday morning when Angela was surprised to see Ted pull up in Clive's beat up old wagon and he had a load of wood in the back with a few crates and tarps.

She wiped her hands of the flour she had been pounding out for biscuits and pulled her coat on.

Ted stepped down from the wagon bench. The wagon squeaked in irritation from the movement.

"Clive let me borrow his wagon." Ted said simply. His smile looked boyish.

"What do you have back there?" Angela leaned over and bit her lip in concentration. She tried to look past Ted's body to see into the wagon with no luck.

Ted just stared for a moment to increase the suspense. "Well..." He said finally, drawing out the word.

"Oh." Angela gasped and playfully slapped his arm. Ted surprised her by pulling her near, his face close to hers.

"I thought perhaps you needed a chicken coop?" Ted asked in a low voice with a hint of a smile. The memories flooded Angela, how he had helped her build that chicken coop in San Francisco, how they had been so silly and frustrated until he had finally gotten the nerve to kiss her. Their very first kiss.

Angela was speechless and felt heat spread across her face. She knew that she was turning a ripe tomato red but she stopped caring. The moment of nearness was sweet, intense and she realized that she wanted to lose herself in his serious blue eyes.

It had been months of sweet visits and he had held her hand a few times over these months but it had been so very long since they had done anything else. He had been biding his time.

His eyes held her captive as well as his arms that were locked behind her back. She would have to wiggle and push away to escape but she had firmly decided that she didn't want to.

Before she thought of anything she whispered. "I love you so much, Ted." The moment she had said it Ted pulled her forward.

His lips met hers to tell her exactly how long he had been waiting to hear those words. His hands were in her hair and in a minute they separated, breathless and exhilarated.

Angela smiled and took a step back to admire the blush on Ted's cheeks. She hooked her fingers behind her back and smirked. She couldn't stop herself.

Ted squinted and took a step forward. "You look mighty pleased with yourself, Angel."

"I am." She said before he placed a sweet kiss on her nose. She could tell by the look in his eye that he wanted to kiss her silly again.

His look changed from silly to serious in a second.

235

"I will wait for you as long as you need me to." He said, and pulled her close again.

"I know you would, Ted, and perhaps that is why my heart is ready. You are so very good to me." Angela laid her head against his chest and listened to Ted's heart thud inside. She was content.

Ted was invigorated by their conversation and after they broke apart he took the time to show her the gift he had brought.

"It is a gift in two parts." Ted's smile was euphoric and he bounded the few steps to the wagon to retrieve the first few crates.

The first crate held a large black chicken with four yellow chicks scurrying below her. Angela squealed and fussed over the fluffy chicks. The second crate had two white chickens with more yellow chicks. Ted received a few kisses on the cheek and began sharing his plan for the second part of the gift.

"I brought supplies to build you an efficient chicken coop. It needs a little more shelter than the one we built in San Francisco, since the winds can be colder here than in it had been in California." Ted said and pulled out a piece of paper. He had drawn out a simple structure with a door and two very small windows for light. The entrance had a small walk space and then a wall of chicken wire and a latch to go in to get the eggs. The chickens would have a shelter from the cold but a hatch and a walk space to the side where they could have their own yard.

Angela followed Ted around the west side of the barn and he paced out the location of the fence.

Angela would be able to see her chickens every day and she knew she would love the walk to the barn every day to see her babies.

With many thank you's and a quick embrace Angela escaped to try and save her biscuits, and Ted began to unload materials.

Angela came back to a crusty blob of dough on her kitchen counter that could not be salvaged. Dolly came down the stairs dressed and ready for her day of work. Angela usually had something ready for Dolly to eat quickly.

"I heard squealing." Dolly said and gave Angela a very subtle smile.

Angela couldn't hide her smile when she explained what Ted had brought for her.

"Do you have time for me to start breakfast now?" Angela asked, wondering if Dolly would go hungry because she dawdled so long over Ted's gifts.

"I am early, I have plenty of time. I want to wash up." Dolly headed to the back room with an empty water pitcher.

Angela tossed the blob of crusty dough in the rummage bucket and she pulled out some bacon and whipped up a quick batch of buttermilk pancakes. She used the eggs she had gotten from Marie and John Harpole and grinned to herself about Ted's gift. Knowing it meant she would be using her own eggs soon.

The bacon snapped and popped in the cast iron skillet and Angela deftly flipped pancakes as she wondered over the exchange. Having said the words of love she felt lighter. The confusion and hiding felt silly now. She just wanted to look forward to many more days to share with Ted.

She called out the back door for Ted to come inside a few minutes later.

She set the table for three and made a heaping pile of pancakes, and a plateful of bacon strips. She retrieved a small jug of dark maple syrup from her pantry and fresh butter she had churned herself a few days before.

Ted and Dolly joined Angela at the table.

Ted was full of praise over the hastily thrown together meal but Angela took the moment as a positive sign. The scene was perfection. This could be every breakfast. She suddenly saw the role she could play in Ted's life and it filled her with joy. She truly was ready for the next step and she would pray that God would bring it about in His timing.

* * *

Reggie Gardner

Reggie rode his horse to work every day. Spending nearly everyday at the Harpole ranch, then at two p.m. he would ride over to Grant's Grove nearby and check in on Corinne. She didn't require as much paperwork as the Ranch did but he somehow made the trip everyday to just see how everything was. He felt foolish but he had to see how Dolly was a fairing. Even if he knew that she was busy and perhaps thought of him as a nuisance.

237

There was just something about that quiet and mysterious girl that unsettled him to his very core.

Violet Griffen, the housekeeper of Corinne and best bread maker in the county, usually brought him a plate of leftovers from lunch every afternoon. She was a kind gal and was the first to mention to him a few clues into Dolly's personality. Violet had noticed his infatuation. He appreciated her advice on how to get through Dolly's silent exterior, and he really appreciated that she hadn't teased him.

Dolly had been difficult to get through. She sometimes showed interest, a few conversations had given him hope, but the daily moments when he would find ways to bump into her had done little to nudge their relationship beyond acquaintance.

Reggie worked everyday with his mind, with his books and accounting figures but every evening he went home to the work on his cabin and patch of land. He lived near the Varushkin family and had a two-acre plot. It was heavily wooded at the moment and he had plans of clearing a spot for a wheat or potato crop.

He had an idea to invite Dolly by sometime to walk the land, knowing she would see things that he knew nothing about. She and Corinne could find anything in the woods. He dreamt about walking with her and learning about everything she knew.

The plans and thoughts of how to approach the shy young woman kept Reggie busy through the long winter months. As the spring flowers made their appearance he began to make promises to himself. He would get through to her. He would try harder.

Chapter Thirty-Six

Corinne & Violet

Violet was not usually in town on Mondays. She made it a point to never be in town on that day, and one other. Corinne had wanted company and Violet had said yes to the outing before Violet had thought it over. She didn't want to make any explanations so she acquiesced. Her new light blue dress was a bit fancier than she was used to but Corinne had insisted that she wear it. Violet was practical and really didn't like to change her clothes for a simple visit to town but again she agreed.

Her usually chipper mood was hidden today. She had a dream about when her husband left and she relived the fight they had had. It had lingered in her mind all morning through her early chores. She had hoped that the excursion to town would help her mood but as she followed Corinne through stores and they visited with everyone they met, she still lingered in melancholy.

The bright sun and spring breeze had everyone in town smiling. Clive's store was getting a coat of fresh paint and a new sign, Corinne stopped to hassle Clive for a few minutes.

Clive tried to recruit both the ladies into painting for him.

"No no no! Violet is in a new dress!" Corinne did all the protesting.

Violet probably would have helped and ruined the dress for certain. She wore her fake smile wearily today. Part of her was tired of pretending that everything was alright when inside it wasn't.

At one point in the conversation Clive tilted a sideways look at Violet and his eyes focused in on her. She was positive that he could see straight through her. With a sympathetic look that made her feel better and want to cry simultaneously, he dropped his stare. She was glad he didn't press her.

Corinne led the way through town, she picked up mail at the post office, bought three yards of lace trim to give to Marie for sewing projects, they poked through new hat designs at the millers, all before they made their way to the new grocers.

Violet was in a daze while at the store. Corinne purchased a crate of oranges that had just arrived from California and she was excited talking with the store owner about oranges and their many uses for the rinds.

Violet felt her body react before her brain had fully acknowledged what she had seen.

She ran from the store at a breakneck pace and was hiding behind the building and shaking for several minutes before Corinne found her.

"Oh, Violet are you ill?" Corinne exclaimed. She was panting from her search of the street then around the building.

Violet shook her head but was without words.

Corinne stroked her back and said soothing words but her look of concern was real.

"I am taking you to Doc Williams." Corinne stated. She gently tried to lead Violet away from her position, flatly up against the wall.

Violet gasped and dropped into a crouch, wrapping her arms around her knees and hugging herself.

"You are scaring me, Vie, please tell why I can do?" Corinne had tears in her eyes. Obviously she had never seen Violet act in this manner.

"A minute.." Violet said weakly. She rocked on her heels a little.

"You need a minute?" Corinne asked, trying to discern.

Violet nodded. She took deep breaths and closed her eyes to try and find a way to calm herself. She found the ability to pray and felt a calm start to fill her.

After a minute she was able to stand.

Corinne gave her a hug and Violet finally let some tears flow.

"You gave me a fright." Corinne said into Violet's shoulder as she embraced her friend.

"I am sorry, I saw…" Violet broke into fresh tears and she shook while trying not to sob.

"Was it Eddie?" Corinne had no clue who else could have affected Violet in such a way?

"No, no."

Violet took deep breaths and once she was under control she decided to break the embrace. She wiped at her tear-soaked face with a handkerchief she'd had up her sleeve. She laughed nervously while she saw the concern on Corinne's face. It wasn't funny but the laugh came out anyhow.

"It wasn't my husband." Violet said with a weak voice, still shaky and filled with emotion. "It was my mother."

Reggie Gardner

Reggie Gardner had been working on a gift to give Dolly for more than a week. He had always been a decent artist, and while he had been at sea he had worked on his painting skills. He wanted to give Dolly flowers but he thought it would be silly to give the girl that was surrounded by flowers every day, more flowers. So instead he thought out ideas for gifts. Finally he came up with one that was hopefully foolproof.

With a purchased frame the gift was complete and he took it with him in his work satchel. After his work with the Harpoles he made his way to the laboratory at the Grant's. He saw Dolly working at a table where she was grinding something at the mortar and pestle.

"Is Corinne working today?" He asked this question of her almost everyday.

Dolly looked up from her grinding with her brown eyes noticing him. She wasn't flirtatious or coy but she gave him a perfunctory smile that could have been friendly to anyone.

"She went to town. I have no accounting work for you today." She said simply.

"That is perfectly fine. Do you have time for a break?" Reggie asked, feeling foolish but wanting to get past the humdrum conversation of everyday with this girl.

"Why yes." Dolly said and took her apron off. She walked to the door of the laboratory and looked to Reggie to follow her. He gladly obliged.

"I like to walk at this time when I can. Especially when the air smells of spring and fresh earth." Dolly said and her dark brown eyes shined.

Reggie swallowed and nodded dumbly.

"I..uh.." Reggie was going to take off on a run if he couldn't get his tongue to work properly. "I made you a gift." He finally spit out.

Dolly had a confused look for a second. She swung her arms down at her sides playfully. Reggie found it distracting.

"What does a gift mean?"

Reggie shook his head realizing perhaps she didn't know the meaning of the word. It was easy to forget that English wasn't her first language.

"A gift is a present, a ...."

Dolly laughed and her wide smile made his heart melt. "I know what a gift is. What does this gift mean?" Dolly asked, she giggled again at his lost expression.

Reggie drew a blank for any answer that wasn't ridiculous.

"Is it a gift from one friend to another?" Dolly suggested.

"Oh?" Reggie caught her meaning. She wanted to know his intentions for the gift. Perhaps it was something from her tradition. He paused, trying to find the words. "Well, yes. I mean, well no."

"No, we are not friends?" Dolly furrowed her eyebrows.

"Well, yes we are. I think." Reggie relaxed when her face relaxed. "I would like to be great friends." Reggie finished lamely. He wanted to court her. Why hadn't he said that?

Dolly nodded, seemingly satisfied with the explanation.

Reggie pulled out the gift, he handed it to her simply. He had wanted to wrap it in parchment paper but he thought that was too formal. He wanted her to see it immediately for what it was.

The watercolor painting was a bluebird on a branch, about to take flight. The fancy frame was shiny black.

Dolly covered her mouth with her free hand and stared at it for the longest moment. "This is magnificent." Dolly said and her eyes expressed that she felt that strongly.

"I wanted to bring you flowers. But I thought this would be better." Reggie closed the satchel and nervously clasped his own hands in front of him.

"It is the perfect gift. Thank you Reggie."

His name sounded perfect on her lips. He was glad that she had finally used his given name as he had asked her to more than a dozen times. Hearing it now was like a sweet song.

They walked toward the creek for a minute and Dolly sat on a log near the water.

Reggie stood not wanting to crowd in.

"Dolly? Would you consider allowing me to court you?" Reggie finally asked, his heart playing a fast beat in his chest.

"Chelsea has explained courtship." Dolly said quickly then she grew quiet.

Reggie nodded and hoped that she would continue. After a minute she did.

"You are a very special man. A man of God, and a man of numbers and wisdom." Dolly stated and Reggie saw that she meant her words. "I am a girl, who is lost between two worlds. When I become a woman I want to have picked a world to be in." She said and looked to Reggie with a pained look.

Reggie replayed her words in his head. He wanted to understand.

"You believe yourself to be too young to be courted?" Reggie knew it was wrong when he said it.

"No, I am not free to pick this world, the place I am now is not promised to me to keep." Dolly seemed confused and she looked at the water. "You are very special. I could say yes to courting." She said the word almost as a question. It felt foreign on her tongue. "But my future is unknown to me."

Reggie thought over her words and remembered back to when she had first joined the wagon train a few years ago. Knowing no English, but Clive had made a deal with Corinne that she would teach Dolly all about her herbal medicines and Dolly would share her knowledge. The chief had promised to send for her once she was educated.

The full weight of that knowledge hit him. She could be forced to go back to her tribe.

"Your tribe is coming back for you?" Reggie almost choked on the words.

"They may, though they are Shoshone, I am half Hopi, my mother was rescued by the Shoshone after a raid. My mother was Hopi."

Reggie tried to remember everything he knew about her and realized he didn't know as much as he thought. "Your father was French?" He remembered a tidbit and decided to ask.

"Yes, Joseph Bouchard. I never really knew him. He taught my mother about God, and taught her some English. She passed some of those things on to me." Dolly said quietly. There was a hint of pain in her words.

"You want to be a woman of God?" Reggie asked knowing that she did. She sang at church with passion in her eyes. She was always carrying her bible.

"Yes." She said then sighed.

"If you go back you would have to give that up?"

"Almost certainly, unless things have changed." Dolly finally looked at him again. "I know in my heart I cannot live without God." She said desperately.

Reggie knew that talk of courtship was done for now. She had bigger decisions to make and he did not want to be another confusion for her.

"I will be praying for you friend," He added to hopefully ease her mind. "God will find a way for you."

Dolly looked relieved that he had understood her. She had said more to him than she had ever expected. He was a good man, and a part of her wished that she could agree to his wishes for this courtship tradition. For now she would pray. She was glad to know that he was her friend and pray for her as well.

Reggie felt his heart calm down, knowing that if this girl was the one God meant for him that it would work out. He could be content to continue on as better friends. Though knowing her better from today made his heart all the more involved.

Corinne & Violet

Corinne and Violet were home just as it was time to make dinner.

Violet was quiet and pale, still shaken from her confession to Corinne. She had been very vague about details.

"How have you avoided seeing them in such a small town?" Corinne had asked when they were riding the wagon home, with all of Corinne's purchases in the back.

"My mother only came to town on Monday's and Thursdays. My father…" Violet had stammered over the words. "He was not one for being around people."

Corinne had let the vague information pass without further questions.

Violet stayed silent through the meal preparation and the meal.

When it was time for bed Corinne stopped Violet in the hallway before Violet escaped into her own rooms.

"I am praying for you my friend." Corinne said simply. Her concern was real but without details she would worry. Her friend had never seemed so down.

The next day Violet was her old self. The haunted look from the day before was gone. Violet seemed sincerely herself, thankful to be blessed with busy hands and a heart full of joy.

Corinne kept Violet in her prayers though. It was on her heart more often now.

Angela Fahey

The governor's wife, Henrietta Pritchlan, had made good on her promise to help Angela with a house-warming party and the event was beginning to take shape.

Angela was excited over everything spring was bringing her way. Joy overflowed in her heart as she prepared her home for it's first party.

She went over the guest list with Corinne and she was pleased to know that more than forty people had responded and were coming.

Angela had a white chiffon dress with red embroidered flowers that she would wear for the event. Corinne brought extra china, and Marie had an extra table brought over with bright white tablecloths that were very elegant.

Angela stressed herself over the outside of the house being yet unpainted but everyone took turns calming her.

Olivia Greaves stayed all day Thursday to be Angela's helper, going over every little detail. It was nice to talk with Olivia too because she talked all day about Ted and his family. Hearing stories was almost as good as having him near her.

"I believe my sister has warmed to you." Olivia said with certainty. "She has really improved in many things lately. All our prayers are making a difference." Olivia placed an arm on Angela's shoulder in approval throughout the day.

With Friday afternoon drawing to an end, Angela was nervous and jittery. Her home was decorated and filled to the brim with food. Her guests were due to arrive at any moment and she was babbling at anyone who would stand next to her.

Corinne was finally the one to calm Angela's nerves. Corinne with very few words reminded her that she was loved and part of a community that welcomed her. Ten deep breathes and a quick peek through the house to make sure everything was in order Angela settled herself by the door.

The Greaves were the first to arrive, resplendent in lace and frills. Sophia looked like a painting in a bright yellow dress that bounced as she ran up the front steps. Olivia and Amelia were wearing their best as well, their reddish blond hair done up fashionably with sausage curls and elegant twists. They all greeted Angela warmly, Amelia even stopping to

245

kiss Angela on the cheek before she moved on to greet Corinne and Dolly.

Ted came with roses and a look of pride as he drank in the vision that Angela made in her new spring dress.

The Greaves were the earliest and Sophia pestered to know when Galina's family would arrive. Everyone laughed over Sophia's energy. She seemed to be all wound up.

Finally the guests poured into the yard. Wagons and buggies filled up the driveway and the hitching post was full in short order.

Everyone brought a housewarming gift of some sort or another.

Clive made everyone come outside in the dusk light to see the saddle he brought for her.

"Your poor horse needs to be ridden, Red." He said with a jest and everyone laughed as Angela's eyes went wide. It was common knowledge that Angela was still a bit fearful of horses. The saddle was handsome and expensive to Angela's eye and she thanked him with a kiss on the cheek.

The Governor and his wife came and the event was officially started.

Sophia and Galina were tight as two peas in a pod, finding their own little corner to talk and giggle while the grown ups told stories and laughed.

Most of the town council had shown up, to be supportive, Angela doubted that they would stay long but she was happy to see that the harsh feelings over the boarding house issue was behind them all.

Ted was beside Angela for the entire event. His attentive gaze always there to calm her. Once everyone had visited, Angela turned to Ted to see if it was a good time to serve the food.

He surprised her by making an announcement.

"I want to thank everyone for coming." He said loudly. Angela wondered what he was doing.

"I know I am not the host of this house warming but I wanted to take this chance to thank everyone here for being so supportive of the woman I love." A few people gasped, others laughed and Angela just looked shocked.

"I have only been here for a few months, but I have loved her for longer than a year. She has enchanted me since I met her. The Angel who saved me in San Francisco." Ted took Angela's arm and gave her a look of affection.

"So now before all her friends and family here in Oregon, I wish to make my intentions known." Ted knelt before her and held out a golden ring with a red ruby sparkling in the lamplight. "Angela Fahey, would you be my bride?"

The crowd cheered and Angela could not hear her own thoughts but she trusted that the nod would suffice. When Ted slipped the ring on her finger she finally found her voice and said.

"Yes, yes, yes!" Then Ted lifted her into an embrace.

The event took on a new purpose to not only celebrate the new home but also the new engagement.

Clive, and the Grant Brothers, Lucas and Russell took turns tousling Ted's blond hair into disarray. Sophia and Galina both squealed and hugged Angela at least ten times.

Corinne had tears in her eyes when they finally got a chance to be alone for a second.

"I could not have prayed for a better way for today to be." Corinne linked her arm in Angela's and shed a few happy tears.

Many gifts were given from simple preserves for her pantry, to a silver tea set from Corinne and Lucas, a lovely quilt from Marie, a riding lesson from John Harpole, bringing laughs when Angela's fear showed again, a fancy chest of drawers from the governor and his wife, and so much more from the community.

Angela was overwhelmed by everyone's generosity. As everyone made their goodbyes for the night Angela said a prayer for everyone as they left her home. May the Lord bless every single one.

———————◆·◉·◆———◆·◉·◆———————

Angela and Dolly had cleaned up the food mess from the night before but had left some of the dishes. Corinne had promised to come by in the early morning to help with the party clean up. Angela was giddy over her engagement and Dolly was happy to hear her friend gush over how much she loved her dear Ted.

Corinne arrived early as promised with an extra washtub, the hot water was poured in with the sudsy homemade soap. The cups and plates were loaded in and left to soak in the hot water.

All three ladies grabbed a cup of coffee and sat at the table for a quick visit before doing more work.

Angela was excited to talk over her feelings. Corinne had questions that Angela couldn't answer about plans.

"I don't know what Ted has in mind but my guess is that we will be talking over these things soon. How can it be possible to be so very happy?" Angela sighed and enjoyed hearing Dolly and Corinne laugh at her silliness. She took a sip of her creamy coffee and dreamt about her future.

The three women made quick work of the dishes and went through some of the gifts, trying to find a home for some of the easy to place items. The canned goods from Millicent Quackenbush made them all start thinking of what they could eat. Corinne stroked the fine leather of the saddle that Clive had brought in. It was laying awkwardly on the davenport.

"You need to give this to me!" Corinne said sarcastically. "It will take you years to work up the nerve to ride." Corinne teased.

"I promised Clive that I would try, and your father said that he would help me to get past my fear." Angela gave Corinne a playful punch.

Dolly and Corinne took the saddle to the barn and Angela followed behind them. Warren was mucking out the stalls until he got a glance at the shining leather of the saddle. He found a temporary place for it to rest but promised to build a place for it to live. He told her he would need a few supplies to keep it well maintained and oiled. Angela promised to get everything he needed.

They all went to visit the newly finished chicken coop and they cooed and clucked to the baby chicks. Angela then walked over to the spot where she wanted to build another cabin for the Sparks family.

"Are you certain that Ted would like to have them sharing the property?" Corinne asked.

"I had mentioned it to him before. I do hope that is something he would agree to. I guess I have a lot to talk over." Angela fretted for a moment but she calmed her heart when she thought about it for a second. God would work this out. If it was meant to be then it would be.

They were all walking toward the back door when they heard Clive's voice holler.

"Hallooo."

"We are in the back." Angela yelled and they picked up their speed to get to the front of the house.

Clive met them alongside the house.

"I have guests out front." Clive said gravely.

Angela frowned after seeing Clive's face.

They walked the few steps to the front of the house.

Two tall men in leathers and feathers were waiting on horseback. Clive sighed then spoke. "They have come for Bluebird."

The End

Wildflower Series

Book 1 – Finding Her Way
(previously released as Seeing the Elephant)

Book 2 – Angela's Hope

Book 3 – Daughter's of the Valley

Coming soon … Book 4 – The Watermill

Also by Leah Banicki

Runner Up – A Contemporary love story,
Set in the world of reality TV.

Connect with me online:

https://www.facebook.com/Leah.Banicki.Novelist

Please share your thoughts with me. leahsvoice@me.com

The self-publishing world is very rewarding but has its marketing challenges. Please remember to spread the word about my books if you like them. By using word-of-mouth you
help to bless an author.
Like – Share - Leave a review

Thank you, Leah Banicki

Character List

Corinne Grant - Married to Lucas Grant. Age 19. Started a business making medicinal oils from plants. Also has built a greenhouse for the cultivating of plants and herbs.

Lucas Grant - Graduate of Yale agricultural school, thrives on farming technology and making improvements in the agricultural field. Married to Corinne.

Chelsea Grant - Married to Russell Grant. Granddaughter of Clive Quackenbush
Russell Grant - Lucas Grant's brother, owns a farm nearby. They help each other often on each other's land.

Clive Quakenbush - Mountain man, fur trapper, Hudson Bay store owner, Government liaison for Indian Affairs, hunter and business man. Widowed twice.

Jedediah Quackenbush - (nickname JQ) son of Clive, works at Oregon City store.

Millicent Quackenbush - (nickname Millie) married to JQ. Rarely works in the store but is active in her community and church.

Gabriel Quackenbush - Son of JQ and grandson of Clive, ran the Hudson Bay store in San Francisco, California territory. Now running the fancy goods store for Clive in Portland Oregon.

Amber Quakenbush - Married to Gabriel, Irish immigrant, came over as a child with her parents. Helps her husband run the store. Befriended Angela Fahey

Dolly Bluebird Bouchard - (Indian name is Bluebird) half Indian, half white. Mother was Hopi and father was a french fur trapper. She was sent by the Shoshoni tribe to learn from Corinne about plants and medicines to bring back and teach the tribe. her father's name was Joseph Bouchard.

Angela Fahey - Irish immigrant orphaned and sold into a workhouse at a young age with her brother. She became a maid in Corinne's Aunt's home and they were fast friends. She attempted to cross the Oregon Trail and was wounded early on and had to recover before continuing her journey.

Sean Fahey - Irish Immigrant who ran away from the work orphanage. Older brother to Angela Fahey. In the company of Ol' Willie. Current location, California Territory.

Henry & Edith Sparks - Henry is the Captain at Fort Kearney, they took Angela in after an unfortunate accident. Edith and Henry are nursing her back to health. Recently adopted three young children whose parents were lost on the Oregon Trail.

Thaddeus Greaves - (nicknamed Ted) – courting Angela Fahey, they met in San Francisco when he arrived after his father had died of scurvy. He returned to Upstate New York to care for his widowed mother, Amelia Greaves, and sister Sophia Greaves.

Olivia Greaves – Ted's Aunt, lace maker. Staying with Ted's family in Oregon City.

John Harpole - Corinne's father, first wife Lily (Corinne's mother) - deceased - 2nd wife Marie Harpole - Mother to Cooper and Abigail Marie Harpole

Warren Martin Jr. - Hired as a spare hand, does milking and odd jobs. Stays with Earl in his cabin during the week.

Mrs. Gemma Caplan- former owner of Oregon City boarding house, hired on as manager and head housekeeper.

Brian Murphy - Manager of Q & F Distillery – in San Francisco

Oregon City residents –

Doctor Vincent Williams
Persephone Willliams, the Doctor's wife

Mr. Higgins - Apothecary

Gomer Hynes – Oregon Gazette owner

Pastor Darrell Whittlan and his wife Helen

Marshall Crispin - school teacher outside of town.

Reynaldo Legales - Manager at Harpole Ranch

Amos Drays - local carpenter

Brian Murphy - Manager of Q & F Distillery – in San Francisco

Orchard House residents

Frieda Warhan

Thank you so much for reading my book:

My Biography -

I am a writer, wife and mother. I live in SW lower Michigan near the banks of Brandywine Creek. I adore writing historical and contemporary stories, facing the challenges that life throws at you with characters that are relatable. I love finding humor in the ridiculous things that are in the everyday comings and goings of life. For me a good book is when you get to step into the character's shoes and join them on their journey. So climb aboard, let us share the adventure!

My writing buddy is my miniature poodle Mr. Darcy, who snuggles at my feet while I write until he must climb onto my chest for dancing or snuggles. My beagle Oliver is more concerned with protecting the yard from trespassers – squirrels and pesky robins.

I love hearing from my readers and try to answer every email personally.

Please share your thoughts with me. leahsvoice@me.com

Website:
http://leahbanicki.wix.com/author

Made in the USA
Monee, IL
10 September 2024

65461900R00148